WILLEMSDORP

THE ANNIVERSARY EDITION OF HERMAN CHARLES BOSMAN

*Planning began in late 1997 – the
fiftieth anniversary of Bosman's first
collection in book form,* Mafeking Road *–
to re-edit his works in their original,
unabridged and uncensored texts.
The project should be completed by
2005 – the centenary of his birth.*

GENERAL EDITORS:

STEPHEN GRAY AND CRAIG MACKENZIE

Herman Charles Bosman

WILLEMSDORP

The Anniversary Edition

Edited by Stephen Gray

Human & Rousseau
Cape Town Pretoria Johannesburg

First anniversary edition, first impression 1998
Second impression 2000

Copyright © 1998 by The estate of Herman Charles Bosman
First published by Human & Rousseau in 1977
Anniversary edition published in 1998 by
Human & Rousseau (Pty) Ltd,
Design Centre, 179 Loop Street, Cape Town

Back cover photograph of Herman Charles Bosman in Johannesburg,
canvassing adverts for *The S.A. Opinion,* late 1940s, taken by a street
photographer, courtesy of the Harry Ransom Humanities Research Center.

Cover design by Robert Meas
Typography by Welma Odendaal
Typeset in 11/13 pt Times Roman
Printed and bound by NBD,
Drukkery Street, Goodwood, Western Cape

ISBN 0 7981 3901 3

HERMAN Charles Bosman was born of Afrikaner parents in Cape Town in 1905. In the 1920s he encountered the backveld world of the old Transvaal Republic as a young teacher, a career abruptly halted by his being imprisoned for the murder of his step-brother and condemned to death. After his reprieve in 1930, he lived as a freelance journalist in London and in Johannesburg, where as the literary editor of various periodicals he became known for his short stories, particularly with the collection *Mafeking Road* in 1947.

During 1943 he was the editor of the United Party-supporting *Zoutpansberg Review and Mining Journal* in Pietersburg in the Northern Transvaal, clearly the original of 'Willemsdorp' with its *Northern Transvaal News*, edited by one 'Charlie Hendricks'. There he met his third wife, Helena, who remained with him to the end, preserving the material he generated in devising his masterpiece.

He died unexpectedly in Johannesburg of a heart attack in 1951, at the age of forty-six, leaving the novel *Willemsdorp* in a completed but unfinalised typescript. When first issued in 1977, it soon established itself as a classic of South African fiction – despite in some places (thanks to censorship restrictions) being glaringly incomplete. This text of *Willemsdorp* is the first to appear in full, uncut, as Bosman intended.

Contents

Introduction

THE surviving typescripts of Herman Charles Bosman's *Willemsdorp* were purchased ten years after his death, together with much other material, from his widow, the late Helena Lake, in Johannesburg in 1961. Thereafter they became part of the holdings of the Harry Ransom Humanities Research Center (HRHRC) at the University of Texas at Austin, Texas. These were later classified, together with some carbon copies, by the doctoral candidate there, Vivienne Mawson, into an earlier 'Version B' (a typescript of 146 pages, breaking off in the middle of the present Chapter 7), and a later, complete 'Version A' (the 218-pager reproduced here) – the most important single item among the Bosman Texas papers.

When Human and Rousseau first published *Willemsdorp* in 1977, courtesy of the HRHRC, Mrs Lake agreed for reasons now unknown to certain cuts in the text. These are listed at the end in the Notes to this edition. Without going into the finer details here, we may nevertheless readily understand that any deletions from a Bosman work do affect his most intricate fictional designs and, for whatever reason, also reduce his reader's potential enjoyment.

From the spiral wirebound notebooks and many other working papers in the Texas collection, it is clear how meticulous that design was. One page he ingeniously folded over and over to form a template of sixty-four squares, each minutely filled in in spidery pencil: for example, 16: "Queer Col. man calls on CH – wants to sell dagga – CH doesn't understand"; 21: "Footballer out with Mavis Clark"; 38: "Principal gets home – suspicious. See notebook." This scheme places the visit of Charlie Hendricks and Jack Brummer to the Wondergat as No. 32 – a sinkhole is literally at the exact centre of the plot. Eight paired chapters thus square out in an exacting kind of symmetry, showing the most careful craftsmanship. This collapses only in the virtuoso final Chapter 16, where all is scuttled for that last hallucinatory rush of action.

With that scrupulous sense of design, Bosman was able to pull the rather inert Version B together and propel it forward into the finished work. Version B told much the same set of stories and in many ways is more blunt than Version A. But, lacking the connecting character of

Cyril Stein and the whole dagga business, its various plots seldom intersected; certainly not in the well-honed way of the later text which is truly a web, an imbroglio of interconnected events. After all, *Willemsdorp* is in the form of the popular murder mystery and needed to be tight. In Version B this tightness was not yet felt, and only a very few patches were lifted from it by him for reworking.

Here is one example:

It was here, on what was now known as Kerk Street, that the first houses were built of sun-dried brick, with their front doors opening on to the wagon-trail. That settlement had grown, of course, during the intervening century – but it had not grown very much. And now, picking his way over the uneven sidewalk, in the heat of the early afternoon, Charlie Hendricks felt that that little street had changed hardly at all since the time when the wagons of Willem Steyn's party had come to a stop by a stream amid thorn-trees, and their leader had announced that he would here found his village, his dorp that was to serve as the religious and administrative and social and commercial – in that order of importance – centre for the members of his trek, and of the treks that were coming after them, who would take up vast tracts of farming land, and till the soil, and breed cattle, and dispossess the kaffirs, and exterminate Africa's Midas-wealth of fauna, and become poor whites.

Compare with the more astringent draft here, in Section 4 of Chapter 5.

As the above extract makes plain, and as the Texas papers confirm, Bosman also had it in mind to be writing a rather American type of work – tongue-in-cheek epic-pioneer in style, hardboiled in outlook, and above all with a recognisable atmosphere (*Willemsdorp* is like Sherwood Anderson's *Winesburg, Ohio*, has the grit of *Tobacco Road* and the William Faulkner of *Light in August* is an influence). Glaring examples of this American bent, retained in Version A, are the use of "sidewalk" for "pavement", "negro" for "black" (and a host of other pejoratives). References to the United States, and comparisons with it, abounded in Version B and are still traceable in Version A. Compared with other deeply local Bosman works, this one is conspicuously international: no glossary is called for here, as the few Afrikaans, South African English, Sotho and Zulu words used are explained in the text.

In 1949 when Bosman commenced work on his *Willemsdorp* project, Alan Paton had recently made a passing but complimentary reference to *Mafeking Road* in the *New York Times Book Review*, prompting a talent-scout at Harper and Bros. to attempt to headhunt the obscure South African. This was in May that year; by September Bosman had found a New York literary agent and *Willemsdorp* was to be their opening attempt to crack the American market. But Bosman was a slow worker; his unexpected death meant his papers were left in disarray. . . Only a decade later, when his reputation was at an all-time low, would the work reach the States at all, and then only in an unsorted condition. (Mawson did not complete her cataloguing until 1975.)

During the two-year period that Bosman worked on his 'American novel', he was also a sub-editor at Johannesburg's *Sunday Express*, so that it is fair to expect impeccable precision in the typescript; manual typewriter work, carefully corrected by hand. There are precious few mistakes.

On only one crucial matter had Bosman not finally made up his mind (in this respect, the text gives mixed signals): does the summer of the action take place just after the 1948 National Party (read: Volksparty) election victory that was to bring in the apartheid period, or indeed *just before* it? A decision one way or the other had to be taken, involving the deletion of no more than a dozen words either way. Now the Willemsdorp community is on the cusp, poised; here its by-election foreshadows what inevitably is to come.

My gratitude to the director of the Harry Ransom Humanities Research Center for allowing me access to its collection, and for the attached Andrew W. Mellon Foundation fellowship which assisted me in completing the editing.

Stephen Gray
Johannesburg, 1998

Chapter One

1

WILLEMSDORP, a small town in the Northern Transvaal, is almost a hundred years old. Its character is bleak, in that the town itself is situated on the furthest edge of the Highveld, on the northern brink of a plateau that stretches south and west for a thousand miles. Just beyond Willemsdorp is the beginning of that great escarpment at the foot of which is the semitropical bush country that reaches to beyond the Limpopo River, where the Transvaal ends and Rhodesia begins.

The Willemsdorp area is grass country. The summers are hot and the winters cold with heavy frosts. Changes in temperature, summer and winter, are sudden and fierce. The winter months are rainless. Only to the eye of the Transvaaler is the landscape not monotonous. Great tawny waves of veld reaching away on every side interminably, with clumps of rocks taking the place of trees, and with empty, immense silences substituting for human habitation.

Even today, when it is a two or three day journey by rail away, the Cape seems pretty remote from Willemsdorp. A hundred years ago, when there were no roads and the Boer's only means of transport was the ox-wagon, the Cape must have seemed at the other end of the earth. Yet even then there were those among the Boer leaders who felt that they had not trekked far enough. They must go still further northward, dragging with long teams of oxen their cumbrous kakebeen wagons through endless grass plains and over rugged mountains in order to get away from the rule of the English.

But the majority of the Boers was content to remain in the area between the Orange and Limpopo Rivers. They set up the Orange Free State and Transvaal Republics there where they believed that the might of the British Empire could not reach them. Afterwards they realised that the old leaders had been right when they said that the trek should have continued a thousand miles further. But by that time it was too late. For by then Cecil Rhodes had annexed to the Crown of England the territories north of the Limpopo, hemming in the Boer republics, with the result that the Boers could trek onwards away from the Cape no more. Instead, they had to stand and fight. Twice the Boer nation with a total population of less than a quarter million souls fought the British Empire, which was then at the zenith of its greatness. In the first war, 1880-81, the Transvaal Republic beat the British Empire. The second war, that lasted from 1899 to 1902, brought about the end of the independence of the two Boer republics.

Today, to the descendants of those Boers, the tremendous yellow vlaktes of the Highveld are more than stretches of soil to grow mealies on. They are the scenes where old commandos rode. Memories of vanished freedom die hard. And in each small town there is a Boer War cemetery: women and children of the concentration camps lie there. Time does not heal all wounds.

Three hundred years ago the Hollanders found a settlement at the Cape. They did it to help trade – trade with India. The riches of the East came to Europe in the holds of the sailing-ships of the Dutch East India Company. There was no Suez Canal, so it was a long voyage. The Dutch East India Company landed a number of officials and colonists at the Cape to start a halfway station between Europe and Asia. They wanted a place where they could provision their ships. Scurvy took a heavy toll of passengers and crew in those days. A few years later French Huguenots, refugees from France following the Revocation of the Edict of Nantes, came and joined the Hollander colonists at the Cape. A hundred and fifty years later, during the Napoleonic wars, the English sent a fleet to capture the Cape. The Hollander forces did not put up much of a resistance.

The English rulers were soon to discover what the Hollander rulers had already come to suspect – and were unhappy about; namely, that the colonists at the Cape had been welded into that homogeneous entity that constitutes a new nation. They were not Hollanders; they were Boers. They had developed a language of their own. Their outlook was different from that of the Europeans. Although living among the negroid peoples of Africa they had remained white. They had a spirit of sturdy independence and their own way of doing things. In many respects primitive, they could nearly all of them read and write. They were strongly attached to the Bible and their church. They were potential schizophrenics through generations of trying to adapt the rigid tenets of their Calvinistic creed to the spacious demands made by life on the African veld.

And they didn't want to be Anglicised. They resisted inducements. The appeal to them to become Britishers fell on deaf ears. A few yielded. The bulk chose to remain Boers.

The star of the British Empire now gleams, alas, less brightly than it did at the turn of the twentieth century. And there are regular air services between Cape Town and Johannesburg and the capitals of Western Europe. Trucks and cars speed on asphalt roads over vlaktes where once the ox-wagon was the only means of transport. On the Magersfontein battlefield the British Tommies' empty bully-beef tins are replaced by the assorted litter of picnickers from the city. The little Zulu herdboy, squatting by the mountain stream of one of his native Ubombo hills, pulls from the inside of his shirt an American comic to while away the blue and yellow tedium of an African summer's day. On a Karoo sheep-farm a grim-faced Boer tunes in his wireless at 6.30 p.m. for the stock exchange report: as he listens to the figures he grows noticeably more sullen-visaged.

But through it all there is still the tawny grass of the Highveld. And there is Willemsdorp, a small town in the Northern Transvaal, almost a hundred years old. It is bleak in character.

2

In the printing works of the *Northern Transvaal News* one Jones, the compositor, was ready to lock up. Quite soon, now, the old-fashioned bedrock cylinder would be set in motion and would run off, stopping occasionally for minor adjustments and inking, the whole edition of the *News*. The cylinder would go bumpety-bumpety-bump-bump (but not quite so fast) 2 738 times, not counting spoils.

The language medium of the *Northern Transvaal News* was English. The paper was published twice a week and had been in existence for over a quarter of a century and boasted of being the most influential newspaper in the Transvaal outside of the Johannesburg and Pretoria dailies. Upwards of twenty-seven bi-weeklies in small Transvaal towns made the same boast. But nobody worried about that much. Noticeably unimpressed in this regard were executives holding key posts with national advertising contractors. The *Northern Transvaal News* was on no account to be confused with *Die Noordelike Transvaal Nuus*, a bi-weekly newspaper published in the Afrikaans language and claiming to be the most influential Transvaal organ of public opinion outside of the

Johannesburg and Pretoria dailies. The *News* was conducted in the interests of the Union Party, which drew its support from the English-speaking section and from Boers with an English orientation. *Die Nuus* was the vehicle of the Volksparty, with an almost exclusively Boer membership.

Jones the compositor was, as always, disgruntled. He was tall, skinny and elderly. One thing he didn't like was editors. Another thing he was resentful of was a banner headline, which involved a quite unnecessary amount of hand-setting. He was also antipathetic towards sub-editors, bartenders, women, linotype operators, Frenchmen, police constables, negroes that pulled rickshaws, Iceland poppies, lead type and the kind of pale sunlight that came in through the window of his boarding-house room on mornings when he had to get up for work. Nobody seemed to know his Christian name. To everybody he was either Jones or, more familiarly, Jonesey. He was unmarried.

"Looks like this new editor is going to start buggering around with the layouts," Jones observed to Sid Fisher, the linotype operator who had got up from behind his machine and, his day's work done, was performing sundry sketchy ablutions in front of a paraffin tin that he had filled at the tap.

"Well, he's entitled to, ain't he?" Sid Fisher enquired. "It's his job, ain't it?" Sid Fisher's voice held neither warmth nor interest. He was thinking mainly of his girl, whom he would be meeting in half an hour – hence the toilet. In any case, he was making merely his stock reply to what was Jones's habitual manner of talking about new editors. (The members of the works department of the *Northern Transvaal News* held their jobs longer than editors did.)

"His job, my arse," Jones replied. "Who does he think is going to set those five-column heads every week?"

"You," Sid Fisher replied mildly, through a thin layer of soapsuds.

"It's all the riff-raff we get here," Jones continued. "Broken-down journalists that can't get jobs in Johannesburg coming here as editors. Drink's his trouble, I suppose. Drink *and* incompetence. And going by his name I should say he's a bloody Dutchman, too. I got no time for that sort. I don't trust them. A Boer working on an English newspaper. There's too much of that. And that woman on the woman's page, too. Lena, somebody. She's another one. Here" – to an apprentice – "take this page proof through to that Mr Hendricks, and tell him it's the last he'll get. I'm not going to pull any more."

In the front office Charlie Hendricks, the new editor, looked across his desk at Lena Cordier, slim, dark-haired, in her early thirties. "Have you been doing the woman's page long?" he asked her.

"Two years," Lena Cordier answered. "I was a schoolteacher here, before."

Her voice was low and smooth. Charlie Hendricks liked the sound of it. It was a dark voice that went well with her hair.

"Is this your only experience of journalism?" Charlie Hendricks asked, his tone faintly patronising.

Lena Cordier nodded.

Charlie Hendricks smiled. It was a particular kind of smile and produced with set purpose. Charlie Hendricks's intention was that Lena Cordier should ask him how long he had been in journalism, thereby giving him a chance to expand. But Lena didn't ask.

Charlie Hendricks went on looking at her – studying her. She was decidedly not unattractive, he thought. A bit thin, perhaps. But that was how he liked them. Long features in a woman appealed to him. He looked at her left hand. No. No engagement ring. And there was a stillness about her – a calm.

"By the way, Miss Cordier," Charlie Hendricks said. "The paper is nearly finished – nearly going to bed, as we say. You've heard that expression? Yes? Well, there's only that last page. Anyway, I've been thinking. There are lots of points that you can still put me wise on. About the people here, and things like that. How about having tea with me when we knock off – in that café across the way?"

Lena said she wasn't free.

"Tomorrow afternoon, then?" Charlie Hendricks asked.

"Yes, very well, Mr Hendricks," she answered, "and thank you. Oh, here's the apprentice with the last page."

Charlie Hendricks took one look at the damp sheet and said he was damned. "Fetch me the layout," he said.

The apprentice withdrew, sullen. If the editor was going to start monkeying about with the last page they'd be late.

Why couldn't she go out with him this afternoon? – Charlie Hendricks wondered. Must be some fellow taking her out. Well, Lena Cordier was attractive enough, he thought. Although he didn't think she would be quite the type to make a big hit in a country town like Willemsdorp, where the men liked their women buxom. But because she wouldn't go and have tea with him he felt piqued.

"What do you think of this, Miss Cordier?" Charlie Hendricks asked when the apprentice had returned the layout. "How's this for cheek? After all the trouble I've taken with the layout, the compositor quietly goes and follows his own ideas. Just because he won't do hand-setting. I know this sort of workman. Can't get a job on a Joburg paper and comes along here. Drinks as likely as not. But just look at it. Who does he think is going to mark all the corrections on this proof?"

Mildly, Lena Cordier told him.

3

The Willemsdorp Town Hall was reasonably full. So was the speaker, Robert E. Constable, the Union Party by-election candidate for the Provincial Council vacancy. But Robert E. Constable was at his best when he was slightly full. He hadn't downed enough whiskies to give him a black-out on the platform. At the same time he had had more than the two or three that you normally have to get yourself mellow. Everything considered, Robert E. Constable was putting up a very good fight for the seat. For he had so much against him. In the first place, Willemsdorp was a predominantly backveld seat, the English-speaking town-dwellers combined with the small pro-English Boer element not being numerically strong enough to counterbalance the practically solid Volksparty vote of the platteland Boers. Another disadvantage under which Robert E. Constable laboured was the fact of his not being bilingual. He couldn't speak Afrikaans. In private, of course, he was proud of this circumstance, regarding his inability to speak a word of the Boer language as a positive social and intellectual accomplishment. But what might have passed as an asset in private life was a distinct drawback on the political platform. Another thing, he wasn't a local man. His nomination for the Willemsdorp vacancy was accomplished through string-pulling at the Pretoria headquarters of the Union Party. In consequence a good few loyal Union Party supporters in Willemsdorp who had themselves hoped to receive the nomination were, understandably, sore.

But the biggest obstacle in the way of a victory at the polls for Robert E. Constable was the Union Party's new Native and Indian policy. How the Union Party expected to get away with a liberalistic policy like that was a mystery. It was even stated in some quarters that the new policy was actually propounded by a pro-Boer element that had smuggled itself into the ranks of the Union Party for the purpose of undermining the party from within. Well, that was quite possible. The English-speaking section of the South African nation had long ago come to the conclusion that there were no limits to the low cunning of the Boer.

Yet, in spite of the obvious weaknesses in his position, Robert E. Constable put up a surprisingly good show. His platform manner was all the more impressive for being slightly aloof. A lot of people were heartily sick of that spirit of cheek by jowl *neighbourliness* that South African politicians were wont, of late, to seek to infuse into their public utterances. And it was of little moment that his glibness of speech was in considerable measure attributable to the quantity of raw spirits he had consumed. For nobody in the audience was sitting near enough to the platform to be able to smell his breath.

The first part of the meeting went off successfully. It was only at question time that Robert E. Constable began to wonder, in all seriousness, whether there was not a measure of truth in that ugly story that the new Native and Indian policy had been foisted on to the Union Party by Boers who had smuggled themselves into the party – sneaking in undetected, no doubt, by cultivating cavalry moustaches and smoking fat imported cigars.

Nearly all the prominent professional and business people of Willemsdorp were in the Town Hall to hear Robert E. Constable. Boer representation in the professions was meagre, in commerce just about non-existent. In the front rows there was, in spite of the heat, a fair sprinkling of furs. And the display of jewellery was on a scale that would have done credit to any Transvaal small town. For with the high prices for farm produce and the upsurge of activity in base metal mining Willemsdorp was experiencing prosperous times.

On the whole it was an audience of satisfied-looking people. It was a group of men and women that exuded, subtly, an air of well-being. You could sense a certain degree of poise about them and, almost, breeding.

It was only the occupants of the back row that did not fit too happily into the Union Party audience pattern. At question time it became clear why.

They were young men. They were not well-dressed, a couple of them even sporting open-necked shirts. They were conspicuously lacking in aplomb. The English they spoke was what they had learnt in school up to standard six. They were young Boers, supporters of the Volksparty, and they had come to heckle. A youth in a faded blazer put the first question.

"Are youse Union Party going to give niggers the vote?" he asked.

"Only the civilised nigg- that is to say, civilised Natives," Robert E. Constable replied.

The young men in the back row laughed derisively. "There isn't no such thing," Faded Blazer shouted.

The next question was put by one of Faded Blazer's colleagues, a fat young man in a soiled shirt.

"Is youse Union Party going to give coolies the vote?" Soiled Shirt enquired.

"Only," Robert E. Constable replied, "civilised cool- that is to say, civilised Indians."

More derisive laughter from the back row. Above the laughter Soiled Shirt called out: "There isn't no such thing as a civilised coolie."

It was Faded Blazer's turn again to put a question. And it was clear that Faded Blazer's bent did not lie in the direction of originality. "Is youse Union Party," he demanded, "going to give the vote to Bushmen?"

At this question pandemonium broke loose in the back row. Robert E. Constable's reply was inaudible. Half a dozen of the hecklers were on their feet, prancing up and down and yelling for the police. One of them rolled up his sleeves and, in between also yelling for the police, was offering to fight. The strong-arm men employed by the Union Party to keep order in the hall made short work of ejecting the hecklers.

"Come on now, you kêrels," the leader of the strong-arm men said to Faded Blazer and Soiled Shirt, speaking to them in Afrikaans, "you know we're with you. But we're getting a quid each from the Union Party bastards to keep order at their meeting. Go out quietly and we'll be with you in the bar just now. They're just going to sing their bloody 'God Save the King' and then it will be all over. Come along now, Old Bul."

The occupants of the back row left quietly.

And those members of the audience who did not understand the

Boer language were suitably impressed. It was comforting to think that the Union Party had as stewards determined men who would brook no nonsense from hooligans.

4

Johannes Erasmus, principal of the Willemsdorp Afrikaans-medium primary school, came out of the Royal Café, accompanied by his wife, Malie. Johannes Erasmus was middle-aged and inclined to corpulence. He had a bull neck and a round face and his hair was getting thin on top. His body looked as though it had been carved out of a solid wooden block, in simple planes, not unlike the primitive images turned out by Native wood carvers along the Zambesi who employed a chopping technique and worked almost in complete darkness. Physically, Johannes Erasmus was not different from the general run of prosperous Boer farmers – a heavy body set on round, sturdy legs. It seemed, in general, to be the other kind of Boer farmer, the unsuccessful kind, the man who as likely as not worked for an employer as a bywoner, who had a long, rangy frame. It seemed to be the leptosome type of Boer that predominated in the drift to the cities, not in order to improve his prospects but to look for work as a miner or unskilled labourer because he had got played out on the platteland.

Johannes Erasmus's wife, Malie, was a good deal younger than her husband. She was pretty with a conventional prettiness. Her hair was dark, her face oval, her lips red.

The sidewalk along which they walked was for the main part unflagged. Most of the single and double-storeyed buildings in Kotze Street, the town's chief thoroughfare, had verandas in front supported by ornamental wrought-iron posts that had been erected in some time long past when iron was still cheap. Johannes and his wife crossed the road in the direction of the Town Hall and saw the motor cars lining the gutters. You didn't have such long rows of parked cars around the Town Hall when the Volksparty held a meeting, Johannes Erasmus reflected. Nor such a swanky class of car. It was obvious where the money was – with the English-speaking Union Party. Johannes Erasmus's sympathies were with the Volksparty. A Boer, he believed that his first loyalty should be towards his own nation. At the same time, in his position, Johannes Erasmus did not consider it advisable to display his political feelings too openly. There was that time during the last war when the Union Party had known years of power. He still remembered his visit to Pretoria, then. It was just about impossible for him to get any favours from the Education Department. Even his old friend, Toons Ferreira, with whom he had in the past more than once pledged the memory of the late President Kruger in brandy – even Toons Ferreira had been scared to do anything for him.

And so, because he was a Boer, Johannes Erasmus would naturally enough not attend a meeting of the Union Party. At the same time, he felt it advisable to keep away, also, from political meetings addressed by Dap van Zyl, the Volksparty candidate for the Willemsdorp Provincial Council seat that the by-election was all about.

Under a street lamp a number of coloured children, ragged, exactly half-white and half-negro, were playing a barbarous form of postman's knock that included kicks and occasional peltings with what looked like cowdung.

"That's through having had that RAF camp here during the war," Johannes Erasmus observed to his wife, Malie, a note of bitterness creeping into his voice. "You can see they're first generation bastards. Raw kaffir and white. They're not like the Cape Coloureds that have been half-castes for hundreds of years."

"I wonder what's going to happen to them when they grow up," Malie mused. "No place for them. They'll all turn out criminals, I suppose."

"The English air force – " Johannes started again.

"We had some half-castes before the English air force came, though," Malie replied.

"The RAF just lived in the locations," Johannes Erasmus continued, ignoring his wife's remark. "And now they've gone back to England it's we who are saddled with this burden. As though we haven't got enough colour problems as it is."

"Well, I don't know, Johannes," Malie said, "but if the Boer girls in Willemsdorp had been a little more friendly to the English soldiers – but they couldn't, though, could they now? I mean, you know some of the things that our people did to Boer girls that associated with RAFs. And remember what the minister said about girls like that, too, in church almost every Sunday."

"Huh, what's that?" Johannes Erasmus demanded. "Would you have wanted the RAF men to have slept with our own white girls instead?"

Malie bridled. "I didn't mean anything low," she said. "I mean, our girls could have been just friendly. They seemed quite nice young men to me, too, some of them. I am sure that they – the nicer ones, of course – wouldn't have anything to do with kaffir women."

Johannes Erasmus did not answer. There was that thing gnawing inside him again. He was middle-aged and he was conscious of it. His wife was still young. There was a lot of red, quick life yet left in her body. At all kinds of unexpected moments he had a sudden sensing of passions smouldering inside her. And it rankled, now, that Malie could think of an RAF as a young man, as a male, and not as somebody in a blue English uniform. In a foreign uniform. And Malie was his wife.

They walked on past the parked cars. The screams of the coloured children grew fainter in the distance. The short strip of paving had given way to the sandy and uneven sidewalk that would eventually lose itself in the stubby grass of the open veld. They drew abreast of the government buildings, a long, low, rambling structure dating back to republican times. In the night air was the heavy scent of pepper-trees. The sky was thickly sown with stars.

Johannes Erasmus's thoughts were centred on the little Western Transvaal farmhouse where he was born and where he had spent his childhood. He thought of his parents and brother. There was the kaffir-path that he and his younger brother had walked along every afternoon back from the farm school. He was a good few years older than his brother. And in other ways, that were more than years, he was still older. Funny that he should be thinking back to those times, now, Johannes Erasmus thought.

In the dark he put his arm around Malie's shoulder and drew her closer to him as they walked.

Chapter Two

1

THE Union Party meeting in the Town Hall was over. Robert E. Constable had said a few final words after the young Boer hecklers had been expelled from the hall. Those few final words had been in the nature of a peroration extolling the future of the Union of South Africa, Robert E. Constable holding the view that, small though its white population was at the moment, South Africa would yet, by virtue of its unlimited resources, develop into a mighty country that would rival America in point of splendour and magnificence.

The audience had filed out of the hall. In the street was the noise of cars being started up. Here and there some people hung about in small knots in the shadow of the Town Hall's jacarandas.

Charlie Hendricks, who had been to report the meeting, recognised some of the members of one group. He had been in Willemsdorp long enough to have been introduced to most of the town's most prominent citizens, who were nearly all Union Party people. But he could not yet relate all names to faces. Anyway, there was Jack Brummer that he knew. Jack Brummer was pretty young to be occupying the comparatively important position of mining commissioner – important because of the quite considerable activity in base minerals in the Willemsdorp area at the moment. What Charlie Hendricks was not aware of, just then, was that Jack Brummer owed his rapid advancement in the Mines Department in no small measure to his prowess on the rugby field. You could see that in his build, of course. And in the glint in his eye. And in the way he walked. Jack Brummer had never got as far as wearing a Springbok jersey, but he had several times played for the province. It was only natural, therefore, that he should have got appointed mining commissioner at an age where most of his contemporaries with only academic qualifications should still be Grade II clerks.

"Oh hello, Hendricks," Jack Brummer said, "meet Cyril Stein. He's the school-board secretary, you know. And this is Mrs Clark – "

"I have already met Mr Hendricks," a plump, matronly woman said. "He was going to stay at my boarding-house, but he got fixed up with that flat at the last moment."

24

"Oh well, you don't know what you missed then, Hendricks," Jack Brummer continued. "I stayed there, once. The best roast lamb and tomato bredie in the country. And her daughter, Mavis. Now, that's something you've missed. Pity I'm her boss. You know, Mrs Clark, if your daughter wasn't working in my office, well, you just don't *know* – "

Jack Brummer ended with a boisterous laugh. What he had just said was a good example of footballer's wit, and he knew it and was proud of it. His hearty manner of laughing was infectious, however, and the rest of the little group joined in. Among them Charlie Hendricks recognised Hershberg, the local chemist, and Louis Bayfield, the attorney.

"What did you think of the meeting?" Mrs Clark asked of Jack Brummer. Then she added, on second thoughts, "But, of course, you wouldn't have been there. Not with you being a fascist, and all."

Jack Brummer laughed again. "No, I was just passing this way," he said. "You know –" turning to Charlie Hendricks – "Mrs Clark is chairwoman of the women's section of the Union Party branch and everybody that doesn't agree with the Union Party she calls a fascist. But it's lucky for you you're a Union Party man – I mean, you're editing their paper. Because otherwise she'd be calling you a fascist also."

Jack Brummer laughed again, heartily, as though he had said something excruciatingly funny. And out of homage to his rugby record – and because a bluff and muscular fellowship goes over, anyway – the little group under the jacarandas joined in the laughter once more.

Everybody started going home, soon after. Charlie Hendricks, before going to bed, had to get back to the *News* office to type out the report of the meeting. It was an important event in the by-election campaign and he had already decided to give Robert E. Constable's speech four columns. And he found Cyril Stein, the secretary of the schoolboard, had apparently elected to walk down the main street for some distance with him.

There was something about Cyril Stein's appearance with which Charlie Hendricks found himself intrigued. Cyril Stein was youngish. He was below medium height and slenderly built. He had an abundance of black hair that had the habit of tumbling forward over his face. He wore a double-breasted blue suit with trousers that, through their unusual width and length, partly concealed his shoes. A gaily patterned scarf trailed over his back.

"Aren't you going this way?" Cyril Stein asked when they reached the corner and Charlie Hendricks continued straight along. "You know, this is the road to our building. I've got the flat next to you – just across from the landing."

"Oh, so that's where I've seen you before," Charlie Hendricks remarked. "In a new town it takes a while to place people. But I can't go back to the flat just now. No such luck. I've got all this" – tapping his notebook – "to put into shape at the office."

"In that case I might as well walk down some distance with you," Cyril Stein replied. "I've got bugger all else to do. How do you find you fit into Willemsdorp? But I suppose everybody else has asked you that question before now."

Charlie Hendricks reflected for a few moments, as they continued on their way.

"Well, it's a town," he said at length. "Like any other kind of town, I expect. Of course, I know Joburg better. But this isn't the first Transvaal town I've been in. I know Klerksdorp quite well, for instance."

It was Cyril Stein's turn to be silent.

"You know, I've been here quite a few years," he said eventually. "I'm school-board secretary. I've got the job through my uncle, who's quite a big noise in the Education Department. But I don't think I've really adapted myself to this place, and I don't think I ever shall. Take my name, now – Stein. It's not really Jewish, you know. As a matter of fact, I think it's just another way of spelling Steyn. The last president of the Orange Free State Republic had the same name. And he was a Boer, all right. Wasn't he, now?"

"Well, of course, yes," Charlie Hendricks replied mechanically. He was puzzled.

Some moments passed before Cyril Stein spoke again. "You haven't got any anti-Semitic prejudices, have you?" he asked.

"Well, no, not that I know of," Charlie Hendricks answered.

"That's what I thought," Cyril Stein said, a note almost of ardour coming into his voice. "I felt that about you, somehow. That's where you're different from just about everybody in Willemsdorp – Boer, Englishman or black man. As a matter of fact, I sometimes think that I must be pretty anti-Semitic myself. Otherwise I wouldn't be so upset at the thought that my name sounds sort of half-Jewish."

"Anyway, what's in a name," Charlie Hendricks answered. He wasn't really interested in the line of conversation that the young man with the black hair had seen fit to introduce. At the same time, he was not as surprised as he might have been at the way in which a complete stranger was laying bare his soul to him. Good Lord, Johannesburg was full of neurotics. He hoped Cyril Stein was not going to be a bore. A pity he should be that way, Charlie Hendricks thought. For there was something out of the ordinary in his appearance. . . something artistic in a town where everybody was cut more or less to the same pattern of conventionality. But if he was just mentally unbalanced – well, Joburg was full of *that* sort.

Cyril Stein seemed to sense what Charlie Hendricks was thinking. "I know you think I'm making a fool of myself, talking to you like this when I don't even know you," he said. "But I just felt I had to say it. There were other things that I wanted to say much more. But that thing just came to the top without my being able to do anything about it. Anyway, this is where I turn off."

"No," Charlie Hendricks said. "I don't think you're making a fool of yourself."

"Anyway, you'll find that there's more in this town than you think," Cyril Stein said as he walked away. "There are undercurrents that you don't know of yet."

The scent of pepper-trees, wafted by a sudden breeze from the direction of the government buildings, lay heavy on the night air.

2

Later that same night – a good while after he had bidden farewell to that little gathering assembled in the shadows in front of the Willemsdorp Town Hall – Jack Brummer, mining commissioner and one-time rugby star, was once more making preparations to take his leave. He had got as far as the door of the bedroom, his shoes in his hand, and he was getting ready to open the door as noiselessly as he knew how, before sallying out on tiptoe down the first floor corridor of Hex Buildings. The girl in the bed admonished him, in tones raised scarcely above a whisper, to for heaven's sake proceed quietly.

This was a nightly feature in the lives of the occupants of the rooms with doors opening on to the passage of Hex Buildings' first floor – the ground floor being taken up by business offices.

Or an almost nightly feature. "All right," Jack Brummer responded, "*all* right."

Neither he nor the girl in the bed was aware that each one of the girl's neighbours knew to the minute each occasion on which Jack Brummer took his departure. For the wooden floors were creaky and worn. And Jack Brummer's walking on tiptoe and carrying his shoes under his arm didn't help much. More than one neighbour, awakening from slumber, would reach for matches and light a cigarette. More than one neighbour, likewise aroused from dreaming, would mutter in nasty tones, "I got to have my eight hours."

Outside the night was vast and star-apparelled. It was a sweet night, grand with old witcheries.

In the corridor of Hex Buildings a weak electric light bulb gleamed on dun-coloured walls and on a brown, uncarpeted floor, the boards of which had for years been innocent of polish. The electric light shone on a man of athletic proportions who was proceeding down the passage with deliberate – and what he guilelessly imagined to be noiseless – steps. Tonight Jack Brummer was observing more care than ever. It was almost as though the fears which the girl in the bed had confided to him made him feel that he had to exercise additional care in his nocturnal perambulation. It did not seem to occur to him that, if what the girl in the bed surmised was correct, then it was somewhat late to start taking precautions. They should have been careful before. Last month, some time, maybe.

Outside was a great quiet. To the day-worn southern hemisphere the hours of darkness had brought the gift of a decorated oblivion – a forgetfulness ornamented with a rich pageantry of dreams.

What Jack Brummer felt, mostly, was fear. What if she was going to start making trouble, he thought to himself. What the hell did women have to be there for? They were all alike. He was scared, all right. And even though he told himself that it was an unreasoning fear, he also knew well enough that that made no difference. He knew that all fears were like that. But what he felt, also, was a lot of disgust. To think that there might be all this trouble, now – and just for *that*. But it wouldn't do to think of *that* – no, it would just make him feel more sick. A girl looked so different when she had clothes on, and when her face was made up, and she was pretty and she smiled. Well, it was easy for a girl to lead a man on, when she was all dressed up, Jack Brummer said to himself. And then what she led him on for, was for *that*, although, of course, all the time what he wanted to be led on for *was* for that, and if the girl didn't lead him on, well, he would lead *her* on, of course.

28

And there she was lying in bed, now – but Jack Brummer felt that he should rather not think of it; he felt quite bad enough as it was. And what she had just told him now – well, he couldn't go to gaol for it, of course. It was silly to have ideas like that. But he knew that the law did come into it, somehow, if the girl was determined to be nasty about it. But not gaol, of course. That was foolish. But there could be a hell of a lot of trouble in it for him, all the same, especially in a little place like Willemsdorp. And he being mining commissioner, and all. One way out naturally would be for him to marry her. Oh my God, Jack Brummer said to himself, at the thought of that. But then why would she have told him if she didn't want him to marry her?

"All right, all *right*," Jack Brummer called out as the girl once more enjoined him to go quietly. And although his progress down the passage was slow and measured and on tiptoe, yet all the same it sounded as though he was trundling some heavy object made of galvanised iron over the floorboards.

In bed, Lena Cordier wondered whether it was right for her to have told Jack Brummer what her fear was.

3

The report of Robert E. Constable's speech put into shape – a job that took him several hours – Charlie Hendricks locked the door of his office in the *News* building behind him and set off on foot down the road to his flat. After a few blocks the paving ceased. Charlie Hendricks was made aware of this circumstance when he jolted his ankle in a rut on the sidewalk. He paused to curse the Willemsdorp Town Council. After all, the town had been laid out a hundred years ago. During that time something more could have been done about putting down pavements.

That was when he encountered Detective Sergeant Brits, of the local police, whom he had met on several previous occasions when he had visited the police station for crime news.

It seemed to Charlie Hendricks that Detective Sergeant Brits, who was flashing a circle of torchlight on the ground, had also encountered an uneven piece of sidewalk.

"Hello, Brits," Charlie Hendricks called out. "What's wrong with your town council? I nearly sprained my ankle right now. It's about time the works committee did something about the sidewalks."

Detective Sergeant Brits did not reply immediately. Instead, he flashed the torch into Charlie Hendricks's face. "You been working, hey?" he asked.

"Oh sure," Charlie Hendricks responded. "I've been typing out old Constable's speech. Why?"

"Oh, for nothing," the detective answered. "I yust asks. I suppose I can yust asks?"

"Well, of course, ask me anything you like. Fire ahead," Charlie Hendricks replied, sounding surprised. Detective Brits seemed a lot less friendly on the street, at night, than when you interviewed him at the police station in daylight hours.

Detective Sergeant Brits, after flashing the torch into Charlie Hendricks's face for a brief moment, returned his attention to the sidewalk. The beam of amber light travelled backwards and forwards over the sandy surface.

"What are you looking at?" Charlie Hendricks asked. "Anything I can make a story out of for the *News*?"

Detective Sergeant Brits shook his head. "Perhaps some time later," he announced. "But not yust yet. You know, we got instructions from some in the government and bime'by you'll get big news. Now that the Union Party's going to get chucked right out, we going to get instructions to clean up the place."

Charlie Hendricks laughed. "I suppose what you're looking for on the sidewalk are Robert E. Constable's footprints," he said. "Well, you'll find him in his room in the Northern Hotel. He's either asleep or drinking."

Detective Sergeant Brits switched off his torch and stood up straight. "Yus," he said, "I know you thinks you's funny. Very funny. But yust you wait. I got nothing on Robert E. Constable, your Union Party's blooming candidate. And I got nothing on you, see? I don't mind telling you I got nothing on you. But if I does gets something on you – well, we're cleaning up the whole South Africa. It's all right that your Mr Constable is asleep in his hotel room. But it's who he's asleep *with*. Mind you, I got nothing on him, so far. It's the Tielman Roos Act."

In spite of himself, Charlie Hendricks found his interest being aroused. "Tielman Roos's Liquor Act?" he asked. "How are you going to clean that up?"

"The Tielman Roos Liquor Law," Brits said, "we've always got. What sort of a newspaper man is you as you don't know that? No, what

30

we's going to clean up *with* is the Tielman Roos Immorality Act. That's what we've got instructions for. And it's three months for the white man. And it's three months for the nigger woman. Maybe more."

Charlie Hendricks reflected for a few moments. "But it's an old law, now I come to think of it," he said. "Remember that scandal down at the Cape some years ago, when a Senator got arrested for having immoral relations with a Coloured woman? Phew, that was a scandal, all right. I mean, even though he got acquitted – God, remember what a stink that was?"

"Yus, he got acquitted," the detective acknowledged ruefully. "It's not too blooming easy to get a conviction. You got to get them dead to rights. You got to get them *doing* it. That's what's so hard. But even if the white man gets acquitted, it's still, like you say, a awful disgrace."

"I don't see what you're getting at, though," Charlie Hendricks said. "I mean, it's been the law for years, hasn't it?"

"The law, yes," Brits replied. "The law is *there*. But for a long time we didn't pinch nobody under it. Not since the last war. It was all them RAFs and Poles and other foreign soldiers coming into the country. You couldn't keeps them out of the kaffir locations. And especially them sailors, too, neither. And so we got orders to go a bit slow. Because otherwise where would the war be, hey? I mean, who would be doing the fighting, hey, with all the Allied soldiers and sailors locked up in gaol in South Africa, doing time, hey? But there is one thing as I must say. And as a Boer I am sorry I has to say it. There has been South Africans as has took advantage."

"Took advantage?" Charlie Hendricks repeated.

"Yus," Detective Sergeant Brits continued. "Because we couldn't really go and put a South African in gaol for doing a thing as we wouldn't put, say, a lousy Portuguese in gaol for, for doing the same thing, see? And so there has been South Africans as has took advantage. But all them things is going to be cleaned up now, when we get the new government."

"Is that what you're flashing your torch over the sidewalk for?" Charlie Hendricks asked. "But, surely, if a white man wanted to go with a nigger woman he wouldn't do it so openly. Not here, on the sidewalk, I mean. He surely wouldn't take all that advantage, just through the police letting up with their enforcement of the Tielman Roos Act for a little while. I mean, no white man would be so degraded. Not even a white man that's so low that he smokes dagga, even."

"Oh no, I don't mean as a white man would go and lie down here with a nigger woman in the middle of the sidewalk," Detective Sergeant Brits replied. "Not as it wouldn't make it a lot easier for us if they did, mind you. But they's too blooming cunning for that. All the same, let me tell you as I suspects that there's more than one nigger woman right here in this town as is in the habit of sleeping with white men. Mind you, no names, nothing. I doesn't know anything for sure. It's only what I suspects, see? And what you only suspects doesn't count for nothing under the law. We got to get them dead to rights."

Charlie Hendricks remarked that that was only fair, no matter how low a white man was.

"Take a look at that, now," the detective said, flashing his torch slowly over the sidewalk again. "But I still got to find out who the man is."

"Man?" Charlie Hendricks repeated, since the travelling beam of light exposed to his view nothing more than a sandy stretch of ground interspersed with small stones.

"Yus, it's a white man, I'm sure," Brits said. "Walking there with that kaffir woman, side by side. The nigger woman's footprints I'll know anywhere in Africa. She's one of the nigger women in this town as I suspects of sleeping with white men. She's got three pairs of shoes. Don't that give the game away, all right, hey? Why, you can convicts her in court yust on that evidence alone, almost, can't you? Three pair shoes. . . where she gets them from, hey, and she a nigger woman? But I won't tell you who she is, because I'm so far yust suspecting her, see?"

Charlie Hendricks found himself getting impressed. "And the white man you've been talking about?" he asked.

"That's yust it," Brits said. "That shoe there might perhaps not *be* a white man's shoe. You doesn't always know. Although I gets a feeling it's not a kaffir's shoe. I don't mean yus because it's new and it isn't fixed up underneath with a piece of motor car tyre. You got some kaffirs today wearing smart shoes, smarter'n any shoes I got to wear. And you also gets white men with their toes sticking out of their boots. But I been following these feetprints, this kaffir woman's feetprints going by the side of the feetsteps of this man that I don't know. Because I don't know everybody's feetprints in Willemsdorp. There's too many strangers that comes and goes, especially with the elections yust now. But the man with these feetprints hasn't got a kaffir walk. He's got a white man's walk. And he been walking alongside of this kaffir woman what has got three pairs of shoes for not more than half a block. Scared he'd be seen with her, see? And then they been standing talking here, right here, for a bit. Not too long, see? And he made off there by the left, and she go straight on. They must yust have talked about where to meet. And although I can't swear about it, I still say, yus, he don't walk with a nigger walk."

Charlie Hendricks told the detective that he thought he was pretty smart.

"Oh, that's nothing," Brits said. "But if it's real class detective work you want, there's a Bushman I come across in South West. Yust with a copper ring in his nose and no other clothes on. Some day when I got time I'll tell you about that Bushman. And the only civilisation he ever seen was a ostrich egg painted blue by the wife of a missionary as lived in the Kalahari. But that Bushman could track a man down like nobody I ever knowed."

All the same, Brits seemed pretty good himself, Charlie Hendricks reflected after the detective had left. And he wondered what his own footprints in the sand of the Willemsdorp sidewalks must look like to Detective Sergeant Brits.

Another thing that struck Charlie Hendricks was that the town councillors of Willemsdorp must be men with pretty clear consciences. They must all be honourable men whose lives held nothing that they wished to conceal from the police. Otherwise they would have seen to it that the streets of the town got properly paved with cement or concrete.

4

The misty light of dawn crept in at the window. Cyril Stein, who was already awake, shuddered. The birds were singing, welcoming the new day with gladness. For Cyril Stein the new day was more hideous than the night, the first light of dawn more dreadful than the dark. He reached out a trembling hand from underneath the blankets and seized hold of what looked like a half-smoked cigarette wrapped in brown paper, lying in the ashtray. He struck a match. His hand shook so much that the flame went out before it could catch the wood. He struck another match. This time it worked. Cyril Stein started puffing at the half-smoked cigarette.

The Zulu watchboy from a neighbouring block of buildings knocked off work, now that it was dawn. On his way home he passed through a narrow passage between two buildings. The window of Cyril Stein's flat opened on to this passage. Even though Cyril Stein's flat was on the first floor, the fragrance of the greyish smoke that came through the window impinged itself on the nostrils of the Zulu watchman who, because he was from Natal, was a connoisseur in certain matters. He sniffed appreciatively. It was good stuff, that. He wondered who was smoking it. It must be the Native servant who tidied the flats, the watchman decided. For there would be no other Native in the building at that hour. And, of course, no white man smoked that kind of leaf. The Zulu watchman wondered if he could get some from the smoker. "Yes, it is good stuff," the Zulu said to himself, again, breathing deeply. "The best msangu, that which grows by the gate."

Cyril Stein crushed what was left of the brown-paper cigarette into the ashtray. He felt that he wanted to sing as the birds were singing, to greet the overpowering wonder of this dawn.

He shared in the timeless ecstasy of the morning. So gay he was that he wanted to shout.

Chapter Three

1

"I T'S queer you should have talked about it, Malie," Johannes Erasmus, principal of the Willemsdorp Afrikaans-medium Primary School, said to his wife at the breakfast table. He stirred his coffee thoughtfully as he spoke. "Yes, it's a queer thing you should have mentioned it."

"Well, you can see it's going to be another hot day," Malie said, half-absentmindedly putting her hand up to her dark hair and leaning her bosom forward over the table. She looked trim and fresh in spite of the heat which was already at that time of the morning making itself felt. In the new light of morning the difference in age between husband and wife was more marked even than usual. On Malie's prettiness there was a bloom so delicate that it seemed as though it might at any moment fade. And then after that it would not come again. Not since her adolescence had she been so good-looking, her blue eyes so limpid under her dark hair, her features so clear-cut, her lips so full and firm. The bloom on her looks was the last of her youth; when that bloom went, middle age would come upon her suddenly.

"When it's a hot day like this, again, in a town," Malie continued, "you can't help thinking of the people on the farms – what it must mean for them. It isn't as though we were born in a town, you and I. We both come from the platteland. We know what a drought is."

Johannes Erasmus thought steadily for a few moments.

"Yes, you are right, wife," he said after a pause. "I will go and talk for him. But, as I was saying, it's a queer thing that you should have brought it up because I was – "

"There was that work you were talking about the other day," Malie interrupted. "Something about driving a lorry for the Education Department school feeding scheme. It shouldn't be difficult for you to get that work for him. With your influence, that is. You could go and see Cyril Stein about it, couldn't you?"

Johannes Erasmus knew, of course, that the man he would go and interview would be Cyril Stein, the secretary of the school-board. And he had no doubt, either, of the outcome of the interview. Cyril Stein would be glad to do a small thing like that for him. But when Malie spoke about his influence – well, that was a thing that he wasn't happy about, somehow. Johannes Erasmus liked to think and feel that he had influence, that he was an important person, somebody to be reckoned with – not only in educational circles and in Willemsdorp, but in a wider field. And yet, somehow, it always came down to this, that in local affairs he wasn't accorded much standing. Old Bayfield, the solicitor, for instance, carried much more prestige than he did. And it wasn't because of Bayfield's personality or anything else, as far as Johannes Erasmus could see. It was just because he himself wasn't in the know, about things, in the way that he ought to be.

That came out particularly at the Club. One couldn't get away from that, of course. But in their attitude towards him – well, you couldn't get away from it that they regarded him as being *different*, somehow. As though he wasn't a man of the world, in the way that the others were men of the world. They looked on him as somebody cut off from the more manly and important sort of activities, just as though he was no more than a schoolmaster. They didn't seem to understand that for a man to be a principal meant a lot more than just being a schoolteacher. You had to be an organiser, for one thing. And you had to play your cards right. There were all sorts of underground jealousies and intrigues in the Education Department that the average person knew nothing at all about. So, for them to think that, just because he was a school principal, he wasn't at the same time a man of affairs – well, he could tell them a thing or two. But, of course, in his position, he really couldn't talk about how he used to take Toons Ferreira out for drinks in a Pretoria hotel. And of how he got Toons Ferreira to arrange this and that for him – right over the heads of even some of the senior school inspectors. But he couldn't mention that in the Club. Somebody might just go and talk about it to an inspector, and where would he be then?

So, when Malie said, now, that he should go and see the secretary of the local school-board about appointing his nominee to that lorry driver's job, Johannes Erasmus didn't feel too bucked about it. Because that wasn't using influence – approaching somebody ordinary through just the ordinary channels, and not going over somebody else's head about it. Not even going over Cyril Stein's head. It wasn't the way that the men at the Club, who were also men of affairs, did things. For them, nothing was worth doing, unless it meant going over somebody else's head to do it.

Thinking along those lines, Johannes Erasmus did not immediately take in Malie's next words. "Have you noticed that Cyril Stein looks sort of different, lately?" Malie was saying. "A couple of days ago I came across him in Kotze Street and, you know, he had almost walked right past me before he greeted me. But, of course, he was very nice when he started talking. He has got a nice way of talking – don't you think so, too? But it looked as though he was worried about something. And when he lit a cigarette I noticed that his hand shook."

"Well, of course, Stein has always been a bit queer," Johannes Erasmus said. "Ever since he's come here, he's never really seemed to have got the hang of the place. And he got the job through his uncle in Pretoria, of course. But I won't say he's not good at his work. But, of course, Stein is not what you would call a man of affairs, really. That's something he'll never be. He's somebody that's all right for routine. If he's left to do things just through the orthodox, everyday channels, he's quite satisfactory."

Malie looked at her husband in surprise. She couldn't understand his making a long speech like that, just over nothing.

"No, he hasn't got much influence," Johannes Erasmus concluded.

Then he realised that he had only a few minutes left to get into his car and drive to school. "It's queer you should have talked about it, though," Johannes Erasmus said as he finished his coffee and got up from the table, "because I was last night thinking about the same thing. I was thinking about how my brother Krisjan and I used to walk home from school together over the veld when we were children. And I felt that I wanted to do something for him. I was thinking about that only last night. And it's queer that you should be talking about the same thing this morning – talking about my getting Krisjan a job."

2

In the way in which Jack Brummer was proceeding to work that morning there was something distinctly unusual. Jack Brummer had been walking, at a normal pace, for some distance through a grove of peppercorn-trees at the end of which were the government buildings. The Mining Commissioner's office occupied part of one wing of the gov-

37

ernment buildings. And then of a sudden, just after he had fanned himself with his broad-brimmed straw hat, Jack Brummer unaccountably changed his gait. He did that immediately on catching a glimpse of a mauve frock passing along the sidewalk at the other end of the peppercorn-trees.

From the manner in which he acted then it would almost appear as though he were trying to hide away behind some of the gnarled trunks of the peppercorns. And he also started walking on tiptoe. In its essentials, his manner of proceeding down his side of the peppercorns did not differ from his habitual mode of obtaining egress from Hex Buildings when the hour was advanced. He fluttered in and out among the peppercorn-trees, taking care not to make a noise. The only difference between now and last night, when he was going down the corridor of Hex Buildings, lay in the fact that *now* he wasn't carrying his shoes in his hand. Maybe, if it had occurred to him to take his shoes off now, he would have done so.

If one of the tenants of a room in Hex Buildings with a door opening on to the passage had seen Jack Brummer then, among the peppercorns, the tenant would no doubt have come to the conclusion that Jack was practising, trying to perfect his tiptoe.

The girl in the mauve frock crossed the road and came on to the near sidewalk. Jack Brummer stopped dead in his tracks, bringing himself up sideways against the rough but somewhat insubstantial bole of a peppercorn-tree. It then occurred to him that somebody – some person other than the girl in the mauve frock – might be watching him, and that to such a person his actions might seem peculiar. Accordingly, Jack Brummer turned his head in the direction of the treetrunk and peered intently at the black ant, thereby seeking to give the impression that he was engaged in nothing more than a spot of harmless naturalistic study. The ant ascended the bark of the treetrunk along a zigzag route and covered the better part of eighteen inches before Jack Brummer wrenched away his gaze. By that time the girl in the mauve frock had disappeared from view around the corner.

Once more Jack Brummer took off his hat and fanned himself. Phew, it was hot. He wouldn't like to be a full-time entomologist on a day like that.

He greeted his typist, Mavis Clark, in so abrupt a fashion that she was still staring for several minutes at the door of the inner office after her boss had passed through.

It was silly, Jack Brummer said to himself, that he should be worrying his gut out like that. But then, what if Lena Cordier went to court about it, and sued him for maintenance or something of that sort? Of course, he didn't think she was the class of girl to do that kind of thing. But then, you never knew where you were with women. The things they did for spite, too, sometimes – out of malice when a man wouldn't marry them. Women. The feeling the word gave him was one of mingled fear and nausea. He would give anything at that moment never to have had anything to do with a woman – with any woman. They landed you in gaol before you knew where you were.

Of course, it wasn't the same thing in his case. It was just silly even to think of gaol in connection with the spot of bother he had got himself into, now. After all, the worst thing that could happen would be Lena Cordier getting a maintenance order against him in the magistrate's court. Mind you, that would be bad enough. Think of what it would do to his position – his position both in Willemsdorp and in the department. And the worst of it was that a magistrate always took the woman's word for it in such a case. What he needed, Jack Brummer said to himself, was a drink to get his nerves right. He was just being absurd, now, getting ideas about law courts and gaol, and so on. Ha, ha, he was just letting his imagination run away with him. What he must do is just laugh the whole thing off.

That was the moment when Mavis Clark came into his office and announced, "There's a prospector to see you, Mr Brummer."

Jack Brummer turned pale. "I can't see him, Miss Clark," he blurted. "I can't, not now."

Mavis Clark returned to her own office more surprised than ever. She asked the prospector, who had called round to register some corundum claims, would he come round a little later. She was unable to fathom Jack Brummer's perturbation. She did not know that it was because he had, for the moment, thought that she had said there was an inspector to see him. And since he had read a few detective thrillers in his time, he associated the word with police headquarters.

A few minutes later Jack Brummer realised what must have happened. Through the state his nerves were in he had heard wrong. The visitor would almost certainly be old Clinkwood from the Kwaggapeul area. In fact, he had a letter from him in his drawer, somewhere. He rang the bell.

"Miss Clark," he announced when the typist appeared in the doorway, "that man that's just been – you said he's a prospector, didn't you? Yes, I thought you did. When he comes again, show him straight in. As a matter of fact, I've been inspecting a prospector, I mean, prospecting an inspector, that is, I've been inspecting – I mean, *expecting* a prospector to call."

"*Well*," Mavis Clark said to herself when she got back to her own office. Mr Jack Brummer was obviously not himself that morning, she said to herself.

Meanwhile, Jack Brummer had just about the same feelings about himself. He must get away somewhere, if only for a few days – to the Kleinberg area, say, where all the corundum mining was going on. He could send in a report about it, too. It would give him time to think, out there in the bush. He'd get his bearings, there. Yes, he must get away soon. Another couple of days here in Willemsdorp, with his imagination making mountains out of molehills – well, he'd go nuts. He'd really believe that Lena Cordier did have something on him. Whereas, what could she do to him? The worst, Jack Brummer said to himself, was a breach of promise case.

Again he was worrying about the law. Hell, he thought, he really was getting impossibly nervy. A couple of minutes later he was able to prove to himself that he was quite right in his diagnosis. He was able to prove to himself that he was perfectly correct in having thought that his nerves were rotten. For when the door of his office opened again, he jumped almost halfway out of his chair. It is doubtful if the thought that he had been proved right afforded him much satisfaction.

"It's only me," Mavis Clark said, "Mr Brummer."

"But I wish you'd knock," Brummer said testily. "I've asked you before, would you please knock."

"I thought that if I knocked you might get more of a fright," Mavis Clark said. "And I'm worried about you, Mr Brummer, to see you like this."

"Like what?" Jack Brummer started bellowing. Then he took a hold of himself. He did it deliberately and even self-consciously. It was almost as though he got up slowly out of his chair and took a firm grip of himself with both hands.

"I am quite all right, Miss Clark," he said in studiously level tones. "And if I need your assistance in any way, I'll ring."

Mavis Clark was somewhat on the short side. Her face was round and she wore spectacles and she had a lot of colour in her cheeks. Her nose was slightly tiptilted. She was, in a dull way, inclined to be pretty. Jack Brummer remembered the humorous observation (or, at least, what he thought was a humorous observation) that he had made about her to her mother, on the previous evening, when he was talking to that bunch of people that had come away from Robert E. Constable's meeting. It seemed ages ago. That was before Lena Cordier had told him –

"If there's anything I can do to help, please let me know. Anything at all," Mavis Clark said, "Jack."

She blushed at having used his Christian name, and went out quickly.

Another woman, Jack Brummer thought, and groaned. When he was sick of women. When the very thought of a woman lying in bed made him sick. Sick with fear and disgust at the woman. Sick with disgust at himself. Sick with dread. He had to get into the Lowveld for a few days. He had to talk to bushveld farmers. And he had to drink. He had to get the hell out of Willemsdorp for a few days before his nerves ran away with him altogether. Gaol. Thinking of gaol in connection with this business with Lena Cordier. He must be going mad, Jack Brummer said to himself.

He reached for his broad-brimmed straw hat and started fanning himself again.

3

At the other end of the government buildings from Jack Brummer's office was the headquarters of the commissioner of police for the area, Commandant Roelf Kolyn. The heat on that forenoon was intense. While Detective Sergeant Brits reported to the commandant, the commandant sat stroking his chin thoughtfully.

Afterwards the commandant shook his head.

"It's like this, Brits," he said. "We're going to clean up this town. There aren't two ways about it. But we don't want anything sensational. Do you get me? We don't want Willemsdorp to get a bad name. Remember that Cape senator that got arrested some years ago for sleeping with a nigger woman? Well, the village where that happened never heard the end of it. The dirty jokes they made about that village – phew! We don't want that sort of thing to happen here."

Detective Sergeant Brits looked upset.

The commandant, to mollify him, spoke in a friendly tone. "Had your training in South West, didn't you, Brits?" he asked.

Brits nodded.

"Well, we all know you're second to none, when it comes to following a track. When you're on the job and following a trail, and you've just seen one place on the ground where the suspect walked – then that suspect is already as good as wearing red stripes and a number on his jacket. Unless – and I am sorry to have to say it – that suspect goes and bribes somebody higher up. But otherwise, when it's just a straight matter of tracking, no man will ever get away from you."

"Well, I won't say on hard ground, now," Brits replied. "But in sand, or where it's not all just stones or cement, sir – then I *knows* as I'm pretty good."

"But who's saying anything about cement, now?" Commandant Kolyn asked, almost petulantly. "I'm talking just about ordinary tracking. There's never been anybody to touch you at it, I suppose? Not even in South West, that is?"

The commandant knew what was coming. But he wanted to give Brits a show – a chance to talk a little. He didn't want him to leave his office feeling too disappointed. At the same time he wasn't going to have Brits focusing too much attention on local contraventions of the Tielman Roos Immorality Act. You never knew where that sort of thing ended afterwards.

"Of the white men, yes sir, I would say that in South West I was the best," Brits said. "But there was a Bushman there what hadn't any clothes on but a copper ring in his nose that could follow a trail what was without a lie three months old. And we also had a trained baboon there that had just no clothes on at all, and that was also better than me. Not much better, I won't say, mind you. I think he had a better eye for a trail than me. But I could smell a trail better'n that baboon could. Still, I don't think as that trained baboon was much of a credit to the Force, if you understands what I mean, sir. I think that Bushman with the ring in his nose was more of a credit to the Force. The baboon never seemed really as he *wanted* to make use of his great gifts. He would steal brandy out of the canteen and go on the booze for a week, even if we was right in the middle of a big diamond smuggling case. That would makes just no difference to that baboon. And then in the end he goes and steals brandy for himself *and* that Bushman with the ring in his nose. And then it would be just too disgraceful, sir, with the two of them on the drunk together. I remember the time – "

"Yes, you should write an article about it for the *News* some day, Brits," the commandant interrupted him. "Now, what I want to say to you is this. Before you do anything further about getting evidence against these men you suspect of having relations with kaffir women, I want you to go and warn them."

"*Warn* them?" Brits ejaculated. "Do you means as I must *warn* them, sir? But it's hard enough to pinch them dead to rights, sir, as the law stands today, and if I've first got to go and gives them the office as I'm on their tail – well, I'll never get them eating carrot soup in gaol."

The commandant smiled indulgently. "Tell you what you can do, Brits," he said. "That's only if you really get stuck, mind. You can telegraph to South West for that trained baboon to come over and help you. I'll pay his railfare down, first class. And I'll arrange for him to be able to sign cards in the dining saloon for as much booze as he likes."

"You will have your little jokes, sir," Detective Sergeant Brits said. "And if I may say so to you as man to man, sir, I want to tell you as how I likes a man to make his little jokes at the right time, sir. Ha ha, sir."

But all the same the detective didn't look very happy. The commandant noticed that.

"What I mean is," Commandant Kolyn said, "you warn a man. See? All right. You have warned him. *Then*, if he keeps carrying on with kaffir women we'll fix him. That suit you?"

"You mean as how, after I've warned him, I can – ?" Brits asked. "You mean as how I really can – ? You mean that, sir?"

The commandant nodded. They both knew what Brits meant without his having had to use the ugly word 'frame-up.'

"Another thing just before you go," Commandant Kolyn said, "I've been getting a good number of complaints lately about dagga-smoking, in these parts. It's supposed to be not only kaffirs smoking it today, but white men also. Have you come across any cases?"

"White men," Brits repeated, "white men? Not as what I knows of, sir. Kaffirs, of course. I mean, you can't pinch a kaffir as hasn't got a pass on him, as you don't finds he hasn't got dagga in his back pocket. Nellie Pope, they calls it. Or the tree of knowledge, they calls it. Or voëls, they calls it, sir. But that you can never stop, seeing as how it grows wild here, sir. But white men? No sir, I dunno about white men."

"What is dagga supposed to do to you?"

43

"Well, from what I've heard, that is, sir," Brits said, "it is supposed to make you laugh, sir. You loses all sense of time, sir, is what I hears about it. And it also – "

"Ever tried it yourself, Brits?" the commandant enquired genially, as the detective got ready to depart.

Brits laughed. "You will have your little joke, sir," he said. "Ha ha. And the way as I'm laughing now isn't the dagga laugh, sir. Ha ha."

When Detective Sergeant Brits got back into the charge office he did a somewhat strange thing. He took out his notebook and spent some time in drawing up a list of the male white citizens of Willemsdorp. It was not a complete list. He omitted a good number of names – the more elderly males he left out altogether, for instance. But he had decided to carry out the commandant's instructions to the best of his ability. The commandant wanted them warned first. Good enough, Brits would warn them. Whether or not they were carrying on with Native women made no difference to Detective Sergeant Brits in so far as the first part of his job was concerned. He would warn them. Just left and right he would warn them. He would warn them good and solid. And then if he caught a white man in the act of cohabiting with a black woman, that white man would have no comeback. That white man had been warned. He had been warned, that white man, whoever he was.

It did not seem to occur to Brits that he was exceeding, if not the actual letter, then almost certainly the spirit, of his commandant's instructions.

4

"No matter if they were just a number of young hooligans that shouted that out about the Union Party wanting to allow Natives and Indians to vote," Louis Bayfield said to the candidate, Robert E. Constable, "it's an argument that must go with the public. Especially with the platteland public. You'll have to explain that they misunderstood you. To most of the people around here there isn't such a thing as a civilised black man. They just won't accept it."

The Union Party's campaign committee was in session in an upstairs room of the Northern Hotel on the morning after their candidate's meeting in the Town Hall. Robert E. Constable felt satisfied with himself. His supporters agreed, too, that his speech had gone over well. As a platform personality, they said, he was as good as anybody they had had. The trouble was just with this votes for civilised people, they said.

"Of course, there's just this about it," Piet Fourie, Robert E. Constable's election agent, said, "it might make them get so wild at places where you'll be talking, like Ribbokrand and Geelwater and Van Tondersdal, that they'll likely – "

"Hold hard," Robert E. Constable said, "that's something I've been wanting to talk about. Have I got to go and address meetings in those places right out there in the bundu? Can't I just talk here in the Town Hall and invite all those people to my meetings?"

But Mrs Clark – Mavis Clark's mother who, in between running the boarding-house, found a good deal of time for political activities – said that that would never work. The one thing that the public objected to, she said, was a candidate who didn't hold meetings in every section of the constituency.

"Even though they don't vote for you," Mrs Clark said, "they still expect you to come and talk to them."

That provided Piet Fourie with the opening he had been waiting for. Piet Fourie was a Boer, one of those many Boers that the Union Party employed in their organisation, since in the difficult task of wooing the stray Boer vote a raw Englishman would be at too much of a psychological disadvantage.

"What I was saying," Piet Fourie remarked, continuing from where he had been interrupted, "is that at a place like Valschdraai the crowd might get so wild that they'll storm the platform and you'll get hit with a bicycle chain. That would be the best thing that could happen to you – if somebody hit you over the head with a bicycle chain at Valschdraai."

Robert E. Constable looked, understandably, indignant. "What do you mean that that's the best thing that could happen to me, Mr Fourie?" the Union Party candidate asked of his paid political agent. "I mean, on whose side are you? If that is the sort of thing that you would like to see happen to me, well, why don't you go and join the Volksparty and have done with it?"

But the chemist, Hershberg, who was also present at this committee meeting, said that Robert E. Constable should not start getting hasty, now. "Take Valschdraai, for example," he said. "Well, there's a rough mob there. And there's nothing damages the Volksparty more than these bicycle chain incidents. Every time a Union Party candidate gets assaulted in this way, his photograph with the bandages and all gets published in every newspaper in the country – in overseas newspapers too, sometimes, with the stitches in his face showing. And that gives the Volksparty a very bad name. You'd be surprised how many people refuse to vote for the Boer candidate, after that. They feel ashamed of belonging to a party of hooligans. Yes, you'd be surprised what a bad name the Volksparty gets through a thing like that. Through a Union Party candidate getting his ear hit half off with a bicycle chain at Valschdraai."

Strangely enough, Robert E. Constable was not convinced. "But surely the Volksparty has got a bad enough name as it is," he said. "What's more, I'm still going to give it a much worse name just through the things I'm still going to say about the Volksparty from the platform right here in the Town Hall. Why, the Volksparty will be just covered in obloquy by the time I've finished saying what I still intend saying about it. I don't see why I should have to go along to the place – what's it called?"

"Valschdraai," Piet Fourie told him.

"And collect a wallop over the ear from a bicycle chain as well," Robert E. Constable ended up.

But the chemist, Hershberg, insisted that it was not the same thing. "Whatever you said that thing is, that the Volksparty will be covered in, Mr Constable," he explained, "I don't know the word, but I can guess what that word *means*, that you've said. But, anyway, that will be nothing compared with how it will be if you come back from the Valschdraai meeting all covered in bandages. You mightn't think so, but to be covered in bandages is even worse than that thing. I'll bandage you up myself, Mr Constable, for the newspapers, leaving a few of the stitches showing out at the side, too. And that'll get your photo into every newspaper as far as Japan, after I've made a proper job of the bandages."

Nevertheless, Robert E. Constable did not seem to enter into the spirit of it all, quite. "By the way," he remarked, "at the meeting last night I heard some of those young hooligans yelling for the police, just before they were kicked out. What was that for? It didn't seem to make sense, really."

Mrs Clark told him. "It's sort of a standing joke among the Volksparty hereabouts, Mr Constable," she said. "It's to do with a meeting that the Union Party candidate who was here before you addressed at a place out on the veld. There were quite a lot of hecklers there that night and, of course, they all swarmed on to the platform, afterwards. And what was so funny about it, and all, was that the candidate started shouting for the police at the top of his voice before anybody had even hit him, or anything. Of course, that *was* funny. I mean, even though he was our candidate, and all, it was *funny*. I remember how the tears were running down my cheeks the way I was laughing, with the candidate shouting for the police. I was there at the meeting. And, naturally, the police didn't do very much. After all, they are all young Boers, the policemen, and they never do very much to protect a Union Party candidate. But it was all so *funny*, if you understand what I mean. And that's why those hecklers last night also started shouting for the police. It was just to copy our candidate, that time. Isn't it a scream?"

"Where was the meeting held?" Robert E. Constable asked.

Louis Bayfield the attorney told him. At Valschdraai, Bayfield said.

Chapter Four

1

MAVIS Clark was worried about her boss, Jack Brummer. There was something on his mind, all right, she thought. And it couldn't be just nerves, she said to herself. *Somebody* must be upsetting him. She wondered who it could be. A man as strong and healthy as Jack Brummer was – such an open-air type – couldn't just suddenly out of nothing become a prey to nerves. And the way he had acted, about an hour or so ago, when she had done nothing more than announce to him that old Clinkwood was in the outer office – why, it was too awful for anything. She wished Jack Brummer would confide in her. What he needed, she said to herself, was a woman's sympathy and understanding.

At that same moment, in his office, Jack Brummer was working out plans for getting away into the Lowveld for a few days. Yes, he had to get away, he said to himself. It would do him good. After all, Lena Cordier had nothing on him, nothing at all. So it wasn't as though he was trying to run away from anything. No, he said to himself, it was just a short health trip. It couldn't possibly look – to Lena or to anyone else – as if he was on the run. And that sudden, inexplicable kind of fear that he had started developing of the police, just of a sudden, well, that was too absurd for anything. Anybody would think that he had a guilty conscience about Lena Cordier. Whereas the truth of the whole business was that Lena was just as much to blame as he was – more, even, if the truth were told. Of course, he did start first, there in his parked car, that night, when he was sitting with Lena – but then, if she was a responsible girl she could have pretended not to have noticed. And he wouldn't have gone any further, either, if she had declined to act up.

And now he was walking up and down his office in fear, Jack Brummer said to himself. And it wasn't so much fear, either, of anything that might arise out of the trouble he had got himself into with Lena Cordier. As far as that was concerned, he wouldn't be at all surprised if he heard nothing more about it. He somehow felt, actually, that Lena was not the sort of girl to make trouble for a man over a thing like that. But then, what was he afraid of? Because he was not good at introspection, it took Jack Brummer quite a while to work out a theory that seemed to account fairly adequately for his troubled mental state. It was because Lena Cordier had given him a feeling of guilt about this one thing, he said to himself, eventually. And so he right away started feeling guilty about all sorts of other things. Silly things that didn't exist, even. He had to do something about it quick, or he'd go crazy.

Jack Brummer recognised that he was afraid, horribly afraid. And what made it so much more awful was that there was no specific thing that he could say he was actually afraid *of*. Except that he was afraid of the police. But he didn't know why. He couldn't go to gaol for anything he had done to Lena. There he was back again saying that to himself, now. It was going round in circles. On and on, all the same thing all the time. Unless something happened quickly, he'd go mad.

And that was the moment when Mavis Clark came into Jack Brummer's office and announced that there was somebody waiting to see him.

"Who is it?" Jack Brummer asked.

"The caller," Mavis Clark told him, "is that policeman, Brits."

Jack Brummer flung a frenzied glance in the direction of the window. But it was already too late. Detective Sergeant Brits, as was his habit, had followed close on Mavis Clark's heels. He was inside Jack Brummer's office almost before Mavis Clark had finished talking.

"Sit down," Jack Brummer, his face very white, said to the detective. Jack Brummer felt on the verge of collapse. But with an effort such as he had never made even in a tight scrum he managed to find his way back behind his desk and to sink into his chair.

Jack Brummer could not know, of course, that Detective Sergeant Brits's visit was merely routine. He could not know that it was part of the new task the detective had set himself – the task of warning the white male population of Willemsdorp of the fate likely to overtake them if they were caught having immoral relations with native women. It wasn't that Jack Brummer was particularly high up on the detective's list, either. It was just that, having his office in the government buildings, he was conveniently near for Brits to call on in the course of his canvass of the town.

In the meantime a strange thing had been happening to Jack Brummer. Seated in his chair, with the familiar feel of it under his backside and against the spine, he was less afraid, of a sudden. And then again, all at once finding that that which he had most feared had now caught up with him, it was as though all his pent-up tensions had left him. The worst had happened. There was actually a policeman sitting in the chair opposite him. And he was still alive.

Moreover, as a man, there was little about Brits that could be considered impressive. Brits's face was on the thin side and his build was bottom heavy. He wore an old sports jacket and a pair of washed-out khaki trousers that made the lower part of his body appear unnecessarily wanting in dignity. At the same time, there was a certain resilience in his step and in the shape of the back of his thighs, below the buttocks, one could sense a highly developed male urgency. Nor did the line of his mouth betray weakness.

Yet for Jack Brummer these were, for the moment, matters of small consequence. It was enough that he himself felt that he could make a meal of Brits just with his left hand, and without trying, even. And he knew he would never allow himself to be seen about in the kind of trousers that Brits was wearing. Jack Brummer felt about Brits merely that he was the kind of person that would try to tackle him low. That sort he could handle.

"Look, Mr Brummer," the detective was saying. "This is just a friendly little visit. I has just dropped in for a friendly chat and to gives you a friendly little warning."

Oh well, that sounded harmless enough, Jack Brummer thought. Brits could be as friendly as he liked. That wouldn't upset *him*. And there didn't seem much wrong with the friendly warning part, either. A friendly warning given at the right time could do a man a lot of good, even. No doubt it had something to do with claim-jumping, again. Or with somebody salting claims. There was a lot of dirty work going on in the bush, among those prospectors and miners. Ah well, it was all part of the day's work. Jack Brummer took up his pen and reached for a notebook. Might as well get it down in black and white, he said to himself. Not that he would do anything about it, of course, but if he wrote it down it would look more official.

The detective held up his hand. "This isn't for you to make no records of, Mr Brummer," he said. "*I* makes all the records that's got to do with this."

For some indefinable reason Jack Brummer found his self-confidence oozing away again.

"It isn't *that* sort of a warning," the detective said, mystery in his voice.

Jack Brummer put his pen down slowly.

"It's about," the detective volunteered, "women. About sleeping with women, if you wants to be exact."

Jack Brummer sat up very straight. He opened his mouth as though to say something. Then he felt that if he spoke he might make a fool of himself. Thereupon he closed his mouth again. Then he gulped. Then gaped. But all the time he kept on saying to himself that it couldn't be. Lena Cordier hadn't gone to the police as quick as all that. It was impossible. He must keep calm. He must think. He saw all his fears coming back again, flooding in on him. But he wouldn't panic. No, he said to himself, he wouldn't panic. What he would like to do, though, would be to land this little upstart of a Brits just one solid smack, though. No matter what happened to him afterwards – just one smack. But even there he found his courage failing him. He had underestimated Brits, until now – until now, when he saw the line of Brits's mouth. He knew he would never have the guts to punch Brits.

But this was all silly, Jack Brummer started saying to himself and, before he realised it, he found himself saying it to Brits, too.

"But this is all silly," Jack Brummer said. "It's not a criminal offence. You – you don't send a policeman round to a man's place of work for a thing like this. It's just an ordinary civil summons – "

Jack Brummer pulled himself up sharply. He realised that he had already said too much. He had panicked, after all. After he had told himself not to.

"Sleeping with kaffir women," Brits continued. "We got instructions to tighten up the Tielman Roos law. I've come round to warn every white man in town that if he's caught in bed – *or* on the sidewalk, doing it, that is – with a kaffir woman, then he's for it. And no matter who that white man is, neither. I got the Commissioner of Police's authority to warn a man before I pinches him for it, see?"

Jack Brummer felt, and looked, stunned. The detective went on talking, but Jack Brummer hardly heard what he was saying. Nor did Jack Brummer make any reply. A long while after Brits had gone out of his office, his mission accomplished, Jack Brummer went on sitting in his chair, staring, unseeing, into space.

And that was how Mavis Clark found her boss. She went up behind his desk and put her hand on his shoulder. "Jack," she called out, "Jack." She shook him, but gently.

Jack Brummer roused himself by degrees. Then he turned his head slowly in Mavis Clark's direction. He looked up into his typist's face. "Women," he groaned.

Mavis Clark did not answer. Anyway, she knew now what the trouble was. And it was what she suspected all along, of course. It was only a woman that could make a man go like that – losing all hold on himself. Sitting there slumped in his chair like that, as though something had happened to his spine. And with his face that greenish colour. She actually despised him, at that moment. Where, in God's name, was his manliness?

But when Jack Brummer spoke, her contempt gave way to genuine pity. His voice sounded so altered. He was clearly in a bad way. She wanted to do something for him.

"Take some of the stamp money out of the petty cash, and go round to the bottle store, and get me a bottle of brandy," he said, "*Mavis.*"

Up to the penultimate part of his speech – up to where he had mentioned the brandy – she felt pity for him. But when he spoke her name he did not seem a wreck to her, any more; he was no longer an invertebrate, slouched and clownish and disgusting. It was the first time he had ever addressed her by her Christian name. She was thrilled.

"It's all right, I've got some money in my bag," she said. "I'll be back with the brandy soon, Mr Brummer."

It was something to do with art and maidenly modesty that served to restrain her, that time, from calling him Jack.

Meanwhile, back in his own office, Detective Sergeant Brits was making the following entry in his notebook: "Brummer has got womman in famly way. Must find out if womman white or black."

2

It was again knock-off time at the *Northern Transvaal News*. The girls who worked at folding and machine-minding and collating and stitching had retired into the ladies' room to take off their pinafores. Jones the compositor and Sid Fisher the young linotype operator were alone in the printing works.

"Editors," Jones was saying, "I've seen 'em come and I've seen 'em go. And I somehow don't give this Hendricks bloke too long here, either. Don't ask me why – I don't know. But it's just a feeling I've got. It's a feeling I've got in my waters."

Sid Fisher, sluicing water over himself from the paraffin tin, did not answer the compositor directly.

"'S a funny thing about that mining commissioner chap," Sid Fisher said, "the way he come to work this morning. I was coming on behind and he didn't see me. But he acted pretty rum, he did. He was walking through them peppercorn-trees, and then he suddenly starts acting like he was going balmy. Walking on his toes, he was – "

"Who?" Jones enquired, thereby letting on that he hadn't paid attention to the first part of Sid Fisher's remarks. "Who? Hendricks? Walking on his toes, hey?"

"No, not Hendricks," Sid Fisher answered. "That mines man. What's his name – you know – Brummer. Blessed queer it was, too. Then he goes and stands right up against a tree. At first I thought he was going to. . . but no, he didn't. Gave me quite a turn, it did, to see him carry on so screwy."

"You mark my words," Jones said, "they'll pitch him out, yet. I don't know why I feel so sure, exactly, but I've seen 'em come and I've seen 'em go. And one of these days he's going out on his neck."

"But they can't fire a man just for that," Sid Fisher said. "Lumme, not just for walking to work on his toes, they can't. Although it's bad enough, mind you."

"Oh, I don't mean *him*," Jones said testily.

Meanwhile, in the editorial offices, Charlie Hendricks and Lena Cordier were also getting ready to leave. Charlie Hendricks had again invited Lena Cordier to have tea with him in the Café Royal. This time she had accepted.

Seated in a grass chair opposite her, watching her pouring tea, Charlie Hendricks wondered what it was about Lena Cordier that made so strong an appeal to him. She wasn't pretty, he thought. No, you couldn't call her pretty. Her features were too long and thin for her to fit into a conventional category of good looks. Her dark hair around her face, like that, suited her, he thought. But then, it wasn't as though her hair was a particularly striking feature on its own. It wasn't black enough for that. Nor was it thick enough. But it did serve to accentuate her pallor. Her hair was like her voice in that respect, Charlie Hendricks thought. For she had a full, deep voice, which she did not raise much in speaking. She had a dark voice. And when she spoke the darkness of her voice contrasted with her long, pale features in a more striking way even than her hair did.

Charlie Hendricks had felt interested in her the first day he had seen her, which was within the first half-hour of his having started on his new job.

And there was an inner quiet that she had. That quite disturbed him. Why he had asked her out to tea was, ostensibly, so that they could talk shop. It was for that reason, too, that she had accepted his invitation.

I wonder what she thinks of me, Charlie Hendricks asked of himself. He knew he was attracted to her, all right. Each day when he came to work he realised it more clearly. Indeed, when he woke up in the morning there was, each morning, something at the back of his mind that made him feel glad. And then only afterwards, when he was getting dressed or was busy shaving, he realised what it was that imparted so subtle a sense of happiness to the quite ordinary things of everyday living. On one occasion he was actually out on the sidewalk, on his way to work, before he again remembered what was the source of the restrained joy that had come upon him of late.

But he wasn't in love with her. Charlie Hendricks kept on assuring himself that the feelings he had for Lena Cordier, that brought warmth and colour to the background of his being, was not love. It was something too peaceful for love, he told himself many times in the course of the day.

Lena Cordier passed him his tea. Awkwardly, he spilt some of it into his saucer. That was something else he didn't like about all this, Charlie Hendricks said to himself. He didn't like it at all. His movements were clumsy when he was with her. Whereas, in everything she did, she was always so collected and cool.

"You seem quite settled down here, now, Mr Hendricks," Lena Cordier observed. "Do you think you'll stay long? Most editors don't somehow. Willemsdorp seems to get too monotonous for them, after a while, it seems. And then they leave."

("Get booted out," Jones the compositor was at the moment saying

to Sid Fisher in the printing works. *"And you take my tip, this Hendricks will get fired out on his neck quicker'n any of them. Drunkenness, as like as not. Or else sticking in a paid write-up and pocketing the dough. Something shitty like that.")*

"Well, I find I like it here, Miss Cordier," Charlie Hendricks said. He wondered if she guessed to what extent her presence was a contributory factor. Did he convey to her, through some nuance of tone, that her being there, doing the woman's page, was the main reason for his being happy in his work?

"Of course, I don't suppose I've found my feet here yet, quite," he added, modestly.

("Feet first," Jones was just about then, too, observing to Sid Fisher. "Remember old Pilkington, hey, two editors before last, hey? Remember how he was carried out of the pub – feet first, hey?")

"But I'm very pleased you're here, Miss Cordier," Charlie Hendricks said. "There is so much help you can give me, still."

Lena Cordier's answer cut Charlie Hendricks to the quick in a way that nothing else at that moment could have done – not even Jones the compositor's observations, if he could have overheard them. For in the words Lena Cordier spoke, and in the unemotional way in which she uttered them, Charlie Hendricks deduced that she did not in any way reciprocate the feelings he entertained for her. It must be some other man, of course, he said to himself, gloomily.

"I'm sorry, but I won't be staying here much longer, Mr Hendricks," she said. "I'm handing in my notice at the end of the month. I've decided to go back to teaching."

She spoke with an air of finality. He wanted to make some sort of protest. But he realised it was useless. The tone in which she made that statement was as cut and dried as was her decision.

And she looked younger to him, then, than the thirty years that he had at first credited her with. Everything seemed a hell of a mix-up to him suddenly. If it was because of a man that she was chucking her job on the *News*, what did she want to go back to teaching for, then? It was no use asking her, either. He felt that she just wouldn't tell him. But there was a man in it, somewhere. He would bet anything on that.

("Give you a laugh, these editors, don't they?" Jones called out over his shoulder to Sid Fisher as he went out of the door.)

Johannes Erasmus, principal of the Willemsdorp Afrikaans-medium Primary School, was ill at ease, seated in the office of the school-board secretary, Cyril Stein.

If you had asked him straight out he would have admitted – for he was honest enough as far as that sort of thing went – that the reason for his feeling uncomfortable was because he disliked Cyril Stein. In the first place, it was perfectly obvious to anybody in Willemsdorp that Cyril Stein would not be holding down the job of school-board secretary if the appointment had gone strictly on merit. Everybody knew about Cyril Stein's uncle; and anybody that knew of Cyril Stein's uncle's standing in the Department would know immediately how Cyril Stein got that job of secretary – a job, incidentally, that put him, as far as the Education Department was concerned, on a footing at least level with that of any senior school principal in the district. Which was absurd on the face of it. Seeing that Cyril Stein had never had anything to do with education before he got that job.

Johannes Erasmus would have acknowledged that it wasn't as though Cyril Stein couldn't do his *work*. He was competent enough as far as that went. In any case, his typist seemed to do most of it, all that Cyril Stein was left with being to make decisions – and in the majority of cases his typist seemed to do that for him, also. Nor did Johannes Erasmus take it seriously amiss that Cyril Stein was in the habit of wearing scarves that were somewhat on the bright side, and that on a hot day, such as today was, he would come to work in sandals. Johannes Erasmus prided himself on being broad-minded in such matters. After all, his own father, Johannes Erasmus recalled, had never throughout the whole of his life worn shop boots – not even to the quarterly Nagmaal service of the Dutch Reformed Church. His father had throughout his life been satisfied to wear ordinary homemade veldskoens. And the difference between sandals and veldskoens wasn't great. But, of course, his father was just a bushveld farmer: he wasn't secretary of the school-board. So that was quite a different thing.

Nevertheless, Johannes Erasmus was prepared to go so far as to say that Cyril Stein could dress as he liked, and he still would raise no objections. Even that ring, now, that Cyril Stein was wearing on the middle finger of his left hand. Well, Johannes Erasmus would not take exception to that ring even, with that big green stone in it. It looked silly, of course, that big green stone, the size of a shilling, just about. But if Cyril Stein wanted to make himself appear ridiculous, that was his own business entirely. In any case, it didn't interfere with his work. And what Cyril Stein got paid for was for doing his job. Even though it was a job he got through influence, Johannes Erasmus found it hard to confess to himself that that was the part about it that rankled: the fact that Cyril Stein had obtained the appointment through influence.

"That vacancy for a lorry driver," Johannes Erasmus was saying to Cyril Stein, after they had spent the regulation ten minutes in talking about the heat and about how busy the town was, with the elections, and in enquiring about each other's health. "I mean, I don't suppose there's much more to it, is there, than just driving a lorry? The people who are really going to have their work cut out to see that this new feeding scheme works properly are the principals of the primary schools. It's going to give us headaches, all right."

"It's a good thing, though, if I may say so," Cyril Stein replied. "Oh, I don't mean it's a good thing your getting a headache. I mean, it's a good thing, this new plan for feeding the children. And I only hope that next year they'll extend it to include all Native children as well. Of course, I suppose they will, after they've seen what a success it's been with White children. Because I'm quite sure that it will be a success."

Johannes Erasmus waved a hand in the air. He was not going to be dragged by this young Cyril Stein into a long debate. He had his own ideas about school feeding and all the rest of it. And he was sure that he knew much more about it, from practical experience, than what Cyril Stein did. If a child was hungry, you couldn't teach him, because that child just fell asleep. At least, that was how it was with white children. With nigger children it probably wouldn't be very much different, Johannes Erasmus thought. Yes, he himself was even more heartily in favour of school feeding than any of those Liberal politicians, with whose attitude on national affairs he entirely disagreed. But if Cyril Stein was going to start a political argument, well, then he, Johannes Erasmus, just wasn't having any.

"Well now, for this distribution business," Johannes Erasmus said to Cyril Stein, "I know that you're looking for a man to take charge of the supplies and to make deliveries to the schools in the district – a man that's reasonably honest and that can drive a truck – that situation is still open, isn't it?"

Cyril Stein looked very surprised.

"It's still open, of course, Mr Erasmus," he said. "But, you know, the pay isn't very much. Not that we wouldn't like to pay much more, that is, but you know how stingy the Department is with funds. But we weren't expecting a man with *academic* qualifications to take on what you have yourself described as little more than a truck driver's position. I mean, Mr Erasmus, if you aren't happy at your present school, couldn't you rather – couldn't you rather – I mean, a transfer as principal to some other school, instead – what I would like to know is, have you thought it *over* – properly, that is, Mr Erasmus – before taking the final plunge, and so on – "

It was Johannes Erasmus's turn to look surprised. And not so much surprised, either, as positively speechless.

"It's not for myself I've come to apply for this job," Johannes Erasmus said eventually, articulating the words with much difficulty. "I'm not so blasted miserable in my work as school principal that I would elect to change over to being a truck driver. I've come to put in a word on behalf of my brother. He's my younger brother. He's a good deal younger than I am. He never had much education. He remained a farmer. And with this drought he's finding things very difficult."

Johannes Erasmus did not consider it necessary to point out that his brother, Krisjan, was not actually a farmer, but only a farmer's bywoner. He did not deem it politic, either, to mention that, if his brother had not had much education, Cyril Stein looked like he had had much less.

"Oh of course, Mr Erasmus," Cyril Stein said, crimsoning. "If you recommend your own brother to the post, that is enough. Can he start right away? Oh, he can? If you'll give me his address I'll wire him immediately. Yes, he can begin at once. The lorry is already here, waiting for him."

Cyril Stein wrote down the address to which the telegram had to be sent.

All the same, they felt most embarrassed, the two of them – the school principal and the secretary of the school-board. It was because Cyril Stein had got his job through influence and not through merit that he had so little sense of reality, Johannes Erasmus said to himself. For himself, considering the sense of inferiority that he went bowed under in any case, Cyril Stein, too, felt that he was called upon to switch the conversation on to something else, to cover up the contretemps.

"Oh, by the way, Mr Erasmus," Cyril Stein said, "there's a former member of your school staff phoned me today to say she wants to go back to teaching. She left your school about two years ago to go in for journalism. Remember her? Miss Lena Cordier? I expect the *Northern Transvaal News* wasn't all she expected it to be. Anyway, she has asked me for the *Provincial Gazette* with the Johannesburg teaching posts. She wants to apply. But do you think it's necessary for her to go all that way? Supposing we just appoint her back on your staff, say? There'll be a vacancy next term. In fact, several vacancies."

Johannes Erasmus did not pursue the subject. It was queer, all the same, Cyril Stein said to himself. For Johannes Erasmus would be stuck for staff next term. And yet he didn't want Lena Cordier back. That meant that Johannes Erasmus had also heard some of the talk that had been going on about Lena Cordier. About Lena Cordier and some man that was supposed to be sleeping with her. Well, if one man could do it, so could another, Cyril Stein said to himself. And all kinds of ideas came into his mind, then, like a swarm of golden-coloured bees.

"I'll send off the telegram to your brother right away, Mr Erasmus," Cyril Stein said.

The two men, the principal of the Willemsdorp Afrikaans-medium Primary School and the secretary of the school-board, rose up out of their seats together, then. And they shook hands.

4

It was in front of Hex Buildings that the Zulu watchman, Mhlopi, encountered the flatboy who worked in the block of flats lower down the road – the block of flats, incidentally, where Cyril Stein and Charlie Hendricks lived. The Zulu watchman, Mhlopi, had been very desirous of making the acquaintance of the Native who worked in that block of flats lower down the road where, on the previous night, or rather at day-break, he had smelt the acrid fragrance of a burning weed that he knew well. It turned out that the flatboy whom Mhlopi was seeking was one Pieta, a Bechuana, whose brown boot polish complexion was several degrees lighter than Mhlopi's own. As was but natural, Mhlopi the Zulu had a deeply ingrained contempt for Pieta, since Pieta was not a pure-blooded Zulu, but was only a Bechuana, which wasn't much better than a Mshangaan and was almost as low as to be a Pondo.

In her room in Hex Buildings, Lena Cordier had put on her dressing-gown and was looking into a night that was thick with stars. Lena Cordier had not been back long from dinner. She had her meals out. Usually – like tonight – she went for supper to Ben's Losieshuis, the boarding-house run by Mavis Clark's mother.

Lena Cordier waited a long time at the open window. Then she went and sat in the only chair in the room, an armchair. She put her cigarettes, matches and ashtray on the pouf beside her. She sat, waiting and smoking. There came no knock on her door. In the passage with its wooden floor and brown walls she heard no footsteps that she knew. From the sidewalk below, an indistinguishable murmur of voices reached her ears. It was Mhlopi the Zulu watchman and Pieta the Bechuana flatboy talking.

"Yes, I know what msangu is," Pieta said. "Is there any man who has come from the kraal that does not know the much good that msangu is for his heart? But it was not I that smoked msangu this morning in the house where I work, my father. I have none of that green grass now. But tomorrow I can buy some from the seller of the green grass. Tomorrow, if my father can wait so long."

Of course, Lena was saying to herself, Jack Brummer would not show up tonight. And she had no reason to expect that he would. Not after what she had told him. He would find any excuse to keep away. He was that sort of man.

She acknowledged to herself that she had never really expected anything else. And yet why was she sitting waiting? Why was she disappointed at not hearing his familiar knock. (He always knocked. He never turned the handle of the door and just walked in: if she had a visitor it would have looked to the visitor as if he was on a footing of undue intimacy with Lena, if he had just walked in without knocking.) But if, as she kept on saying to herself, she had known all along that that was the kind of man he was, why did she feel so desperately unhappy, of a sudden, waiting there in her room for him in vain? Why was she so lonely, all at once?

And everything was so still. The only sound was the blurred accents of those Native voices, speaking in a Native language she did not understand.

"It is the best kind of msangu that there is, with long red heads and with leaves of the greenness of rain that I will get for my father," Pieta was saying. "It is msangu that will make my father laugh much in his belly."

Mhlopi the old Zulu watchman looked pleased. His eyes shone and his lips parted in a smile that revealed a number of broken teeth. He didn't feel so bad about Pieta any more, then. Maybe Pieta was only a dog of a Mshangaan and almost as low as a Pondo. Maybe Pieta wasn't a black Zulu, with the blood of kings and warriors in his veins. But when Pieta could speak with so much appreciation and understanding of the powers of the green weed – and, above all, when Pieta could talk of procuring him some – then he could almost overlook the vileness of Pieta's heritage.

"And could you furnish me here, in the inside of my hand, some shreds of that green weed when I come to you tomorrow, holding the inside of my hand open with my fingers upwards?" Mhlopi asked of Pieta. "Tomorrow, my son, when my hand is open?"

"Tomorrow, my father," the flatboy, Pieta, answered, "if my father will but now hand over half a crown."

Mhlopi looked his disgust. Once a Bechuana, always a Bechuana, he thought. A Bechuana was lower even than a Basuto. It was on the tip of his tongue to tell Pieta as much, too. But on second thoughts he decided not to. He might miss that msangu altogether if he started cutting up rough.

Well, anyway, she had already asked Cyril Stein for a list of vacant teaching posts in Johannesburg, Lena Cordier reflected. It was no use staying on any longer in Willemsdorp. One thing, at least, it wouldn't be difficult to pack. She was staying in a furnished room. There wasn't much in it that belonged to her. The few books she had she would make a present of to the school library. In a way, it came almost as a relief to her, the thought that she was going.

And she was glad, actually, that Jack Brummer hadn't come round. After a while, the thought that she had lost him wouldn't even give her pain, any more, she told herself. And the trouble that she was in at the moment – well, it wasn't the first time that a thing like that had happened to a woman. And in Johannesburg, where nobody knew her, she could take steps and do something about it. She was getting courage again, to face life with. And it was then, while she was looking around the room, thinking out what to pack, that her eye fell on the folded slip of paper under the door.

"Au, my son," Mhlopi was saying. "I am an old man and a poor man. My work is but to keep watch at night in front of a house. Where will I obtain half a crown, my son, and at this time of the month?"

Pieta relented.

"Okay, big boy," he said, talking in the language of the cinema, which he attended regularly. "Make it two bob and I'll get you the dope, my father."

Without getting up out of her armchair, Lena knew what was in that note. And she could guess, with lightning swiftness, when it was pushed under her door. It was while she was having supper at Mrs Clark's boarding-house. And she could guess, too, who had played postman. She knew that Jack Brummer would never have had the nerve to come up the stairs himself to slip that note under her door. He must have got Mavis Clark to do it for him. Lena Cordier could picture Mavis Clark sneaking out of her mother's boarding-house dining-room the moment Lena sat down to her plate of sausage and mash. And that awful cold gravy.

Even before she had gone to the door and had stooped down to pick up the note, and to open and read it, Lena knew its contents. Some ridiculous lie about Jack Brummer having been called away to the Lowveld about vermiculite claims.

The note ended: " . . . confounded vermiculite. In haste – Jack."

Lena Cordier had only her woman's intuition to guide her. But her reconstruction of the manner in which the note came to find its way under her door was very accurate. Detective Sergeant Brits himself couldn't have done better. Not even with the help of the trained baboon. Or of the Bushman with the copper ring in his nose.

"My father will laugh long in his belly," Pieta said when he pocketed the two shilling piece. "It is msangu of a sort that makes one forget great trouble – that makes one forget all trouble."

5

" – that makes you forget all trouble," the queer little coloured man who called himself Josias was saying to Charlie Hendricks.

Charlie Hendricks had come to his office to work, in the evening. And it was while he was sitting in front of his typewriter, with the door open on to the passage that separated the *Northern Transvaal News* building from the café next door, that that little coloured man had come ambling in. His skin was a light copper colour. He might have been Cape Coloured, with a strong strain of European blood in his veins. But from the fine wrinkles on his face you would think of him as having a Koranna ancestry. For the Kalahari desert dwellers acquire wrinkles before they are out of their teens; with them, wrinkles are not necessarily a sign of age. What also suggested a Koranna origin was the way his buttocks protruded. But from his speech and mannerisms, and also, to some extent, from his name – Josias – you would be more inclined to classify him as a Cape gamat. In any event, he was a mixture, all right; Mhlopi the Zulu watchman would have put him pretty low in the scale.

"What makes you forget all your troubles, Josias?" Charlie Hendricks asked, laughing. He had no idea that the coloured man had called on him of set purpose. He thought Josias had merely walked in because he had seen the door open, that he had come in to waste a few minutes of Charlie Hendricks's time and his own.

"The bloo-drimms, master," Josias said. "What we calling Nellie Pope, master."

When Charlie Hendricks still showed no sign of comprehending, Josias lowered his voice slightly. "The green grass, master," he said.

But Charlie Hendricks still made no response.

Well, that was that, Josias said to himself. If the esoteric approach to the subject, which was understood throughout South Africa wherever men who smoked dagga came together, elicited no knowledgeful answer from the white man sitting there at the desk, then it was clear that the white man was not an habitué. So there was no point in pursuing the matter any further. It was not Josias's job to introduce people to the practice of smoking dagga. All he did was to supply the drug to such as were addicted to it.

"Well, I'll be going, now, master," Josias said. "Good night, master."

"Oh, good night," Charlie Hendricks said. "But I still don't know what you're getting at. What you've been trying to tell me, that is."

Josias decided to have one more shot at it. Not that he really expected it to bring him results, however.

"Baas Esselen – " he began.

"Oh yes, Mr Esselen," Charlie Hendricks said. "He was editor here before me. Did you know Mr Esselen?"

"Baas Esselen," Josias said, "he was one of my customers."

"Sounds like he must have been a pretty queer customer," Charlie Hendricks interjected, pleased with his own wit.

No, it was a waste of time, Josias decided. This new editor didn't understand the dagga-smoker's talk. This white man didn't know what he meant when he came to offer him a weed that would make him forget all his troubles.

"You said something about Nellie Pope, Josias," Charlie Hendricks remarked as the coloured man was turning to go. "Who is she? I can't say I've ever heard of her. Does she live in these parts?"

Josias felt that he wanted to laugh. That a man should think that Nellie Pope was the name of a woman! How on earth a man could be as ignorant as all that was a matter passing Josias's comprehension. And he seemed quite a clever white man, too, having a work in which he sat in front of a writing machine to write. He must be as clever as a witch-doctor, almost, that could tell you what was the matter with you by throwing the bones. And yet he didn't know what Nellie Pope was – didn't know that you mixed a few grains of Nellie Pope with cigarette tobacco and rolled a smoke of it in brown paper and. . . oh my God, you were more clever than any witch-doctor, then, when the smoke was burning you in your nostrils (unless it was a witch-doctor that also smoked Nellie Pope, of course: then it was, naturally enough, different). And you were also much more clever than any policeman, even (unless, of course, it was a policeman who was also smoking dagga, then).

And the white man had asked him, thinking that it was a woman, if Nellie Pope lived in these parts. Well, he could say to the white man that she did live in these parts, of course. But that she was really better when she lived by the gate, in Swaziland. And she had a red head, he could have told the white man. And she had a green dress.

"Here," Charlie Hendricks said, taking half a crown out of his pocket and pitching it across to the coloured man as he was moving off towards the door. "Go and buy yourself some dagga with it. I believe you coloured people smoke a lot of it."

Could you beat that for ignorance? Josias said to himself as he got into the passage. Here was he going to *sell* the white man some dagga. And the white man didn't *know* that he wanted to sell him dagga. And the white man threw him half a crown, which was the *price* of a packet of dagga. And all the time the white man hadn't even *guessed* what he had been talking about.

Perhaps Charlie Hendricks might have come nearer to fathoming the reason for Josias's call if Josias had spoken so that Charlie Hendricks could have understood him better. When Josias had said that he was peddling 'bloo-drimms', for instance.

Not anybody would be able to interpret that, just straight off, as 'blue dreams.'

Chapter Five

1

I T was not long after he received the telegram from Cyril Stein, appointing him to the job under the school feeding scheme, that Johannes Erasmus's brother, Krisjan, arrived at Willemsdorp. He alighted at the station carrying a battered suitcase and eating a banana. Through dint of enquiry he found his way to the school-board office, where he reported for duty. Since he had come from a farm, Krisjan Erasmus felt that he had a good deal to learn about how to comport himself in a town. At the same time, he didn't want anybody to think he was just a yokel. After all, he had been in towns before, and in towns bigger than Willemsdorp, for that matter. Why, on one occasion he had even spent the better part of a week in Zuurdal that had a population of at least five thousand white people, not counting the niggers. So, while he was willing to acknowledge that he didn't know quite everything that a city dweller knew, maybe, at the same time people hadn't to think that he was just a backvelder with kraal manure in his trouser turn-ups.

Krisjan walked with a jaunty stride. He was a good deal younger than his brother. He had a good figure – tall and slender; his being loose-limbed imparted grace to his movements, as well as a suggestion of gaucherie. He had a pretty elevated opinion of himself, and just for what he was, on his own merits. This did not, however, prevent him from taking a measure of secret pride in the achievement of his elder brother, Johannes. He liked to think that his brother had got as far as being a school principal. Not that he didn't have it in him to do as well, or perhaps better, even. Only, he hadn't any ambitions along those lines.

Krisjan found his way to the school-board office. He told the typist who he was. The typist went into the inner office to announce his arrival. She was away a few minutes. When she came back Krisjan had started on a second banana. She told him he could go through into the next office. He felt suddenly overawed at the thought of the importance of the man in the next office. So he put down his suitcase next to the wall and balanced his packet of bananas on the suitcase next to one side of the handle. On the other side of the handle he put his half-eaten banana, leaving it there so that he could come back and eat it some more when his interview with the important man in the next office was over.

Krisjan Erasmus was not only surprised at Cyril Stein's appearance. He was disappointed beyond measure. He had expected to see somebody looking like a boss – somebody imposing and solid and with an air of authority. Instead of which, he was confronted with a man not much older than himself who had a weak chin and an untidy head of hair and was wearing, of all things, an open-necked shirt. Why, his own brother, Johannes the school principal, looked a lot more like a boss than this Cyril Stein did, Krisjan Erasmus thought to himself. And so he did not feel at all nervous when Cyril Stein motioned him to sit in the chair opposite him. And when Cyril Stein asked him about the drought in the part of the country that he had come from, he was able to answer expansively. And by the time Cyril Stein came to explain his duties to him and asked him was it within his capacity to perform them, he was able, again, to reply with an airy gesture of affirmation, which brought the fingers of one hand shooting smartly against the brim of his hat.

It was then that Krisjan Erasmus realised that he had been sitting with his hat on, all the time, sitting talking with his hat on in the office of the man who was giving him a job. His ears started turning red under the hat brim. He wanted to take his hat off straight away. But he felt it would be silly to do it now. He sat there in two minds, uncertain whether to take his hat off or to leave it on his head, seeing that it was already on his head, and had been there all the time. And now he came to think of it, it seemed to him as though Cyril Stein had been doing nothing but look at the hat that he had on his head from the moment he had come into the office. And he himself had had the cheek to think that this man who was giving him a job was wearing an open-necked shirt.

He hardly heard, any more, what Cyril Stein was saying. All he could think of was his hat, with sweat stains that he knew about on the band. With his first pay he would buy himself a new hat. Or perhaps he would go without a hat altogether. He would never be able to wear a hat again, he didn't think – not after all this. He felt beads of perspiration coming on to his forehead. Within a few minutes that moisture would come through and show in a dark stain in front, for it was a cheap hat, and old, and the sweat-band had torn out long ago. He couldn't stand it any longer. The hat on his head had become the size of a roof. It was like he was holding up the whole roof with his head, and it was pressing him down. He made up his mind. Sheepishly, he put his hand up to his head and removed the hat.

That was the moment Cyril Stein stood up to shake hands with him, to signify to him that he had got the job and that the interview was over. Krisjan Erasmus shuffled his hat from his right hand to his left so that he could take Cyril Stein's hand. And he felt worse than ever, then, when he stood up and shook hands with Cyril Stein. For it must seem to Cyril Stein that he had taken off his hat to *him*. Just as though he, Krisjan Erasmus, brother of the school principal, was a kaffir, who had to take off his hat when he greeted a white man.

Krisjan Erasmus never quite knew afterwards how he got out of that office and picked up his suitcase again that had a packet of bananas balanced on it and also a partly eaten banana. What smarted most was the thought of how Cyril Stein must be laughing at him. Krisjan Erasmus felt that there was indeed much that he had to learn yet of the ways of a town.

He did not know that Cyril Stein was very favourably impressed with – and felt slightly inferior because of – the firm and straightforward manner in which that young fellow from the country gripped his hand.

When he left the school-board office he enquired his way to Mrs Clark's boarding-house, where his brother had arranged accommodation for him. He would call on his brother and his sister-in-law, Malie, in the evening.

On his way to the boarding-house he had to walk some distance along the main street, where there was a cement paving. He started eating another banana. He flung the banana skin down on the pavement. Then he stopped and looking in at a shop window that displayed bright-coloured ties.

A few moments later an elderly Zulu woman came past, carrying a bundle on her head. With her bare foot she stepped on the banana skin. She slithered, tried to save herself from falling, and then landed flat on her backside on the paving, her bundle ricocheting off a veranda pole into the gutter.

Krisjan laughed. He laughed until the tears rolled down his cheeks. He laughed to hear the elderly black woman emit a long string of Zulu swearwords. After she had risen to her feet and had retrieved her bundle, he was still laughing. In laughter the sense of his own humiliation in Cyril Stein's office was erased from his mind. Of all the inhabitants of Willemsdorp, white and black, there was none then that felt more at home in the town than did Krisjan Erasmus.

2

Charlie Hendricks had come back to his office after supper to put the final touches to an election leader. But the words and the ideas didn't come the way he wanted them to. He felt sick of the old clichés. The most vital by-election in the history of the Northern Transvaal. Save the country from fascism. The attention of the whole world centred on Willemsdorp. A Volksparty victory would mean the end of our cherished democratic freedom. The South African way of life. . .

It was not good. The leader was getting him down.

Then he started thinking of Lena Cordier. She had left the paper. She would be leaving for Johannesburg shortly, getting there in time for the beginning of the new school term. She would, however, until she left Willemsdorp, continue to send in copy for the woman's page. He had persuaded her to agree to that. Actually, of course, he could have done it just as well himself – that part of it, anyway, which consisted of little more than cutting out articles of feminine interest from the American and English magazines. She was no longer doing the socials and personal notes or reporting meetings of women's organisations. Charlie Hendricks knew that the reason why he had asked Lena Cordier to keep on with the paste and scissors part of her job was because he did not wish the last link that bound her to the *News* to be severed.

He was interested in her. She had made an impression on him of a sort that went beyond the momentary expectations of feeling. At least, that was what he said to himself. And there were times when he thought of her that the emotions he experienced came near to intoxication. It was almost as though he were again in his adolescence, then. But it was only when he was away from her, and thought of her, as he was doing now, that there came moments when – well, it was no use

69

trying to get away from it – when saying her name over to himself was a joyous thrill. But mostly it was the beauty of a great calmness that the thought of Lena Cordier brought to him. And when he was in her presence, then there was no sense of intoxication that he was aware of at all.

He thought he knew the reason for that. Lena Cordier was not very much interested in him. If she had guessed at all that she had made an impression on him, she certainly didn't show it in any way. Or was it perhaps that her aloofness towards him was a pose? – Charlie Hendricks started wondering. Might it not be that she had divined his feelings for her, and that she herself was in two minds as to how she should respond, and that that was the reason for that air of cold detachment that she observed in her relations with him?

But it couldn't be that, Charlie Hendricks told himself. For otherwise she couldn't have been so matter of fact in the way she acquainted him with her decision to resign from the *News* and to leave Willemsdorp. In the way she was going about it, cutting herself loose from Willemsdorp, she was as unemotional as if what she were cutting was a piece of string. Although there was something too, now, Charlie Hendricks thought, suddenly. Even in cutting a piece of string tied round a parcel – and in this case the parcel that she was on the point of opening was the City of Johannesburg – she should still be expected to display some sort of feeling. Excitement at going to a new place. Hope for the future. Trepidation and qualms about the fate that the City of Johannesburg held in store for her. A light in her eyes at the thought that a change at least meant something different, something new.

But in the manner of Lena Cordier's taking her departure from Willemsdorp there was no sparkle.

She was leaving Willemsdorp. In her leaving there was neither exhilaration nor despair.

He had several times invited her to come and have tea with him again, or to have a spot with him in the hotel lounge. Each time she had refused.

Charlie Hendricks pushed aside his typewriter. It was no go. The leader would have to wait for the morning. He would turn out the column of slush in between subbing the cables.

He had locked the back door of the office and was stepping into the passage when he heard footfalls. They were coming nearer. It was somebody taking the short cut to Kotze Street. They were quick, light steps. A woman's. Charlie Hendricks saw who the woman was the moment she emerged from the shadows. He walked down the passage towards her. They came face to face alongside the whitewashed wall of the printing works. A light from Kotze Street shone on that part of the wall, the rest of the passage being in darkness.

Before he realised what he was doing, Charlie Hendricks reached out his arms towards her. She drew back against the wall, looked frightened. But only for a moment. In the next instant Charlie Hendricks saw, in the light from Kotze Street, the sudden change that came over Lena Cordier's face as he put one arm around her shoulder, the other about her waist. He pressed her against the whitewashed wall of the printing works. It was a quick kiss. He dropped his hands to his side the moment he had kissed her. It was a salt kiss, tasting of blood and the sea. Charlie Hendricks was intoxicated. For the first time he was, actually in her presence and not just at a distance thinking of her, transported. His arms at his sides, he stood looking at her, staring stupidly.

Lena Cordier slipped out with lithe grace from where she was standing between him and the wall. Charlie Hendricks made no attempt to stop her. In a moment she was gone. Just before that, in the same second of time in which she was turning to run, she had brushed her lips against his cheek.

Charlie Hendricks could feel her light kiss on his cheek all the way back to his flat. And he remembered it for a long while after that, the touch of her lips on his cheek and the sound of her footsteps scurrying off down the passage. And afterwards he wondered whether he hadn't imagined it, perhaps dreamt it.

For, next day, when he encountered her in the street, in daylight, she informed him coldly, aloofly, that she would be sending along the copy for the woman's page soon. Not by as much as the flutter of an eyelid did she betray any kind of knowingness of her meeting with Charlie Hendricks, on the previous evening, in the passage next to the printing works, where there was a whitewashed wall on which a light from the street was shining.

3

Detective Sergeant Brits was still on his rounds, warning members of the male population (white) of Willemsdorp as were not obviously impotent of the penalties laid down by the law against miscegenation.

A queer thing had happened at the butcher shop. The proprietor was a Lithuanian who had not been long in the country and was consequently linguistically handicapped. When the detective had finished talking, the butcher presented him with a couple of yards of sausages and polony. The Lithuanian butcher took Sergeant Brits's remarks about white and kaffir people to have some reference to the quality of the meat he supplied. He took it to mean that somebody had been complaining that he was selling, to white people, meat that was fit only for a kaffir to eat. Well, that was something that the butcher wouldn't have bothered to deny. For that matter he knew perfectly well that he was selling, to kaffirs, meat that was unfit for kaffir consumption. And so, rather than waste unnecessary words in a language that was strange to him, he made the detective a small present. It was something you could understand in any language.

Actually, Brits was not nearly as au fait with the underworld activities of Willemsdorp as he gave out to be. And so he was a good deal surprised suddenly to receive a lot of sausage and polony, like that. All the same, he took the parcel home to his wife and many children.

Next on his list was Dominee Van Rooyen, the Dutch Reformed Church minister. The minister's housekeeper informed the detective, simply, that the Reverend Van Rooyen was not at home. He had gone to visit a sick parishioner, the housekeeper said. Brits accepted the housekeeper's statement and withdrew. His reason informed him that she had in all probability told him the truth. But because he had been in the force so long, his detective instinct made him jump to all sorts of conclusions. And so, in his mind's eye, he pictured Reverend Van Rooyen as having seen him come up the garden path. He pictured Reverend Van Rooyen as having peered through the curtain, conscious of his guilt and in momentary expectation of the arrival of the police, and as having then fled to the back of the house. His reason told him that it was absurd to get hold of such an idea about the minister sitting in the lavatory, in frock coat and stiff white collar, waiting in terror for his housekeeper to stall off the police.

Thwarted by the Dutch Reformed Church, Detective Sergeant Brits turned his attention to the Church of England. He went to call on the Reverend Thorwell Macey. Alighting from his police motor bike side-car, which had a few years before come to replace his horse, Detective Sergeant Brits surveyed the home of the Anglican parson with a good deal of distaste. For one thing, there was no veranda to the house. Then, the doors and windows needed painting. Above all, the minister answered Brits's rat-a-tat in person. He didn't even have a kaffir that he could send to open the door. To the detective's mind that was a lot lower than if Reverend Thorwell Macey's servant had come to the door and had said the master was out – even if by the word 'out' the servant meant that Reverend Thorwell Macey was a fugitive from justice and was at that moment skulking in a Fordsburg hotel under an assumed name and wearing dark spectacles.

It was clear to Brits that a Church of England clergyman didn't get nearly as good pay as what a Dutch Reformed Church predikant got. Brits smelt poverty about Reverend Thorwell Macey's house. Because he had but little culture, the detective could not distinguish readily between genteel poverty and the cruder, starker kind. It all smelt the same to him.

Seated in the English clergyman's study, Brits decided not to beat about the bush with him. He explained in his own words the implication of the Immorality Act, No. 5 of 1927, to be read in conjunction with the Girls' and Mentally Defective Women's Protection Act, No. 16 of 1916. He explained, also in his own fashion, that the law was going to be more strictly enforced.

"So I just come here to do my dutty," Detective Sergeant Brits ended up.

There were certain subleties in the detective's accent to which the English clergyman's ears were not attuned. He looked at Brits in surprise.

"I just come here to do my dutty," the detective repeated, challengingly, almost.

Well, that decided Reverend Thorwell Macey that he wasn't mistaken. He must have heard right the first time.

"You can be as dirty as you like, my good man," Reverend Thorwell said. "But please, not here. My house is dirty enough as it is. So I'll be grateful if you'll – er – go and do your dirty somewhere else."

It was patent to the detective that the parson had misunderstood him. So he began again, slowly and patiently, to acquaint the minister with the nature and purpose of his call. He covered the provisions of the Tielman Roos Act quite fully. And the authorities were going to take strong action, he said. Because there was a lot of that sort of thing going on – immoral relations between white men and kaffir women, and some of them in high places, too. It was the white men, he explained, that were in high places – not the kaffir women. It was all very filthy, the detective said, and the worst of it was that it was hard to prove that sort of charge, since the guilty parties had to be caught dead to rights. And now the Commissioner of Police was making things even more difficult for him by insisting that he had to warn a person before he pinched him. But there was a *lot* of it going on, Detective Sergeant Brits insisted, adding that it was really awfully disgusting.

"Yes, it is truly disgusting," the Reverend Thorwell Macey said, after a few moments of reflection. "It is, in one word, vile."

Detective Sergeant Brits was not prepared for quite so vigorous a reaction on the part of the clergyman.

"Filthy is what *I* calls it," Brits declared.

"It's a beastly disgrace," the Reverend Thorwell Macey continued, "to any country's statutes, a law like that. It's about the most iniquitous Act I've ever heard of. If you'll pardon me, I think it – it stinks."

Out on the sidewalk again, Detective Sergeant Brits made an entry in his notebook opposite the Anglican minister's name.

"Anyway," the detective said to himself as he wrote, "he's the right man to talk about what stinks. His whole house stinks."

4

Well, she could go and get —, Charlie Hendricks said to himself.

It was just after his encounter with Lena Cordier. The daylight encounter, in the street. Not the meeting of the previous evening in the passage that ran alongside the printing works. She was so stiff and stuck up now. All she could talk about was sending the copy round for the woman's page. And she seemed in a hurry, too, as if it was too much for her, even, to exchange a few commonplaces with him in the street. Well, she *could* go and get —, then. He repeated the word to himself.

But where was that intoxication of the senses that came to him for that brief moment – and only last night it was, too – only last night – when her lips brushed against his cheek in the darkness? He had walked home in a dream. And he had said her name over and over to himself. And there was heavy witchery abroad. And there was a joyousness in everything – in the pavement that his feet trod, because he thought of how often she must have walked just there, too, in the years

74

that she had been in Willemsdorp. And the shops in the street, with their iron veranda poles: they all took on a new sense of wonder for him, because she had passed them often and often, her dress whisking against a veranda pole lightly, just as her lips had –

Lena Cordier could go and get —, Charlie Hendricks announced to himself.

He was now in an unpretentious looking street that intersected Kotze Street at right angles. It was said to be the oldest street in Willemsdorp, and it did not appear to have a name, even. It was along that way that the Voortrekkers were supposed to have come in the early years of the last century, trekking a thousand miles into the wilderness to escape from British rule. And in the end the thousand miles turned out not to have been enough. A thousand miles by ox-wagon was very far. And that was the only form of transport that the Voortrekkers knew. And they thought that a distance of a thousand miles between themselves and the English – an ox-wagon's thousand miles – would be enough. They could not foresee the day of steam and then the petrol engine.

Walking along that street, Charlie Hendricks felt that it had not changed very much since the time the Voortrekkers laid it out to be the main street, Kotze Street having long since taken its place. And for more years than anybody could remember Willemsdorp had ceased to be the chief town of the Northern Transvaal. But it seemed as though some of those houses of sundried brick had in their time faced on to a wagon trail. The weather-beaten facades of other buildings spoke of a time when around them there was just open veld, with here and there a thorn-tree, with here and there a hippo.

In the middle of that old street, the name of which seemed to have been forgotten with the years, was a pub. From the outside it did not look attractive. Single-storeyed, it was topped by a series of ornamental cupolas. From the facade the plaster had crumbled in patches, revealing areas of brickwork of a shade that did not delight the eye. Charlie Hendricks walked in through the green curtains. Coming in from the bright glare of the afternoon, he was unable, at first, to get his eyes accommodated to the gloom of the interior of the pub, with the result that he stumbled slightly in making his way to the counter. The bartender stared, unfriendly. He did not approve of a customer coming into his saloon stumbling. It was bad enough if he was unsteady on his feet when he left.

Charlie Hendricks ordered a brandy, carrying the glass over to a small table in a corner. Seated at the table, he was able to take stock of the pub. He hadn't been in it before. The brass rail, worn by many feet, sagged in the middle. The spittoons looked like museum pieces. With its elaborate old-world carvings, the barcounter bore witness to a short-lived period in the history of Willemsdorp when there was thought to be gold in those hills. Today, prospectors in the area had given up searching for the nobler metal. They contented themselves with corundum and manganese propositions. Also asbestos and tin.

Charlie Hendricks recognised the bartender in the sense that he remembered having seen him about the town: bull-necked, his jaw dark and jutting. And Charlie Hendricks guessed, for that reason, that the bartender would know who he was, too. He would in all likelihood already have been pointed out to the bartender as the new editor.

But Charlie Hendricks was sure he had not previously set eyes on the two men standing drinking at the bar. One was biggish and bald and had a yellowish moustache terminating in fierce spikes. He was addressed as Jim by his companion, a wizened, undersized man with his features so tanned by the sun that, if he didn't know him, the bartender would have been quite justified in refusing to serve him a drink in a white man's bar. The bartender addressed one of the men as Mr Clinkwood – Charlie Hendricks wasn't sure which one, for by that time he had had a few more brandies. He also gathered from the talk of the two bar patrons that they were prospectors from the Lowveld. His first instinct was to enter into conversation with them. A base metal story would not come amiss in the next issue of the *News*. But somehow Charlie Hendricks didn't feel that he had the heart for it. He felt sore about the way Lena Cordier was treating him. Getting the inside dope on manganese deposits did not hold out much of a thrill for him just then.

Charlie Hendricks went up to the counter for yet another brandy. This time when he carried the glass to the table in the corner the glass was shaking visibly. And he wasn't uncertain on his feet now simply because he couldn't see his way properly.

"Too much ash content," one of the prospectors was saying.

"What about this new cyclone washing system for heavy medium separation?" the other asked. "Where we fail is the way we smelt our titaniferous magnetites. Look at all the ferro-vanadium we lose."

Charlie Hendricks was surprised to hear that kind of talk. He remembered that when he had come into the bar he had stumbled. . .

Stumbled on to a regional scientific conference, he thought, now.

"Too much bone coal and carbonaceous shale, that's the trouble," the bald-headed man with the spiked moustache was saying.

Ah well, it all seemed very pleasant here, in the pub, Charlie Hendricks thought.

He began to feel that it didn't matter so very much, any more, that Lena Cordier wasn't taking any notice of him. It was a happy world, and there were worse things in it than getting filled up with booze. By and by, after he had had a few more brandies he would go up to the counter and have a chat with those prospectors. They seemed to know a thing or two, all right. What was more, they seemed to know just about an equal amount, the big bald-headed man with the yellow moustache that ended in spikes, and the little wizened man whose face was so suntanned – blackened, even – that he could easily pass himself off as coloured, if he wanted to: that is, if any white man would be so silly as to want to pass himself off as coloured, Charlie Hendricks thought, laughing to himself. The idea seemed very funny, somehow.

It didn't seem so funny to the bartender, however. For the bartender had at that very moment looked over in Charlie Hendricks's direction. And, since he had his licence to think of, the bartender was not exactly tickled to death at the sight of the man sitting in a corner of the pub, over a glass of brandy, laughing to himself. He wouldn't supply him with another drink, the bartender decided.

A little later Charlie Hendricks again approached the counter. The two prospectors were conversing earnestly. And it was clear that they had deserted the more austere paths of industrial chemistry. "There was her husband coming up the stairs and I couldn't get my trousers on" – Charlie Hendricks heard – "although it was all right for *her*. She'd kept her dress on all the time."

"Ferro-metallurgical *science*," Charlie Hendricks announced, lurching up to the counter. But when the bartender refused to serve him, he left without making any fuss.

"Can't carry their liquor, these writing blokes," the bartender said to the two prospectors after Charlie Hendricks had gone out.

Chapter Six

1

THE motor car slowed down after it had crossed the bridge. There were whitewashed stones placed at regular intervals on each side of the road to mark the approach to the bridge, which was quite an unimposing structure, since it spanned but a narrow stream the bed of which was dry for the greater part of the year. After passing over the bridge, the car turned off a little way into the veld, coming to a halt under a clump of thorn-trees.

"If people see us here," Mavis Clark said, "what will they think?"

Jack Brummer looked undecided.

"What can they think, anyway?" he asked, after a while. "It's still broad daylight, isn't it? And if – I mean, dash it all, if there was anything about sitting here that wasn't right – well, we wouldn't come and stop right next to the bridge, here, would we now? After all, every car coming into Willemsdorp from that side has got to pass over this bridge, hasn't it? I mean, cars coming even from as far as Rhodesia – why, there's no other way for them to come. And a man would be mad to bring a girl out here in broad daylight and everything, pulling up here under these trees right next to the road, if it wasn't all *innocent*, that is."

Jack Brummer's voice was raised. He was shouting, almost, by then.

"It's quite all right, I mean," he said, his tone more subdued, "to be sitting right here, where everybody can see us, looking just at the scenery. Isn't it?"

After due reflection, Mavis Clark said, yes, she supposed that was so.

She had taken off her glasses and had put them in her handbag. As she always said, she needed her glasses only for reading and typing with. Otherwise, she didn't need them at all, for seeing either far away or for close to. Only, of course, if she kept her glasses off for a long time, her eyes would start watering slightly. But that was only natural, since she had got into the *habit* of wearing them – for typing and reading, that was.

"If you don't think we should come and stop here, of course," Jack Brummer said after a pause, introducing into his voice a deliberately waggish note that didn't suit him for the reason that it sounded arch – womanly, almost: and he was, after all, a footballer – "well, then, perhaps you would like it better if we went further down into the kloof, perhaps, where nobody would see us."

He laughed lightly, artificially.

Mavis Clark felt foolish. No, she said to herself. That wasn't what she meant at all. And yet, if it wasn't that, what did she mean, anyway. Yes, she knew she wanted him to take her into his arms. But it had to be nothing more than that. And she had looked forward to coming out on this drive with Jack Brummer. And it wasn't working out in the way she had expected it to. She wasn't getting any real happiness out of it. It was not turning out in the way she had expected. She wondered if that note hadn't had something to do with it, perhaps – that note that on Jack Brummer's instructions she had gone and pushed under Lena Cordier's door, while Lena was having dinner in her mother's boarding-house. She did it gleefully enough, then, she remembered. But she hadn't felt too good about it since. It wasn't the kind of thing she would like to have done to her, Mavis Clark had since then felt more than once.

It was almost as though at that moment, sitting beside him, Mavis Clark had, with her woman's intuition, fathomed the reason for Jack Brummer having chosen so public a spot, right next to the bridge with its whitewashed stones, in which to pull up his car. Nevertheless, however much of his feelings she might have divined, it is doubtful if she would quite have been able to put herself in his position – if she would have been quite able to share his feelings of dread on that morning when she heard that Detective Sergeant Brits was waiting in the outer office to see him. For, in spite of everything, Mavis Clark was still more courageous than was Jack Brummer. So it is reasonable to suppose that she would not have been able to identify herself with that exact degree of abject terror that had gripped hold of Jack Brummer's vitals then.

And it was because of the fear that had overcome him then that Jack Brummer was now holding back all he knew. He was dead scared of going too far with a woman again, soon. That was why he had picked that particular spot for pulling his car up in. It was a spot that was at the same time secluded under the trees and yet public through being near the bridge. It was a spot remote from the world and yet within sight of any traveller coming from the north – coming from as far as Rhodesia. In daylight.

"The grass should be more green than this," Jack Brummer observed after an interval of silence. "At this time of the year, I mean."

"It's because of the drought, I suppose," Mavis Clark replied. Not only in their action, but also in their conversation, was there nothing to which anybody passing along that road from the north could take exception.

The truth of the matter was that Jack Brummer wanted a woman. And he wanted a woman badly. But he had had the guts frightened out of him by Lena Cordier's revelation about her condition. And so, while he wanted a woman, now, he was also afraid to have a woman. What was more, with all his physical desire for a woman, there was also more than just a hint of repulsion in the thought of a woman. It was a sense of physical repulsion, even. And that was the reason why he was sitting with Mavis Clark with his car parked just in that spot. He felt safe there. Safe and also irritated.

Actually, he felt that he didn't like Mavis Clark – that he never would like her. He still thought of her as having her glasses on. It made no difference to him that she had taken off her glasses and put them in her bag. It was a usual thing, when he went out with a girl in his car, that she would take something off and put them in her bag. And in the tumult of his feelings he would hardly even notice then what was happening. Anyway, he knew he didn't like Mavis Clark, in her short white frock and all. But as a woman she would do. Only, he was too scared, still.

That was how it came about that Mavis Clark and Jack Brummer went on for quite a while talking inconsequentialities. And long before it got dusk he started up his car again. And he drove Mavis Clark back to her mother's boarding-house.

But a time would come in the near future when Jack Brummer would be less frightened. And then he would take Mavis Clark in his car to that same spot under the trees beside the bridge, where the road was marked off with stones whitened with whitewash. But it would be night-time, then. And no matter what traffic passed down the road – people from Rhodesia, even – nobody would be able to see what went on between him and Mavis Clark, in his car parked among the thorn-trees. And for a long while afterwards Mavis Clark would remember those whitewashed stones – how they looked under the starlight. And when those stones seemed to grow blurred it was not because she had taken her glasses off. For she had not taken her glasses off, that night. What she had taken off and put into her handbag were not her glasses.

And about one part of her memory there would be a serenity. But about another part of it there would be a thing as heavy as those stones.

2

Charlie Hendricks sat up with a jerk.

She had walked into the bed-sitting-room of his bachelor flat without knocking.

For a few moments Charlie Hendricks sat looking at her in a daze. On his return from the pub he had flung himself down on the divan. Drunk, he had dozed off. Now he woke up to see this girl standing in the doorway. And she had come in without knocking. Rising unsteadily to his feet – for the effect of the brandy he had drunk in the bar had not yet worn off – he looked at the girl more closely.

She had small features, a tilted nose that gave piquancy to her face and lips that were inclined towards fullness. She had the kind of face that could smile readily, or that could just as easily turn petulant. Her eyes – well, there was a thing, now, Charlie Hendricks thought: her eyes were large and dark and lustrous and her eyes betrayed her coloured ancestry in a way that her skin did not. Her skin was no darker than many a white girl's skin. But her eyes gave her away. The lashes were thick and coarse; the lids protruded slightly; the blackness of her pupils was unlike the blackness of a Spanish girl's eyes, say: it was a streaky blackness: it was a coloured woman's eyes.

But, of course, at first glance you would take her for white, Charlie Hendricks reflected. She was just the kind of girl, born in a Coloured family, who later on 'passed over' and got accepted as White. All these things Charlie Hendricks was thinking as he rose shakily to his feet. And afterwards he wondered if he would really have thought that the girl was Coloured if it wasn't for the words she had spoken.

"My name is Marjorie," the girl said, "I have come to look for Baas Esselen."

Well, of course, that told you everything, didn't it? Her talking of him as 'Baas' Esselen. Who but a coloured person would talk of a white man as boss? And then Charlie Hendricks realised, also, that she spoke the words heavily, with a fullness of accent. Her voice wasn't *white*.

Anyway, he seemed a queer customer, all right, Charlie Hendricks was thinking – this Esselen, who was editor of the *News* before him and whose flat Charlie Hendricks had taken over along with his job. First there was that little coloured man, Josias, who had come into the *News* office that night and had spoken in mysterious terms of his dealings with Esselen – hinting at more things than he put into words. And now here was this coloured girl walking straight into the flat without knocking, just because she thought Esselen was still occupying it.

"Well, Mr Esselen has left," Charlie Hendricks announced, standing upright by then. "I am in his place."

In saying in Esselen's place, Charlie Hendricks was telescoping his position both as editor and as the occupant of the flat. The coloured girl, Marjorie, seemed to think that he implied still more. She smiled. Charlie Hendricks was embarrassed. He had not yet recovered from the effects of the drink. He felt he wanted another brandy.

He went into the little kitchen of the bachelor flat and came out with a tumbler half-filled with water. From the wardrobe he took out a bottle of brandy and poured himself a stiff tot. He downed it at a gulp. Now he felt less shaky. At the same time, he didn't know what to say to that girl standing there. There were several chairs in the flat. But he couldn't offer her one. He couldn't invite a coloured person to sit down in a chair.

Standing up, facing her, Charlie Hendricks saw that the coloured girl was wearing a doek, a gaudy silk scarf fastened over her head. He could guess why. She wouldn't have proper long hair like a white girl's. Her hair would be frizzy. She probably didn't know enough to comb out her hair with a heated brass comb and with the application of a patent hair-straightening cream much favoured by coloured women in the cities who passed themselves off as white. It was when Charlie Hendricks saw her shoes, a pair of tan-and-white high-heeled shoes, that certain smouldering doubts he had had about her became certainties. No respectable coloured girl could afford to wear shoes like that. Immediately he remembered what Detective Sergeant Brits had told him about the coloured woman with pairs of shoes. He wondered if this Marjorie was that coloured woman.

By that time he had gone back into the kitchen and got more water in the tumbler. Back in the sitting-room he poured himself another drink. He was satisfied about Esselen, anyway, now. He was sure that Marjorie was not the wash-girl that called at regular intervals for Esselen's laundry.

Instinctively Charlie Hendricks began to feel for Esselen that repugnance that any South African feels for a fellow White man that has immoral relations with a Coloured woman. And he began to feel that he himself shouldn't go on drinking brandy like that, going backwards and forwards into the kitchen for more water and coming back and pouring out more tots of brandy and swilling down the stuff while that coloured girl went on standing there, smiling and not talking. And he couldn't invite her to take a chair because that would be out of the question.

"Did Mr Esselen owe you any money, Marjorie?" Charlie Hendricks asked.

The coloured girl smiled again. It was a half-impudent smile, knowing and over-familiar. Nevertheless, Charlie Hendricks had to acknowledge that it was a pretty smile. And he realised that he had referred to Esselen as Mr Esselen. He couldn't bring himself, in talking to this coloured girl, to refer to Esselen as boss. In that way he removed one part of the barrier that was between them of race. It was an important part of the barrier. And it was he himself, and not the coloured girl, that had removed it.

"He does not owe me anything," she said, smiling again.

Smiling seemed to come facilely to Marjorie's lips and eyes. So would she frown effortlessly, also. It would appear that there were no deeps to her. She had a good deal more European blood in her veins than negro or Malay blood. And that easygoing, surface-living part of her nature might have come to her just as readily from some carefree white sailor forebear of hers as from a Malay ancestress singing "Sussie Parmela" when the Cape wine flowed red.

It was Marjorie's smile that drew Charlie Hendricks then. Almost before he realised what had happened, he had put his brandy glass down on a spot on the sideboard where he would find it again, afterwards, and he had gone up to her and put his arms around her.

When he took up his brandy glass once more he realised that he had been right about Marjorie's hair. For when the scarf came off her head, on the divan, it was apparent that she had taken no steps to straighten out her hair's natural frizziness. She had not combed out her hair with a heated brass comb and a hair-straightening cream.

But otherwise, when he lay with her on the divan, Charlie Hendricks could not detect that she was essentially different from a white girl that might have come to lie on the divan in his arms. And – although of this he was unconscious – he had also solved the problem as to how a white man had to act when a coloured girl came into his room. He couldn't offer her a chair, but he could the divan.

After Marjorie had left, Charlie Hendricks remained standing at the sideboard, drinking brandy. And when he looked at the depression in the divan he was filled with self-loathing. He understood then how far he was from being free of prejudice. He had lain with a nigger woman. For the first time in his life he had lain with a nigger woman. And he felt low.

3

Send the visitor in, Cyril Stein said.

And so Detective Sergeant Brits, still on his rounds, entered the office of the secretary of the school-board. It was taking him longer than he thought, to warn the male whites of Willemsdorp that the Tielman Roos Act was going to be more strictly enforced. To a man more gifted with imagination than Brits was, the task he had taken on himself would have appeared stupendous. Brits was also coming to realise that it was a pretty formidable undertaking. But he went ahead with it, stolidly.

"Funny thing," Detective Sergeant Brits said, affably and by way of making conversation, as he sat down at the desk to face Cyril Stein, "but what I thought, coming in here – what I thought was as how I thought I smelt somebody smoking dagga. That's a funny thing for you, now, hey? Somebody smoking dagga at the school-board. Makes you laugh, hey? Next thing you'll be smelling is the minister smoking it in the Upper House of Parliament."

Brits chortled at the absurdity of the idea.

"Dagga?" Cyril Stein enquired. "Dagga, did you say? What is that exactly, Mr Brits?"

The detective's amusement gave way to a look of surprise.

"Dagga? Never heard of dagga?" he said. "Well, that just shows you.

Here's a man never heard of dagga – and you know what? The Commissioner of Police himself says to me only the other day that he hears as how the dagga-smoking habit is spreading among white people in Willemsdorp. Well, that's a lot of balls, of course, I know. I means, it just makes me laugh, of course. Here's you now, for instance, never even heard of it. That's what I say. It's just kaffirs smokes it, and you can't ever stop kaffirs smoking it, not with it growing wild like a weed everywhere – except, they says, the good kind, and that they got to get from Zululand. But that just shows you, don't it? He must have dagga on the brain, the Commissioner of Police must have, thinking as there's white people smokes it. Wouldn't be surprised if the Commissioner comes at it a bit now and again." Brits slapped his leg and laughed.

"Do you really think he does – ?" Cyril Stein began.

"Gawd, no!" the detective ejaculated. "Can't you see a joke, man? I just says it for a joke, man. Just for a laugh. It's awful stuff, dagga. Nellie Pope, they calls it, too. Or just Nellie. Or American green grass, they calls it. Or a kaffir name, msangu. But it's all the same stuff. Makes you stone mad, it does. You goes right off your rocker with it. But I hasn't much to do with it – not smoking it, I mean – ha, ha – but pinching the niggers what smoked it. The Narcotics Squad deals with that. I only pinches a nigger smoking it when he does it right in front of me and I got him dead to rights."

"Oh, so you have a Narcotics Squad?" Cyril Stein asked, looking interested.

"Not here," Brits replied. "In Joburg. They comes in from Joburg only when there's a big lot of dagga smuggling going on, say."

"And what is the effect of this stuff that you call – er – dagga?" Cyril Stein enquired. "I mean, there must be some reason why it's smoked."

"Well, you got me there," the detective answered. "I think it's only when a nigger is so low – real *low*, that is – that he comes at it. But what it does to him, no, that I dunno. I've even thought of trying it myself, once or twice, just to see. But I never done it. For one thing, the authorities might get to hear of it, and think how I'm also a rooker. That's what they calls among themselves a man that smokes it. And another reason why I've never tried is because it's just low, that's what."

"Is there any way you can tell if a man has been smoking it?" Cyril Stein hazarded.

"You *can*," Brits replied. "But it's none too easy. No, none too easy.

For one thing, the pupils of your eyes gets bigger – but not a good piece bigger, if you knows what I means. And it's not too easy, always, to tell if a man's pupils is always that size or if it's only big that way because he's at the moment steamed up full of dagga. Take your eyes, now. See what I mean? I can't say as your eyes is bigger now than what they is normal, like. Although a doctor, of course, I suppose, could tell. And a Narcotics Squad man would know, also, I should say. Why, he wouldn't take more than one look at your eyes, just, and he'd be wise to what you does sitting here in your school-board office in your spare time – ha, ha."

Brits seemed to enjoy the joke. The incongruity of Cyril Stein's being addicted to a disreputable kind of drug – and of all things smoking it on the premises of the school-board – made a very strong appeal to him. He could go on laughing about it for quite a long time, seeing still further angles to it, each time.

"Anyway," he continued, more soberly, "the best way as I know for spotting if anybody smokes it is just going by the smell. You can't miss the smell. It's like a smell of chocolates what's burning, almost. Or not so much chocolates as – oh well, I dunno, it's hard to explain. It's a half sweet sort of smell, sort of. But it's also not sweet. It's a green smell, like, if you knows what a green smell *is*. But it's no good. You got to know the smell for yourself if you wants to know what it smells like. And anyway that's how I tells mostly if somebody is smoking old Nellie. I goes by the smell. But I knows as I'm not always right, mind you. Like just now, when I comes into your office – if I didn't know, mind you – if I didn't *know*, I could almost have swore as what I was smelling was dagga being smoked. So you see, you can't always tell."

Cyril Stein looked as though he was getting sleepy. The subject of dagga addiction among the more degraded section of the Coloured community seemed no longer to interest him very much.

And before he left, Detective Sergeant Brits delivered his message about the enforcement of the provisions of the Tielman Roos Act.

"Oh, that's all right," Cyril Stein replied. "I don't need to worry about that. I've given up sleeping with Coloured women. I've found something better. I get more of a kick out of smoking dagga, instead. You know, Nellie Pope."

When he got out on to the sidewalk, Detective Sergeant Brits was still laughing. He just couldn't get over the idea of Cyril Stein being so funny. Anyway, he liked a man that could make a joke.

Willemsdorp citizens were proud of their club. For one thing, the building itself was new and up to date. The architect was the same architect who had drawn up the plans for a famous Johannesburg club when *that* had come to be rebuilt. Not that the fifty-year-old premises that had to be torn down to be replaced by the new Willemsdorp Club did not perhaps have advantages in respect of comfort, say. Indeed, some of the more conservative members of the Willemsdorp Club had at the start taken anything but kindly to some of the innovations with which the new club building confronted them. Old Bayfield, the senior attorney of the town, for instance, had for a brief spell seriously considered resigning his membership because of the oval bar with its chromium fittings that was right next to what they called the committee room. If you wanted a drink, you'd ring for it, Bayfield said. Sitting on a little round stool with just anybody coming and sitting down next to you might be all right if you didn't care about things like –

In his protestations, Bayfield had never got much beyond veiled hints and innuendoes. For one thing, he dared not. It wasn't as though he couldn't still, if he liked, recline in an armchair and press a bell and a whisky and soda would be served him at his elbow. And it wasn't as though, if he did stand up at the chromium-fitted bar – or eat against it on a high stool – it wasn't as though the person he would have next to him would be just any sort of Tom, Dick or Harry. For if there was one thing that the Willemsdorp Club prided itself on, it was that its membership was exclusive. And that applied no less to town members than it did to country members. And so, even seated against the oval bar, there wasn't much risk of Attorney Bayfield finding himself sitting cheek by jowl with somebody who was just nobody. For it was only if you were a pretty important person in the professional, commercial, industrial, religious, social or educational life of the town that you could become a member of the Willemsdorp Club. (The fact that the literary, artistic, philosophical, musical side of human activity was not represented served only to impart a tone to the club.)

Consequently, taken by and large, Attorney Bayfield didn't have much of a squeal.

"Can you beat that?" the Reverend Thorwell Macey, the Church of England clergyman, remarked that evening in the club. "Just as I've been telling you, it happened. Either I'm drunk, or that policeman is drunk. Or else the Members of Parliament who passed that piece of legislation were, at the time, drunk. But that is exactly what took place. He warned me – I am not exaggerating – he actually had the audacity to warn me of the consequences likely to ensue upon my having sexual intercourse with a black woman. The legal consequences were what he dwelt on, of course. He didn't, that is, well, you know what I mean – other consequences – yes, thanks, I don't mind if I have just one more brandy and soda – but, as I was saying – a bit de trop, what?"

"You mustn't take that too much to heart, padre," Jack Brummer said, trying to talk not in his natural manner but in the way that he imagined an Anglican parson not too well acquainted with South African conditions would expect an ex-rugby forward to talk. "You mustn't get too much upset by that sort of thing, I mean."

And because the Reverend Thorwell Macey had heard that Jack Brummer had just by a hair's breadth missed being capped for the Transvaal, he also decided that it would be expedient to play ball.

"But nevertheless it's not quite – the rules of the game, is it, what?" he asked. "A low tackle – ha, ha?"

There was general laughter.

Johannes Erasmus, who formed one of the little group taking part in that talk, didn't feel altogether happy, somehow. He wanted to fit in. With his whole soul he wanted to have a place, not only in that small group but in the Willemsdorp Club. But he couldn't forget that he was principal of the Afrikaans-medium school. He wasn't just a teacher there: he was principal – the headmaster. And he couldn't just bring himself to laugh when a minister of the church – even if it was of the English Church – said a thing like that. The fact that Reverend Thorwell Macey hadn't meant to infer quite that – and that he had said it mainly because he was nervous in the presence of a distinguished footballer, in the same way that the distinguished footballer was nervous in *his* presence, going so far as to commit the gaffe of addressing him as padre – these were urgent realities that Johannes Erasmus, in his capacity as school principal, could not identify himself with on the spur of the moment, for the simple reason that he had had a hard life as a child.

Nobody who had had a hard life as a child should ever presume, in later years, merely because of adventitious success that has come to him, to arrogate to himself a place in the community. Let him content himself with being a self-made man. Let him content himself with being a genius. But let him not try to make the awful blunder of pretending that he *belongs*. That was what Johannes Erasmus thought then.

"Ha, ha," he said, joining in the laughter. "Very good, I must say. A low tackle. Ha, ha."

And immediately afterwards he felt that he could have cut his tongue out for that. When he realised that he had so easily betrayed both himself and his people.

It was at that moment that Robert E. Constable, the Union Party candidate for the Willemsdorp Provincial Council vacancy, came into the club, accompanied by his election agent, Piet Fourie.

" – and soda," Robert E. Constable announced in a large voice. "Just come back from a political meeting. How d'you like that, eh? Just come back from a political meeting on the backveld. Where was that meeting, Piet old boy? You tell the boys. Blessed if I can remember the name at all."

"Swanepoelsrus," Piet Fourie, Robert E. Constable's election agent, informed all and sundry within earshot. "At Swanepoelsrus the meeting was. And a first-class meeting, too, if you ask me."

Hershberg the chemist went up and shook hands with Robert E. Constable. For Hershberg had been to Swanepoelsrus. And he knew that if Robert E. Constable had pulled off anything like a successful meeting in that notorious Volksparty stronghold there must be a considerable swing of public opinion back to the Union Party.

"Except, perhaps, at the end, it wasn't so good," Piet Fourie the election agent said. "That was when some roughs started asking him would he let his sister marry a nigger. But we always expect a bit of that sort of thing, of course."

"But I got a lot of applause, right through," Robert E. Constable declared triumphantly. "What was more – no bicycle chains. I've still got both my ears on."

"And they asked would he go to bed with a kaffir woman," Piet Fourie was saying above the din of voices.

Meanwhile, Reverend Thorwell Macey was enlarging to Jack Brummer on several further implications of the detective's call. Jack Brummer did not think it necessary to mention that Detective Sergeant Brits had but recently visited him as well.

And, listening to all that talk, it was as though Charlie Hendricks realised then, for the first time, what sort of a white man he was. A white man who went with coloured women. He hadn't realised it quite so clearly while the girl Marjorie was in his flat. While she was lying on the bed, even.

And, ordering another brandy in the Willemsdorp Club, Charlie Hendricks started worrying, then. In spite of himself, he began to feel his conscience troubling him. He told himself that it must be living in a small town that was affecting him that way. But telling himself that didn't help. He felt low. He was a white man who had gone with a nigger woman. It was as though he suddenly felt his whole world rocking. Even though he told himself that he was just being silly.

"I wouldn't be surprised if people like that carry on with kaffir women themselves," Piet Fourie was saying. "Otherwise, how do they always come out so pat with it?"

Johannes Erasmus, the school principal, was not very happy in the Willemsdorp Club. Nor was Charlie Hendricks.

Chapter Seven

1

I T wasn't the actual words that the compositor Jones had used, Charlie Hendricks reflected. But it was the way he had spoken them. There was something positively insulting in his tone. And Charlie Hendricks realised that there was nothing he could do about it. If he took any notice of Jones in that particular way, then he would only succeed in making himself look ridiculous. Still, it was galling. Secretly, Charlie Hendricks began to wonder if Jones had any suspicions about the coloured girl's visit to his flat. That might account for Jones's impudence, perhaps. But in the next moment Charlie Hendricks dismissed the idea.

(He didn't know that that was Jones's way of treating all editors.)

Charlie Hendricks drew his car up at the side of the road. He was on the way to Kleinberg. Kleinberg was not very far from Willemsdorp in terms of miles. But Willemsdorp was Highveld. It stood on the edge of the great plateau. As far south as you cared to go was rolling grassland. But Kleinberg was north of Willemsdorp, and it was in the Lowveld, a good way down towards the foot of the plateau. The climate of Kleinberg was, in consequence, tropical, with the grass-covered uplands giving way to thick bush. In the luxuriance of the vegetation in the Kleinberg area there was also a fierceness.

The spot where Charlie Hendricks stopped his car was already a good distance into the bush. There was a shallow stream with yellow water. Some yards away from the new concrete bridge were the crumbled foundations of the old – a pile of broken masonry strangely silent, somehow. Since this was a time of drought, the yellow water in the stream had been reduced to the narrowness of a furrow. Across one side of it stood a barbed-wire fence, the wire being carried on crooked poles. Two gnarled willows served as gateposts; willow leaves were floating on the water. It was queer that willows should be in that place, when all around there was just African bush, soetdorings and moepels and withaaks and kameeldorings. Where the ground sloped, big roots of the willow stuck out.

The car was halted in the shade of a deep cutting. The road to Kleinberg had been hacked through dense bush and blasted down a mountainside. A wall of ironstone rose up sheerly. Above it, stiff spikes of tall brown grass speared the sky. Beyond lay the bush, that was old and Africa.

Charlie Hendricks looked at his watch. It was yet early afternoon. He did not need to get to Kleinberg for a long while, yet. There was plenty of time. He got out of the car. He took off his jacket and flung it on the seat. Yes, there was quite an easy way up the side of the cutting. A ledge or two that afforded footholds; a couple of saplings that he could pull himself up by. In a few minutes he had clambered out over the top of the cutting. A strip of tall grass – last year's grass, brown with the drought, and then, beyond, the bush.

Charlie Hendricks did not go far into the bush. If he had left the engine of his car running, he would still have been able to hear it distinctly from where he stood in what was not so much a glade as a niche in the thick jungle. He might have penetrated ten yards into the bush, maybe twenty. And what he saw there, in that irregular opening, was nothing. What he saw, standing in the bush, with the thorns plucking at his shirt, was a grey anthill, with next to it a prickly pear, broad-leafed and steadfast: Turkish fig was the name the Boers gave to it. There were some fragments of cowdung. Red ants scurried over the grey sand.

No more than that, Charlie Hendricks saw, standing in the bush only a few yards off the road and with the thorns plucking at his shirt. He may have stood there for two minutes or for five minutes, or for five hours he may have stood there. Or he may have stood there for years, with his hair and beard growing to a length as he stood, and his shoes and shirt and trousers falling into decay, and his car, a little distance away on the road, rusting and becoming with each year more out of date.

And suddenly Charlie Hendricks grew frightened. In the air he breathed there seemed to be the smell of blood. But what frightened him was not the veld's blood smell. It seemed like a very ancient fear, something he could not define. The leaves of the prickly pear seemed ancestral. The fragments of weathered cowdung were timeless. The anthill had always been there, and always it had been that same shade of grey. The weathered cowdung was more primeval than the Triassic rock that had been exposed by the cutting. About the anthill there was

92

a vast antiquity that went beyond all geological reckonings. The prickly pear seemed alive in an awful, whilom sense, in that aeons ago it should have been extinct.

Charlie Hendricks turned away. Before he realised what had happened, he found himself fleeing. He had only a few yards to go through the bush, to get back to the edge of the cutting. But if somebody told him that they were years instead of yards he would not have disputed it. In the hot sun of early afternoon, with the thorns tugging at his shirt, Charlie Hendricks found himself shivering.

And when he had clambered down the side of the cutting and had got back into his car, and had started it up again, Charlie Hendricks did not at first notice that his jacket was missing. And when he did discover his loss – discovering that while he was in the bush some passing piccanin had stolen his jacket out of the car, in that interim that might have been a few minutes or many years – Charlie Hendricks did not worry about it overmuch.

All the same, the feelings that Charlie Hendricks experienced during those few moments in which he had found himself in the opening in the bush were in actual fact of a very commonplace order. Indeed, you can't, anywhere in the bushveld, turn away off the road and go a few yards into the bush and *not* get those feelings. It is impossible not to come across an opening, after a few yards. And it is of course impossible for that opening *not* to be decorated with an anthill and some prickly pear leaves and a handful or so of weathered manure. And any Boer with a look of distance in his eyes and a lot of wrinkles on his face will tell you that it is the most natural thing in the world to get frightened – and very frightened, for that matter.

The name the wise old Boer applies to it is 'Ouma bangheid' – fear of your grandmother – implying thereby that it is a terror not rooted in modernity, but that it is something going back pretty far. But if that same old Boer has taken to you, he will also try and put you right, winking as he delivers himself of this statement. Why you get frightened, he will tell you, is because in that narrow opening in the bush, cut off from all human companionship, you actually meet yourself. You encounter yourself face to face, the wise old Boer will say, and before God, is not that the most frightening and spinechilling meeting that any man can have?

Well, of course, you'll turn and run. What man in his proper senses wouldn't?

If Charlie Hendricks had known this, it might have helped to console him for the loss of his jacket – with a few pounds in the inside pocket – on the road to Kleinberg. In actual fact, however, he did not worry about that loss as much as he might have.

2

It was that same afternoon that Cyril Stein, school-board secretary, picked on for the execution of a project that he had been turning over in his mind for several weeks. He knew that Lena Cordier was leaving Willemsdorp. She was going back to teaching. She had come to his office for a list of the Johannesburg vacancies in the *Provincial Gazette*. He had spoken to Johannes Erasmus, principal of the Willemsdorp Afrikaans-medium school, about his taking her back on his staff. Johannes Erasmus had declined. Cyril Stein could guess the reason for that, all right. No doubt the school principal had heard the same stories that he himself had heard, about Lena Cordier and that footballer man who had been appointed mining commissioner because he had come so near to being selected for the Springbok rugby team, that time.

Well, he fancied Lena Cordier quite a bit himself, Cyril Stein did. And he said to himself that if she could allow a brainless oaf like Jack Brummer to have all those privileges – well, what was wrong with him, himself, him, Cyril Stein, himself? At least, he felt that he had brains, which was a lot more than what anybody would ever credit Jack Brummer with.

So, that afternoon, Cyril Stein walked out of the school-board office early. He informed his typist – doing his best to make his voice sound casual – that he wouldn't be back for the day. He hurried home to his flat. It was in the same building and on the same floor – on the other side of the landing – as the flat occupied by Charlie Hendricks. On the stairs he encountered a girl with a gaily coloured square of material wrapped round her head. Cyril Stein's first interest was in the silk square. He liked bright-coloured stuffs. Then he looked at the girl. He had seen her on those stairs before. He had some idea that she had been in the habit of calling on Esselen, the previous editor of the *Northern Transvaal News*. He wasn't sure, though. She was quite a pretty girl, he thought. He looked at her more closely. Aware of his gaze, she cast her eyes down demurely. It was when she went past him that he realised that she was a Coloured. In the movement of her hips there was, for all the world to take note of, Africa.

The coloured girl, Marjorie, finding that Charlie Hendricks was not at home and that that other white man she had met was not, apparently, disposed to enter into conversation with her, continued on her way down the stairs and along the Willemsdorp sidewalk. But Cyril Stein kept thinking of her for a good while.

The African woman's backside, Cyril Stein was thinking to himself. It was like the shape of the African continent on the map. From the loins of the negro woman would spring all the future generations that would people the African continent. The white man would come and go. His brief sojourn and his passing would leave behind few traces. In the loins of the black woman the history and the destiny of Africa were wrapped up. The white man would come and go and be forgotten. Africa, wombed in the negro woman's pelvis, was secure. Africa would go on forever.

But she was quite pretty, Cyril Stein thought, that girl. If she stood still, now, and didn't move – if there was no vibration in her buttocks – you would take her to be white. It did not occur to him, then, that if that gaudy square of silk material came off her head you would be able to tell too, then, from her hair, that Marjorie was not a properly white woman.

In his flat, Cyril Stein changed quickly into a blue pinstripe suit with lapels that were of an unusual width. The breast-pocket of the jacket was also pretty high up. Those had been among Cyril Stein's special instructions to his tailor. Longer than to change his suit it took him to select the right tie. In the end he was satisfied. Then he sat down on the edge of his bed and took out his cigarette case. In the case were half a dozen cigarettes. He was very methodical about what he did, then. Starting at the end of a cigarette, he rolled it slowly backwards and forwards between thumb and forefinger until a fair amount of the tobacco had come out. He introduced into the vacuity thus created a small quantity of greyish-green leaves that he took out of a brown paper parcel. Finally, he stuffed back some of the cigarette tobacco that he had first rolled out. He did it all very expertly. Even though his hands shook, his performance of the operation betokened long practice. Only with one of the cigarettes did he fail, a bulge forming where the greyish-green leaves were inserted and the paper tearing slightly. Annoyed, he struck a match and smoked that one himself. But with the remaining five cigarettes he was one hundred per cent successful.

He slipped the cigarette case into his inside jacket pocket and, locking the door behind him, sauntered down the stairs and into the street. He was still smoking the stub end of the doctored cigarette. Even though there was none of that packing of greyish-green leaves left in the part of the cigarette that he was smoking, the inhaling of it nevertheless seemed to afford him a good deal of satisfaction. It worked as a chaser.

The sidewalks of Willemsdorp and the blue skies above them seemed to Cyril Stein ecstatically and indescribably lovely. Much too soon he found himself on the first floor of Hex Buildings, knocking at the door of Lena Cordier's room. He would rather that he hadn't got there so quickly. Ah, could he only have dawdled longer, savouring, as he walked, the entrancing loveliness of the sidewalks and feeling that he wanted to laugh outright, that time when he passed a uniformed policeman. His walk to Hex Buildings and up the stairs formed part of a smooth and deep-breathed trance.

His knock on that wooden door was like the beginning of a spell being broken. But he desired Lena Cordier. He had to knock at her door. And he had to wait for the door to be opened. And he had to go through with his project just as over the past weeks he had planned it. But he almost regretted it, in a way, that his monarchy in the kingdom of heaven should have to end thus – in the arms of Lena Cordier. Almost, he would have liked to linger longer in the Elysian fields where the flowers had the fragrance not just of common day roses, but of paradisiacal asphodels. A rose smelt *dirty* next to an asphodel. And as for Lena Cordier –

Still, he told himself, he had to have that, too. No matter how Lena Cordier *smelt*.

The door opened. The wooden door in the passage on the first floor of Hex Buildings that he had knocked on went ajar.

Lena Cordier invited him to come in. Lena Cordier looked ineffably lovely. She was fabulously, supernaturally beautiful, no matter how she might smell afterwards.

"I have come to talk to you about why you should not have to leave Willemsdorp and go to Johannesburg, when I can fix you up easily in the district with a school," Cyril Stein found himself saying, mechanically, because he had gone over the introductory (and the finalising) stages of that interview in his mind so often.

He said all that after Lena Cordier had invited him to sit down. She had indicated the armchair for him to sit in. He had, without quite knowing what he was doing, seated himself on the pouf, upsetting the ashtray in the course of it. Lena Cordier sat down on the edge of the bed, facing him.

"*Have a cigarette,*" Cyril Stein said, passing over his cigarette case. He watched Lena Cordier extracting a cigarette. He took one himself. He watched her eyes as he lit her cigarette.

And the first sensations Lena Cordier had were extremely pleasurable. Softly curved and sweet and far-off, life seemed to her, then, all of a sudden, and about the mere fact of existence there seemed to be the colours of bright stripes. And for a moment she felt peculiarly drawn to this young man who had come from the Education Department with the request that she stay on in the Willemsdorp area. And then, almost immediately afterwards, a reaction set in.

It was something that Cyril Stein had not calculated on. And yet he should have been forewarned against that possibility. He knew enough about the green weed and its effects on different people. He knew there were those who, at the first time of smoking the greyish-green leaf, were not able to yield themselves in entirety to its embraces. It would be different the third or fourth time. But there were some people – a relatively small proportion, maybe – who, inhaling for the first time the acrid fumes of the cannabis indica plant that grew wild in Zululand – experienced, after some transient moments of bliss, an intense and uncontrollable nausea. Next time they smoked it they would be all right, of course. But the results of a first experiment could be quite devastating. Mostly, you got sick like that only if you were pregnant.

And it just had to be Cyril Stein's luck that Lena Cordier belonged to that small minority that couldn't take the drug straight off, first time. She, least of all, would have been able to explain afterwards, coherently, exactly what happened, or how it happened. For, in the first place, she had no idea that she was smoking a drugged cigarette. All she knew was that she felt happy, suddenly, for no reason that she could explain. And then, shortly afterwards, and also for a reason that she could not fathom, she all at once felt bilious. That was about all she knew as to what happened. Secretly, she thought that her physical condition was the cause of it.

For Cyril Stein, in that new Jerusalem that he was in from the dagga, the thing that happened to Lena Cordier then was singularly horrible. It looked much worse to him than it would have looked to a man in a normal state of mind. He walked out of Lena Cordier's room, of course, when that happened. But for long afterwards the whole thing stayed very vivid in his memory. A girl, indescribably and ethereally beautiful, and with her mouth wide open, as though she were singing a soprano love aria, and what came out of her mouth was not song but green- and apricot-coloured vomit.

Afterwards, when he was back in his flat, and the influence of the drug had dissipated, Cyril Stein might have thought that he had imagined all that, and that he had never even called on Lena Cordier. But how he knew that it had really happened was from the state that the wide lapel of his pinstripe jacket was in.

3

You got into Kleinberg suddenly. You saw it once, from above, and then the road wound through some more bush and in the next moment you were driving through the main and only street of the village. There were a few scattered stores and whitewashed houses and a church hall with a baobab in front of it. Nailed to the baobab's trunk was a placard announcing the arrival of the famous Afrikaans actress, Sarah Wessels-Wessels, and her distinguished company.

There was already a sizeable crowd on the church square when Charlie Hendricks got there. Kleinberg had been selected as that year's venue for the Waterberg's celebration of Kruger Day. The air was sultry. It was not yet sunset. Everywhere was rugged growth. The village council could not keep the sidewalks free of poisonous, spiky tendrils or of thick, voluptuous vegetation. There was no doubt that Kleinberg was in the tropics. The flowers flaunted an unhealthy scarlet. The green on broad and ferny leaf had an unnatural hue. Trunks and stems looked as though they had been dipped in sulphur. Sores on men and animals took a long time to heal.

The fact of Charlie Hendricks being minus a jacket did not attract notice. Many of the men were in shirt-sleeves. Others wore suits of corduroy. The cut had been fashionable a century ago: those 'dopper' suits with embroidered jackets were worn in homage to the Voortrekkers and the Transvaal's historic past. A sprinkling of women had also come in

Voortrekker costume – in sunbonnets that protruded brusquely from their foreheads and long wide skirts that descended to their shoes. An ox-wagon decorated with the flags of the long vanished Transvaal and Free State Republics was drawn up in the centre of the church square. It served as a plinth for the speakers.

Charlie Hendricks, making his way towards the ox-wagon, recognised the orator. It was Dap van Zyl, the Volksparty candidate in the by-election. Charlie Hendricks knew that Dap van Zyl was coming to the end of his speech. For he also recognised the peroration. "Already there is the dawn of a new greatness, a new era, for the South African people," Dap van Zyl was saying. "In the fullness of time – "

It was just the way his opponent, the Union Party candidate, Robert E. Constable, spoke.

Floridly handsome Dap van Zyl was. Clean-cut features and mobile mouth. And long, gracefully curved chin. And yet if you drew a line horizontally across the middle of his face, the upper half would not seem to fit in with the lower half.

Dap van Zyl sat down to thunderous applause. The sun was by that time near setting. It had all been admirably timed. A cavalcade approached – old men riding side by side with young boys, just as it was in the Boer War – greybeards and penkop youngsters taking up their rifles against the English. In the gathering dusk the horse commando circled the plein, fine-looking horses and fine-looking men. Young and old, they sat in their saddles with negligent ease. Bushveld bred, they had grown up with guns and horses. In spite of the fact that he was on the other side – that he was a newspaper man in the employ of the Union Party – Charlie Hendricks felt a tightening at his throat. They were his people. That was how the men of his people had ridden to war half a century ago – Transvaal Boers and Free State Boers and Cape rebels – a handful of burghers ranging in age from schoolboys to octogenarians, with no uniform but their farm clothes. With their bandoliers and their Mauser rifles they had ridden out over the veld to challenge the might of the British Empire. And it took the British Empire three years to win the Boer War. "Hoera, hoera, ons burgers is getrou; hoera, hoera, ons sal ons land behou." The crowd around the wagon took up the chorus. Fifty years under a foreign flag did not seem so long, then, in a nation's history. The foreign flag of England might not have been floating above the government buildings at all, then.

"If they did not burn down all our farmhouses and if they did not put our women and children in concentration camps," Charlie Hendricks heard a voice say at his elbow, "the English would never have won the Boer War."

Charlie Hendricks turned round. The speaker was Jack Brummer. Charlie Hendricks did not answer. He felt that he was being carried out of his depth. The Union Party argument about forgetting the past and looking, instead, to the future, did not come out very pat, then. He knew Jack Brummer was a republican. Of his own sentiments he did not at that moment feel too sure. So he said nothing to Jack Brummer.

Suddenly it was night. Night came to Kleinberg, as to all tropical places, with annihilating swiftness. Then the flaps of the wagon-tent were parted from the inside and a figure in a top-hat and black frock-coat, with the red-green-blue-and-white presidential sash of Paul Kruger draped across it from right shoulder to left middle, emerged from the interior. A motor car's headlights were trained on to the figure. Then, from inside the tent, booming and sonorous on the stillness of the night air, came the last message (played on a gramophone) of Paul Kruger, last president of the Transvaal Republic, dying in exile in Switzerland: "Take from the past that which was good. . . I was born under the English flag. I do not wish to die under the English flag. . . "

There seemed no incongruity in the pause, halfway through the speech, to enable the gramophone record to be changed.

Kruger's last message came to an end. The headlights were switched off. The top-hatted, frockcoated figure with the huge false beard withdrew inside the tent. The horse commando fired a volley into the air. The crowd struck up the old Transvaal Volkslied. A Dutch Reformed Church minister pronounced the benediction. The Kruger Day celebrations were at an end.

All that was left of Kruger Day were orange peels and banana skins and pieces of paper littering the church plein. Charlie Hendricks mentioned the loss of his jacket to Brummer. Jack Brummer said that he knew the local shopkeeper, who would unlock his shop and get Charlie Hendricks a sports coat. Jack Brummer also lent him a few pounds. The night wind blew a piece of newspaper against them as they walked off in the direction of the hotel.

4

"Why didn't you say all that to me before?" Malie Erasmus asked, stung. "Before I went to the trouble of getting Johannes to have you fixed up with this work here, in Willemsdorp, and all, I mean?"

They were in the bedroom of Johannes Erasmus's home. The wife and the brother of the principal of the Willemsdorp Afrikaans-medium school were seated together on the bed. It was night. Johannes Erasmus was at the club, wondering what he was doing there.

Krisjan Erasmus, but recently elevated from being a starving bywoner to a position of what he regarded as eminence, turned immediately to face Malie. Immediately after she had said those words about his job. His face twisted into an expression that might as easily have been pain as malice. He didn't care tuppence for women. On the back-veld, girls had run after him. There was something about him that girls couldn't resist – a certain type of girl, anyway. There was a certain air and backveld grace about him. A red masculinity that girls fell for. And he knew they were attracted to him. And so he despised them. Krisjan had a raw, crude sex, of a sort that could rouse women's passions. His brother, Johannes, had nothing of that. That was why Johannes's own wife, Malie, and his own brother, Krisjan, were at the moment sitting in his bedroom and on his bed. While he was at the Willemsdorp Club, unhappy, wondering what on earth he had come there for.

But for all the contempt that he might have for women, one thing that Krisjan Erasmus respected was his job. To be a lorry driver was to be a king. That was how he felt about it, after the poverty and the misery and the degradation of his life as a bywoner. And Malie mustn't start talking nonsense, now. He wouldn't stand for her saying anything that might imply his job was imperilled.

"You cut that out about my work, see?" Krisjan Erasmus said to Malie. "I'm good at my job, see? Mr Stein the school-board secretary said to me only yesterday that I'm good at driving the department lorry. I'm always on time, he said. And I'm never drunk on my work, he said. And he said on that sort of job it was hard to get a man that keeps sober, seeing that he's on his own so much, with no boss to see if he's walking into a bar or not. And so, all right, I don't say you didn't get me this job. But it's me now that's keeping this job, see? And so I say you've got to lay right off my job." On his face was a look of hatred, mingled with fear.

Malie was surprised at the violence of his reaction – surprised and taken aback. And he had been so arrogant a few moments before, in what he had said to her. Anyway, it was good to know that there was a point she could get him on. Although she would go no further with it now. But there was satisfaction in the thought that she would know how to set about it to have him cringing.

"But it wasn't nice of you to have spoken to me like that, Krisjan," Malie said. "After everything that has been between us, that is."

"But I didn't mean it," Krisjan answered. "Before God, I don't mean it the way you seem to think. It was you that asked me, first. And I wasn't thinking when I said that. I didn't say you weren't as good as any woman I've ever had. I only said you weren't the worst I'd ever slept with. I mean, there really isn't much difference between one woman and another *that* way, and all I said – "

"That's all right, Krisjan," Malie said coldly. She got up from the bed. She despised herself. She could sense the disdain in which Krisjan held all woman. But she felt that all that was nothing compared with the contempt she had for herself. It was unbelievable that she could have been so weak. A pitiful creature like this Krisjan, now. Sitting there on the bed, bewildered – not knowing whether to be impudent or to fawn. And that cheap hairoil that he plastered on his head. It was horrible. She had all her life felt that she was low. This proved it, now. And the worst of it all was that she didn't feel any more guilty, now, after she had lain with Krisjan, than she had felt all her life. All her life she had felt guilty, anyway. If it wasn't because of one thing, it was because of another. It must have been that she had always known she was low.

To think that she could have sullied herself with a man like that. Just look at him, she thought. And just imagine what he is, she thought. And that awful hairoil. Suddenly, Malie felt that she wanted to laugh. It wasn't a tragedy that she had got herself mixed up in. It wasn't even very filthy or very disgusting. It was something just funny – funny. Oh, screamingly funny. But she dared not allow herself to start laughing, because there would be no stopping herself, after that. She would just want to go on laughing. On and on laughing. Rushing right out into the street, laughing.

That was one thing that served to control her – the thought that there would never come an end to her wild mirth. The other thing that restrained her was the knowledge that her body would again desire Krisjan. She might laugh at him as much as she liked. She could despise herself for being an abandoned whore. But her body would again betray her. And when that happened she would have no rest until she had lain with him in bed, in his arms once more. The laugh was on her.

"Button up your clothes, now, Krisjan," Malie said. "Let us go back into the dining-room."

Krisjan adjusted his apparel quickly, furtively. Not that he cared how Malie saw him, of course. But it was as though in his imagination he suddenly pictured the secretary of the school-board looking at him, seeing his nakedness exposed.

When Johannes Erasmus arrived back from the club a good while later, his wife Malie and his brother Krisjan were sitting in the dining-room talking.

The three of them engaged in a desultory discussion. Then Malie went out to make coffee.

"Are you getting on all right, with your work?" Johannes asked of his brother when the two of them were alone. Krisjan replied affirmatively. His job again, he thought. His job seemed to be mixed up somehow with his brother and his brother's wife. He didn't like it. Krisjan felt it was one thing that he himself should be mixed up with his brother's wife. That wasn't anything very important. But he didn't want his job brought into it. After they had coffee, Krisjan left.

"That stink of Krisjan's hairoil is all over the place," Johannes Erasmus said to his wife as they got into bed. "What he wants to stick cheap stuff like that on his head for I don't know. I can smell it right here in the room, almost."

Once again Malie felt that she wanted to laugh.

Chapter Eight

1

M AVIS Clark informed her mother that she was being beastly. Mother and daughter were talking in a room in Ben's Losies-huis, the boarding-house that Mrs Clark ran.

"I'm sure I don't know where you get ideas like that from, Mother," Mavis said, her naturally vivid colouring accentuated by two crimson spots high up on her cheeks. "It's all right saying that you were also a girl once and that you're talking to me like this for my own good. If you can see anything wrong in my having gone out a few times with Jack – "

"He's your employer, for one thing," Mrs Clark interjected.

"He's not," Mavis replied. "The government is my employer. And Jack Brummer is in the service of the Mines Department, just like I am. And he gets his cheque every month from Pretoria in the same way that I do."

Mrs Clark was in no mood for quibbling. "Has he said anything – " she began.

The two spots on Mavis's cheeks, on a level with her eyes, turned a darker red. "Why should he?" Mavis Clark fenced. "I don't even know how he feels about me. And – and I don't know how I feel about him, exactly. And just because I've been out with him a few times, you're starting to upset everything. And *spoiling* everything, that's what you're doing."

She took off her spectacles and began to polish the lenses on a handkerchief, keeping her eyes down as she rubbed.

"Don't think I can't understand how you feel, Mavis, darling," Mrs Clark said, her voice gentle but also tinged with a worldly practicality – as befitted somebody who was at once a woman and a successful person at business, at once a mother and a prominent committee member of the local branch of the Union Party – "and I want you to believe me that I went through all that too, when I was young. I had all those same emotions, darling. You young people seem to think that we older people don't know – that we can't share in – oh dear, oh dear – can't you see that I'm only trying to help you? Don't think of me as your mother. Try and think of me just as a woman. Just as another woman – somebody that has had a little more experience of life than you have had, perhaps."

That was something Mavis Clark couldn't stand for. In her heart she resented that suggestion. Her mother. Experience of life. Her mother knew how to run a boarding-house, maybe. She could organise little fund-raising functions for the Party, perhaps. But what did that have to do with life? Had her mother ever felt anything like what she was feeling now? Had her mother in her life ever known real bliss – the real thing, though? And had her mother ever known real torture? Mavis Clark thought of her father. Smug was what he was, she thought. And even when she had seen him lying in his coffin (sinful though it was of her to entertain ideas like that) that was one thing about the way he lay there that she just couldn't help noticing. Dead, he seemed just as complacent, as serenely self-satisfied as he had been when living. Well, that was something that she didn't want. Wouldn't her mother understand that she didn't want that? – Mavis Clark said to herself. She didn't want to be a successful and respected boarding-house proprietress. She didn't want dull contentment and to be comfortably and unexcitingly married. It hurt, what she was going through now with Jack Brummer. She wasn't a fool, Mavis Clark said to herself. Except perhaps at the start. But God, how much she had learnt! Oh, she knew what Jack Brummer was, all right. And if her mother's idea of the right way to live was that you had to play safe, well, her mother could have it. That wasn't wisdom, it was just cowardice. If that was the philosophy of old people, they were welcome to it. Maybe they weren't worthy of anything better.

Mavis Clark put her glasses on again.

"If you want to know has he asked me to marry him, Mother," she said, "well, then the answer is that he hasn't. And I'm not sure if I want him to. After all, how long have I known him – known him to go out with, I mean? I feel it's so stupid of you to talk about it at all. After all, as I've said, I've only been out with him a few times. And he's away, now. He's at Kleinberg. He's got to send a report to Pretoria about what's going on in the district. And I don't know exactly when he'll be back. Or how he'll feel about me when he gets back. Or – or – how I'll feel about him."

"It's not only what I'm saying, Mavis," Mrs Clark answered. "It's what other people are saying, also. About your sitting alone with Jack Brummer in his car under the thorn-trees other side of the bridge."

"Well," Mavis said, drawing in her breath, "if that isn't the limit. That's the worst of living in a dorp like this. Where there's nothing to do but talk scandal. And what's wrong with it, I'd like to know? I don't mean, talking scandal; I mean my sitting with Jack in his car by the bridge – in broad daylight. What's wrong with it?"

"The time people are talking about," Mrs Clark replied, calmly, "or at least one of the times, was when it wasn't broad daylight. It seems it was pretty late at night, too."

The high colour left Mavis Clark's face. "Who – who – " she started.

"I'll tell you later, Mavis," Mrs Clark said. "Not now. And, of course, it wasn't told to me directly. But I want you to understand that I've also been young. And I've also – "

Mrs Clark pulled herself up. Maybe she had said more than she had intended. On the other hand, it was just possible that she had worked out exactly which words to give utterance to, and which to leave unspoken.

A long silence followed. And during the silence it seemed as though Mrs Clark was still going on talking. But she wasn't, of course. It was just that in those three words she had spoken, in her having said, "And I've also – ", that there was revealed to Mavis more than she had ever known before, about her mother. But not more than she had unconsciously suspected, maybe. At the same time, it was more, also, than what Mavis Clark wanted to know.

It was hard for Mavis to ask the obvious question. She would rather not have asked. The thought of that love story of long ago at which her mother hinted held for the daughter no element of faded romance. It gave Mavis a feeling of repugnance more than anything else, really. It was a fragrant secret that it would have done her mother no harm to have kept to herself, Mavis thought. Next thing, her mother would be producing a packet of yellowed love-letters. Nevertheless, and almost dutifully, Mavis put the question.

"Was it Father?" Mavis asked.

And before her mother spoke, she knew the answer. She knew it from the pink colour that came into her mother's cheek, high up.

"No," Mrs Clark said. "It was another man."

How flat that sounded, Mavis thought. Here was her mother just busy dramatising herself. It was tiresome. Sickening, even. She wouldn't be surprised, now, if her mother hadn't brought up that whole argument just so that she could relive a bit of a romance of her own. Thrusting on to her daughter something that her daughter could not even try and feign interest in. Mavis found herself getting angry.

"Who – " she started to ask again.

"Who the man was?" Mrs Clark interjected. "Well, you see, it was like this – "

"No," Mavis almost shouted. "Not *that*. Who was the infernal busybody that told you I was with Jack Brummer in his car and under the thorn-trees after dark?"

Mrs Clark did not reply. She looked staggered. . . stunned.

2

After dinner at the Kleinberg Hotel the guests trooped into the lounge. It was a large room and it smelt musty. There were cracks in the floorboards and in the low walls. A couple of sporting photographs hung on the walls – determined-looking men holding long fish: the fish were naturally enough not nearly as long as what the fishermen claimed them to be, but they were pretty sizeable, all the same. There was also a faded picture of Boer leaders and British generals meeting at the end of the Second Boer War to make peace.

A number of round tables, their tops liquor-stained, had been pushed together in the centre of the lounge. To Charlie Hendricks they seemed all locked together, like the wheels in a complicated piece of machinery.

In the kitchen the naked kaffir cook, dinner over, was preparing a quick dish with a French name for a couple of late arrivals. He had a natural talent for cooking. And because he belonged to the Mchopi tribe – the male members of which were permitted, at certain seasons, to give the women a hand with the preparation of food and drink – he had not been completely frustrated in the old days, when he was still a tribal warrior. Coming home from an inter-tribal battle, he could get self-expression out of doing a ragout or an en casserole or a galantine just right. Or a meat gateau. If it had been a victory, the meat part would have consisted of some portion of an enemy that he had brought home with him. Otherwise just a lump of crocodile brisket would have to do. In the kitchen of the Kleinberg Hotel this naked Mchopi warrior had found himself. His buttocks and belly glistened regularly with grease. That was from wiping a knife or a spoon on them. If there was curry on the menu, that day, his belly and buttocks would be streaked with yellow – a bright yellow. He was an artist.

There were numbers of introductions. Raw brandy flowed, in the Kleinberg Hotel lounge. Charlie Hendricks found himself sitting next to Dap van Zyl, the Volksparty candidate for the by-election. Jack Brummer was also somewhere in the vicinity. So were other people. Charlie Hendricks wasn't very sure of their identity. The brandy the waiters brought was heady stuff.

"How's your paper getting on?" Charlie Hendricks heard Dap van Zyl asking. And it didn't seem so much as if Dap van Zyl really did belong to the other side. Charlie Hendricks felt more at home with Dap van Zyl, somehow, than he would ever have done with Robert E. Constable. The man he was busy fighting tooth and nail was also a man he felt nearer to, in a human sense, than he felt to his party's official candidate.

"What you boys so serious about?" Charlie Hendricks heard Jack Brummer calling out, suddenly, above the stridency of numerous raised voices. "Are you trying to get Dap van Zyl to do something for you after he gets elected?"

There was a lot of laughter. But Charlie Hendricks didn't think it so funny. Although Robert E. Constable was his own party's candidate, he would never be able to turn to him for help, if ever he got stuck, Charlie Hendricks felt. Robert E. Constable was too aloof for that sort of thing. But he wouldn't find it very difficult, if he was ever in trouble, to go to Dap van Zyl, Charlie Hendricks thought.

"We Afrikaners have got everything," Dap van Zyl was saying. "We've got a feeling for the country that's part of our blood. I can pick up a clod of earth, red Transvaal earth, between my fingers and crumble it. Where's your intellect and economics then? What I feel about that handful of soil is the guts of nationhood. What English-speaking South African has got that? It's only we Boers that have got it. We've got to win. Show me where the Englishman with his 'God Save the King' is in Africa, next to that?"

More talk and more brandy.

People came in at intervals, from outside of the charmed circle of the round-topped tables and Dap van Zyl's talk. By that time the round-topped tables seemed as though they actually were turning, and forming part of a machine – part of Dap van Zyl's political machine, maybe. Farmers' hands were extended from out of the shadows. Dap van Zyl addressed the owners of the hands by name, by their Christian names, and he enquired after those farmers' children by their Christian names. That he didn't always get those Christian names right was only a trifle.

Afterwards it seemed to Charlie Hendricks that there was another voice, there at the group of massed round-topped tables, that was gradually putting Dap van Zyl's voice out of business. It was a newly-arrived voice, and it was female. Only after a considerable while was Charlie Hendricks able to take it all in. The speaker was sitting next to him. She was feminine, after a fashion. Her name was Sarah Wessels-Wessels. That meant it was getting late. The play was over. The audience had streamed out of the hall. The gifted actress who played the star role had shed her stage costume and had found her way into the hotel lounge. By degrees you heard less and less of Dap van Zyl's voice, and more of Sarah Wessels-Wessels's. The politician, good though he was, couldn't compete with the actress when it came to sheer blah. In sheer hooey, Dap van Zyl the politician was outclassed.

It was part of his greatness that he knew when he was licked. Shortly after Sarah Wessels-Wessels's arrival, he withdrew.

People's faces swam in coloured mists. Sarah Wessels-Wessels's face also. She must be drunk, too, Charlie Hendricks thought. In any case, she was drinking a lot. The upper part of her face was wide and her eyes were set far apart. And she had black hair that fell forward over her face. She had to keep brushing the hair out of her eyes with a hand that fluttered like a flag; her long, slender fingers were like the stripes on the flag.

"Yes, my own grandfather was Surveyor-General of the Free State," Charlie Hendricks heard Sarah Wessels-Wessels say. "I was in Venice last year – or was it Milan? I forget, now, but they called it the Queen of the Adriatic. All history and palaces." – Again she fluttered some stray hair from her mouth to make room for the brandy glass, and her narrow fingers were blowing in the wind – the slender bars on a haughty pennon winging from some ancient battlement of the Doges. – "That was when I acted in my first Italian film. They've got a cathedral with two thousand column things and a lion in front. A man sang operas to me on a mandolin. The newspapers were full of it."

This time the steward merely enquired, "The same again, sir?" So

109

Charlie Hendricks knew that the rest had left. He and Sarah Wessels-Wessels were alone in the lounge. It was only then that he realised there were no more faces around, swimming in coloured mists.

"I am a pathological liar and an egomaniac," Sarah Wessels-Wessels was saying. "My psychiatrist, Dr Kumpfel, says he can't do much about it, because if he changes me from a pathological liar and an egomaniac it might break out in other ways. Maybe massage or electric treatment might help – might help him, I mean. With that awful bull neck he's got. All bulging with suet."

They went on drinking. Then, afterwards, Charlie Hendricks helped her down the passage to her bedroom. She leant sideways, drunkenly, to kiss him. Almost, they both fell.

"How did you like me in the tableau tonight?" she asked. She sounded quite sober. Obviously, the part of her brain in control of her speech organs was the last part of her to get drunk.

"I didn't see your play," Charlie Hendricks said. "But I've seen you act in Johannesburg. I think you're good."

"No, not the play," Sarah Wessels-Wessels said, as they continued down the passage. "The play was lousy. I mean the tableau, on the ox-wagon. How did you like me as President Kruger?"

Although his brain was fuddled with drink, Charlie Hendricks was still sober enough to be startled. He was also sober enough to be able to recall that that top-hatted, frockcoated figure standing on the wagon in the light of the car lamps did – making due allowance for padding and the rest – bear some sort of a resemblance to Sarah Wessels-Wessels's own figure.

"Good God," Charlie Hendricks said.

3

With the moonlight streaming in through the windows of her bedroom in Hex Buildings, Lena Cordier lay asleep. She was dreaming.

Lena Cordier dreamt that she was back home, on her parents' farm. It was afternoon. Two pigeons came fluttering on to her shoulder. There was a queer light about the afternoon: the afternoon seemed to have the same colour as the pigeons' plumage. Then she remembered what a long time she had been away from the old farm on which she had grown up. The pigeons must be thirsty by now, she thought. It must be a long time since they had last drunk water. She would go into the kitchen to fetch water for the pigeons. But then she remembered that in the kitchen she would meet her mother. And she did not want her mother to see her. She did not want her mother to see her now. She would go and look for water for the pigeons out on the veld instead.

But when she turned away from the kitchen door she saw that the pigeons had changed into white ducks. The two pigeons had got transformed into quite a number of white ducks that were lying on the ground. And they were dead. She stooped down to find out what the white ducks had died of. And what she saw then made her recoil. It was very horrible. For the reddish-yellow beaks of the white ducks were enlarged to a size greater than their bodies. And their beaks were twisted into frightening shapes. That must be why the ducks had died.

The dead ducks should be buried, Lena Cordier said to herself in her dream. They must be buried before her mother found out about them. So Lena started burying the dead ducks, shuddering as she did so. The enormous yellowish-red beaks were twisted and leering. They would poison the soil where they were buried, Lena thought in her dream. Or they would grow again, out of the soil, and then her mother would know. For if you planted tomatoes there, then there would come up tomatoes with twisted yellowish-red beaks. And her mother would know. There was only one thing to do, Lena Cordier said to herself in her dream. Then, the next thing, she found that she was actually doing it. Yes, she was burying those dead ducks in her own body.

Lena Cordier awoke from her nightmare with a scream. Her forehead was damp with sweat. She fumbled in the dark for the matches and cigarettes on the pouf beside her bed. She lit a cigarette. It didn't help. All the details of the nightmare remained vivid in her mind – terrifying, loathsome, disgusting. It was as though the actual taste of the nightmare was in her mouth. She got out of bed and walked over to the window through which the moonlight streamed. She opened the window wide.

The fresh air made her feel better. From the passage below voices floated up to her. They were talking in a Native language she did not understand. Even though they were black men, conversing down there in the passage at the side of Hex Buildings, the sound of their voices brought comfort to her. After the shock of that nightmare it was comforting to think that life was still calm and normal – that people still continued in their ways of life peacefully. The sound of talk and laughter coming up from that passage below steadied her nerves. Even though it was kaffir voices, Lena Cordier said to herself, it was good to hear them.

"This is truly of the number one msangu, my son," Mhlopi the Zulu watchman was saying to the Bechuana flatboy, Pieta.

"It is the best green grass, my father," Pieta answered, accepting the dagga cigarette from the hand of the old Zulu and taking a number of deep puffs, drawing the acrid smoke far down into his lungs. It went very deep down. Deeper than any well. Deeper than the shaft of the Wit Nigel gold mine. Pieta staggered slightly, after the third puff. He passed back the cigarette to the Zulu, who took it gratefully.

"That is one thing in which you are not like the other low class Bechuanas," the watchman said. "There, you are almost a Zulu. Almost, you have in your liver the blood of kings. It is that you do not keep the msangu cigarette a long while, my son. But after you have pulled at it for a sufficiency, you pass it back to the man with whom you are smoking, and you wait then until he gives it back to you. You do not keep smoking it until it is half finished. As we say in Zululand, you do not put the names of your wives and your children and your grandchildren on it. . . This is indeed very good msangu, my son."

Pieta felt not a little flattered. It was much that a full-blooded Zulu should speak thus well of him. It was much that a Zulu should say of him that he, a mere Bechuana, was almost of royal blood. Nevertheless, Pieta could not help but observe that the Zulu was addicted to that very weakness that he praised Pieta for being free of. For the Zulu had the habit of hanging on to the cigarette, all right. He would take a few puffs. And then he would wait. And then he would puff some more. And then he would talk. And then he would have another few puffs, and only a good while afterwards – and then almost as an afterthought – it would occur to him that he had a companion. And so, when he did eventually pass back the msangu, there was a great deal of it dissipated in smoke. The Zulu seemed to put not only his own family on it, but his chief's wives and children as well.

Meanwhile Lena Cordier, awakened from sleep by a nightmare, remained standing at the window, drinking in the night, calmed by the sound of voices uttering words in a language she did not understand.

"It gives one dreams, my son," the Zulu Mhlopi said, then. "Truly the msangu brings one great dreams. It is not for nothing that we say of it in Zululand that it brings one blue dreams. Is it not indeed good stuff, this msangu?"

112

"But it brings another kind of dream, too, my father," Pieta responded, a touch of acerbity in his voice – for Mhlopi really was hanging on
to the cigarette that time, "especially if one smokes too much of it. Too
much frightening dreams, my father."

They started reminiscing, then, frightening each other with stories of
terror that had descended on them when the dagga had brought the
wrong sort of visions. They made their own and each other's flesh
creep, Mhlopi and Pieta, in the tales they unfolded under Lena
Cordier's window of the ghouls that had visited them in dagga night-
mares on such occasions as the drug had acted perversely.

4

Charlie Hendricks was tolerably familiar with the modus operandi on
the Witwatersrand gold mines. Shafts going straight down into the
earth for ten thousand feet. Sand dumps and slimes dumps that were
the size of young mountains and formed Johannesburg's most distinc-
tive topographical feature. It was difficult for him to accept the activities on the corundum propositions as being in the category of mining
operations, also. Jack Brummer had brought him along, into the bush
area of the Kleinberg district, to have a look around.

At dozens of places in the bush were those diggers' camps. There
would be no more than two or three families working on each proposition. The diggers lived in tents, or in galvanised-iron shacks. They also
favoured a type of lean-to that could be taken apart in sections and
moved to some other part of the bush as occasion required. The corundum was near the surface. At no place were there holes more than
about six feet deep. Only in rare cases did the miners use dynamite. It
was practically all pick and shovel work. Charlie Hendricks looked at
a pile of newly-recovered corundum stacked in a heap awaiting transport. What he saw were greenish-black boulders. Some were about the
size – and shape – of a man's head. Others looked as though they could
weigh several tons.

At each of the encampments Jack Brummer stopped the car and
went up to speak to the diggers. He seemed to know them all. Several
of the men Jack Brummer spoke to had grievances, which they were
not particularly hesitant about airing. Generally, their complaints had
to do with the price they were getting for their product – which they
referred to as 'the stuff.' What they also seemed to be unhappy about

was the state of the roads to the nearest railhead. Recovering the stuff was nothing, one digger said to the mining commissioner. Most of his work went into moving it.

At one place, where Jack Brummer got out of the car to talk to some miners, Charlie Hendricks thought that he recognised the two men that he had seen a couple of weeks before in the pub at Willemsdorp. The two men who had stood at the counter drinking and whom he had taken for prospectors because of their metallurgical line of conversation. One had called the other Jim, as far as he could remember. But they looked different, now, because they were dressed in shorts. Still, he didn't think he was mistaken in that one man with the yellowish moustache ending in fierce spikes. Charlie Hendricks remained seated in the car. It wasn't a matter of sufficient interest or importance for him to find out if they were the same two men. And in any case he felt that he would rather not meet them. He knew he had been drinking that afternoon. And he had a slight suspicion that he might have made a fool of himself in the pub.

It was then that he remembered having made a fool of himself in another way. That was the afternoon Marjorie had come into his flat. . . He made a conscious effort to thrust the recollection of Marjorie's visit out of his mind. He tried to think of something else. But it was no good. There was no escape. A sense of self-loathing came over him. He was a white man and he had lain with a coloured woman. It was awful. He felt hot, sitting in the car. He opened a window. But there was no fresh air that could come in. The day was sultry and oppressive.

He was glad when Jack Brummer came back to the car. But all the way on the road to the next diggers' camp, Charlie Hendricks kept on thinking of Marjorie.

As it turned out, the next camp that Jack Brummer stopped at was the last. And this time, too, Charlie Hendricks stayed behind in the car. There was a monotony about these camps. Tents and galvanised-iron huts. Fat, barefooted women and ragged children. Men in khaki shorts or disreputable-looking flannels making holes in the earth with pick and shovel. Their eldest sons helping them. And the same talk about bad roads and unfair prices. And the women carrying buckets to the spruit for water. And washing hanging on the line – their dresses pulling up and exposing their fat, white buttocks: for they had nothing on under their cotton frocks.

Actually, digging corundum was more like farming than mining, Charlie Hendricks thought. When you thought of a gold mine, that was – when you thought of a stooping, sweating army of nigger laisha boys, shovelling the broken rock backwards between their legs down a stope. It was a human machine with a hundred carbide lamps on its forehead. The twisting galleries thousands of feet below the surface were like the lost labyrinths of a disordered brain. A Johannesburg gold mine was at once splendid and terrible. But here – they weren't corundum miners, these people: they were corundum farmers.

"I thought you said that place we stopped at under the koppie was the last," Charlie Hendricks observed to Jack Brummer. For Jack Brummer was again bringing the car to a standstill beside the road.

"The last corundum proposition, yes," Jack Brummer said. "But what I want to show you here is something else. Would you like to see it?"

Charlie Hendricks followed the direction of Jack Brummer's gaze. Just a few yards from the road was a barbed-wire fence. It was square. It enclosed an area about the size of a living-room. There might be a grave there, in the middle of that barbed-wire fence. Or there might be a monument there. That was the feeling you got from seeing a barbed-wire fence right on its own like that, in the bush, and away from all other barbed-wire fences, and enclosing an area the size of a small living-room. Charlie Hendricks's curiosity was piqued. Something historical – to do with the Boer War, possibly, he thought. But before he had climbed the barbed-wire fence – Jack Brummer raising a strand to help him through – he knew it wasn't that.

"Quite frightening, isn't it?" Charlie Hendricks said, peering down into the abyss. "Especially on a hot day like this. I must say it gives me the creeps. How did it come here?"

It was a hole in the ground that went sheer down. A black hole of which you couldn't see the bottom.

Jack Brummer picked up a stone and dropped it into the hole. At first there was silence. Then there came the reverberations of a stone striking against the sides of the hole. Finally there was a noise like the ringing of metal against metal. But it wasn't that, of course. Your instinct told you that it was the sound the stone made falling, very far down, into water.

"It gives most people a bit of a turn," Jack Brummer said. "They call it the Wondergat, in these parts. Old Jim Clinkwood says the Phoenicians sunk this shaft. He reckons that what they took out of it was gold. You must meet the old guy, some time. He's very interesting. A good cut above the average corundum miner. Had some sort of an education, too, I believe. You get some queer characters in these parts."

Never mind about queer characters, Charlie Hendricks thought. That hole was queer enough.

"What puzzles me is how they got it so deep," Charlie Hendricks said, after a pause. It was a long pause. About as long as it would have taken another stone, dropped into the Wondergat, to reach the spot where it would send echoing up the sound of metal striking against metal. "Without explosives and without machinery, I mean."

"Old Clinkwood reckons they did it with heat," Jack Brummer said. "They'd light a fire on the rock and when it was just about red hot they'd pour on water. They still do the same thing here, on the corundum diggings, when they strike a rock they can't shift, and they're out of dynamite. Pouring water on a hot rock splits it as neat as high explosive."

For some queer reason, standing on the edge of that black shaft, Charlie Hendricks found himself, in the heat of the tropical sun, shivering.

Charlie Hendricks was still thinking of the Wondergat when he and Jack Brummer got back to the hotel at Kleinberg.

"I suppose why that hole makes such an impression on one – just a few yards off the tarred road and only a couple of miles from here: I know just where it is, and I'd like to go and have a look at it again on my own, some time," Charlie Hendricks said to Jack Brummer. "I suppose why you get those feelings is because – what did you say those old miners were, Carthaginians?"

"Phoenicians, supposed to be," Jack Brummer answered. "Anyway, some sort of Turks, as far as I can make out from old Clinkwood."

"Well, whoever they were," Charlie Hendricks continued, "why you get such a strong sensation, looking into that Wondergat hole, is because what they dug out of there was gold. You wouldn't get stirred that way if what they had been mining there was only copper, for instance. It's because it was gold that it gives you such an unearthly sort of feeling, I'm thinking."

Jack Brummer did not answer right away.

"If you take my tip," he said to Charlie Hendricks, eventually, "you won't go in for getting that sort of ideas. Thinking that sort of stuff isn't healthy, here, in the bush. It doesn't do anybody any good, getting too fanciful in this part of Africa. What'll you drink?"

Charlie Hendricks gave his order.

But meanwhile the picture of a whole series of corundum diggers' camps was passing through his mind. Men and women and greenish-black boulders and children. And yellow canvas and corrugated iron. And lines of washing hanging out to dry. And white women drawing water at spruits, exposing their bare backsides to the bushveld sun.

Chapter Nine

1

FOR the first few minutes – for as long perhaps, even, as the first ten minutes – Charlie Hendricks felt decidedly nervous. For Detective Sergeant Brits had come into the editorial office of the *Northern Transvaal News* and had seated himself at the desk opposite Charlie Hendricks and had begun to talk.

The worst of it was that Charlie Hendricks felt guilty when the detective came in. And his sense of guilt had to do with the coloured girl, Marjorie. Had the police found out? – was the question that came into his mind in a flash. And in that same moment he remembered the story that was going around town. The story that Detective Sergeant Brits was calling on Willemsdorp's men to warn them that the police would take action if they were caught cohabiting with black women. At the worst, Charlie Hendricks said to himself, that was the reason for the detective's call. Well, there was a farcical side to this new line of activity of Brits's of course. It was very funny, and all that. Slapstick comedy. Somebody falling off a stepladder into a bucket of whitewash. Yes, it was humour, all right – although perhaps not of a very subtle sort. The custard-pie throwing kind of comedy.

All the same, it could make you feel pretty uncomfortable, a detective calling on you and telling you that the eye of the law was steadfastly fixed on you. The eye of the law that never closed in sleep – that never as much as dropped a lid, even, when coal-dust got into it. The most innocent man could feel a trifle shaky. Charlie Hendricks felt that even the Reverend Thorwell Macey, ridiculing the detective's visit when he spoke about it in the club, would have had a more contented mind if Brits hadn't come round. Even if it was only a routine visit.

And Charlie Hendricks could not believe that his own life was not nearly as unblemished as the clergyman's. There was Marjorie, for instance. . .

Gradually, though, as Brits went on talking, Charlie Hendricks began to feel more at ease. It was the kind of stuff Brits was talking that brought relief to Charlie Hendricks's mind. For Brits was talking about murder. Well, that was harmless enough. Brits could go on talking about murder until he was blue in the face. There he himself was safe enough, Charlie Hendricks reasoned. As long as he laid off the subject of white men and coloured women, Brits could go on talking as much as he liked. All the same, in spite of the heat, Charlie Hendricks felt himself shuddering, slightly, at the detective's stories. It was much like the way he had found himself shuddering on the edge of the Wondergat, that day, in spite of the heat.

"You can't stop crime," Brits was saying. "Whether it's me or a hundred other policemen just as good as me. But what we can do is bring the criminals to justice. And we gets big crimes here. Don't you think as we don't. What about the shopkeeper, Vermaak, that got murdered at Klipspruit and that I got eight kaffirs hanged for? And most of them married kaffirs with wives and families. What about that, hey?"

"Oh, you did?" Charlie Hendricks enquired mechanically.

"Eight swunged in one bunch," Brits repeated with satisfaction. "And I bet you don't guess what was the hardest part of the case – to get them swunged, I mean."

"Well, finding them, I suppose," Charlie Hendricks said. "Tracking them down. Proving their guilt. All that, I should think."

"Finding them was the easiest part," Brits said. "We got a informant to lead us right to the hut where all them niggers was lying drunk on the floor. Less than half a mile from the scene of the crime, too. They couldn't wait to open the brandy they had stole from the store. And did they get a shock to hear Vermaak was dead? They thought they had just done tied him up and gagged him. They didn't know as he had fell forward and choked himself. Just my luck that happened, too. Else where would I be with my first big case and him not dead?

"And getting them kaffirs to confess wasn't too hard, either. At the end of a week they all squawked. Except one nigger that I had to do up pretty bad with the sjambok. He just wouldn't come his guts. Claimed he was just passing the hut and seen there was a brandy-drinking party and got drinking also. He knowed nothing about Vermaak, he said, never having been near the store. And today I still think as maybe he was only telling the God's truth. But of course, I wouldn't have none of that. What's the good of swinging only seven, when there's eight as you can have swunged? Hey, what do you say?"

"Oh yes, certainly," Charlie Hendricks said, his voice sounding a bit faint. "Oh yes, indeed."

"Anyway, this one nigger as claimed he was innocent," Detective

Sergeant Brits continued, "and for all I know, he could have *been* innocent – well, him I really had to give a solid doing with the whip. I would have to start on him some time after breakfast, and then work through till lunch time. *My* breakfast and *my* lunch time, that is. I mean to say as that kaffir, of course, couldn't eat a bloody thing. He just left his mieliepap in the cell all the time untasted. Sometimes when I gets tired I calls in a couple of kaffir policemen to help me. But I done my share with the whip, too, all right. I have my promotion to think of. It was one of them short-handled whips and sometimes it broke. But you should of seen that kaffir's shoulders and backside. It was a real treat, man. And I'm not talking now about his guts, where I kicked him a couple of times. Or what I done with his face. You can say what you like, but there's nothing as tough as a kaffir. If it was a white man, he would have been dead end of the first day. But you should of seen that kaffir, the places where that whip got him.

"After you been laying into a kaffir pretty solid for a few days – just knocking off to go and eat, now and again, or going out for a drink, so's to get strength – well, a kaffir turns all green. He don't go black and blue like a white man. He goes all green, and yellow-green. When a young police recruit as hadn't been in the force too long comes walking into that cell, not knowing what's on, he gets sick on the stomach right away. He takes just one look at that kaffir and he vomits all over the floor.

"But the hardest part of the case wasn't getting them niggers to make confessions. What *was* hard was to keep it from the court that Vermaak, the shopkeeper, wasn't properly white. Because if the court and the jury and the judge was to have knowed that Vermaak wasn't a white man, them eight niggers wouldn't have got swunged, see?"

Detective Sergeant Brits went on talking for a good while. And after he had left, Charlie Hendricks was still in doubt as to the exact reason for his call.

Charlie Hendricks felt that he didn't like it, altogether. When the detective first came into his office he was worried. He was worried that it might have something to do with Marjorie. But then, when Brits went on talking, and stuck to the theme of murder, Charlie Hendricks started feeling at ease again.

It was only after the detective had gone, having dropped no hint as to the reason for his call, that something disturbing crept into Charlie

Hendricks's mind once more. But as the day wore on that feeling went. He was prepared to dismiss Brits's visit from his mind completely.

Only, at intervals, naggingly, the memory of it came back.

2

Since the contretemps in Lena Cordier's room, Cyril Stein had been trying to pull himself together. He'd got a fright. This wasn't the way to carry on in a small town – calling on a young woman in her room and inveigling her into smoking a drugged cigarette. That was one of the disadvantages of living in a small town like Willemsdorp, Cyril Stein thought. You got no scope in it.

He was trying hard, now, to break himself completely of the dagga habit. He hadn't been smoking the stuff very long. And he had started on it, actually, in a spirit of devilment. He had heard a lot about Indian hemp, and the effect it was supposed to have on one. And so, when that queer coloured man, Josias, had come to him with a packet, Cyril Stein had bought it. The coloured man hadn't asked him straight out, of course, if he wanted to buy dagga. He had approached him in a round-about way, speaking in esoteric terms, in the same way as, walking into Charlie Hendricks's office one night, he had made indirect references to the weed that brought you blue dreams. Having a quick brain, Cyril Stein had tumbled to what it was about.

And the dagga had turned out to be all that Cyril Stein could have conceived of it in his imagination. Yes, and more. For that reason he was becoming afraid of it. He didn't want to become a dagga addict. He was scared of his personality disintegrating under the influence of a drug that could transport him to imaginative ecstasies. And that could also make him do things that he didn't want to do.

But was he so sure of that? – Cyril Stein asked himself that evening when he was walking in the black shadows of the jacarandas back to his flat. Was he really so sure that he hadn't really wanted to call on Lena Cordier in the way that he had done? Well, to be honest with himself, he had to admit that he had for long entertained feelings like that about her. Only, he had never had the guts to make advances to her. And all that the dagga had done was that it had given him guts. It was unfortunate that things had turned out in that particular way, of course. . .

121

With a jerk, almost, Cyril Stein started pulling himself together again. He refused to let his mind go along that path. All he was doing, reasoning along those lines, was to try and convince himself, in an insidious fashion, that there was nothing wrong with dagga, after all. And he knew that there was a lot wrong with it. In the first place, it was habit-forming. If you smoked enough of it, you became addicted to it. You became a slave of dagga. You couldn't do without it. And how easy it was to fall under the spell of Indian hemp was only too apparent to Cyril Stein. That was why he found it hard to give it up.

What he needed was sympathetic human companionship, Cyril Stein felt. He needed somebody, man or woman, that he could really talk to – somebody that he could understand and that could understand him. But it was hopeless, trying to find any sort of intellectual or spiritual oneness with anybody in this awful Willemsdorp, where everybody was narrow-minded to the point of intolerance, and everybody was a Philistine. That thought gave him a measure of satisfaction – but not much. It did not ease his sense of loneliness at all. He might chuck his job and go to Johannesburg. That was the worst of having got a job through influence. That kind of job could never be any good. Not if it was through *family* influence that you got it. If it was through the influence of a stranger, that you had to battle yourself, personally, to do something for you, it might perhaps be different.

Cyril Stein went on to tell himself that his real reason for having called on Lena Cordier was because he wanted to talk to her. He wanted friendship. But he was too shy to tell her what he had come for. And he had the feeling that she would have laughed at him. And that was why he had armed himself – putting those drugged cigarettes into his case.

And there was that Hendricks, the newspaper man. Cyril Stein felt that Hendricks was a cut above the average Willemsdorp citizen. Hendricks seemed to have a sensitive face. And that was why he had waited for him, in the shadows of the jacarandas, and had got into conversation with him, and had walked with him down the sidewalk. Cyril Stein squirmed when he thought of that, now. He felt that he must have made an awful fool of himself. And he felt that he was always making a fool of himself. That was where the Indian hemp was so marvellous – he felt a king, after a few puffs, an emperor: a man one with his fellow men and as good as the next man. But he wasn't going to smoke it again, Cyril Stein told himself. No, no matter what wonderful stuff that dagga was, he wouldn't touch it again.

Just ahead there was a bright light shining on the sidewalk. It was shining through the half-open green curtains of the pub. Not a bad idea, Cyril Stein thought. He'd go in and have a beer.

The bar was crowded. Quite a number of people standing up against the counter knew Cyril Stein. They waved at him. They shouted greetings to him. He waved back and wished them good evening. But he noticed that nobody signalled to him to come and join them. But he didn't really resent it. He knew he wasn't one of them. Secretly, too, he didn't wish it otherwise. Deep inside himself Cyril Stein knew that he would be nothing if he wasn't different from them – and if he didn't stay different. Never mind how desolate he felt sometimes, feeling lonely. It wasn't just the mob he wanted to be friendly with. Hell, no.

He found a vacant place for himself at the counter, next to a young man in a cheap but gaudily coloured blazer. He ordered a beer.

Cyril Stein was halfway through his beer when he realised who that young man in the cheap blazer, standing next to him, was. And, judging from how red his ears were, that young man who hadn't been in town long from the platteland knew who Cyril Stein was.

"It was the Gawd's truth, the Gawd's own truth, Meneer Stein," Krisjan Erasmus, brother of the school principal, declared, "but it's only very seldom – not more than perhaps two times in a month – that I come into a bar. I don't like drink, Meneer Stein. But I just come in to be friendly."

"But so do I, Meneer Erasmus," Cyril Stein found himself saying. "I also just drop into a bar now and again for the sake of companionship."

It was going to be embarrassing, Cyril Stein felt, if Johannes Erasmus's brother – who had apparently had quite a lot to drink already – should start feeling that he was drinking in the presence of his employer, and that he had to be conscience-stricken about it.

"After all, I'm also in the bar, here, aren't I?" Cyril Stein said. "What are you worrying about?"

Krisjan Erasmus guffawed – partly because he did, like most people from the backveld, have a sense of humour, and partly because he was drunk.

"In any case," Cyril Stein continued, trying to indulge in light banter and thereby (as was not unusual with him) saying the wrong thing, "you needn't be afraid that I'll go and tell your brother on you."

Krisjan bridled. "How do I do my job, driving the lorry, Meneer Stein?" he asked. "Do I do my job good?"

Cyril Stein admitted, truthfully, that he had had no complaints about Krisjan's work.

"Well, my brother has got nothing to do with my work, or with me, that's what I say," Krisjan Erasmus continued. "Just because he got me the job, he mustn't think that he's my boss, see?"

Cyril Stein saw more in the young man's statement than Krisjan Erasmus would have been able to realise, even if he were sober. Cyril Stein saw in him a fellow sufferer insofar as getting a job through influence, through *family* influence, was concerned. That was a thing they had in common, he and young Erasmus. It was the same kind of frustration. Cyril saw the signs of it on Krisjan already. But it didn't make him warm to Krisjan Erasmus, for that reason. Rather did the fact that they were in this respect in the same boat make him feel contemptuous of the principal's brother.

"And his boss isn't my wife – I mean, and his wife isn't my boss either, see?" Krisjan continued, in between downing another brandy. "What's more, my brother wouldn't think he was somebody if he knew what's going on with me and his wife, that's what. Yes, every time he's away in the night – at the club, or somewhere – yes, there am I on the bed, sleeping with his wife. And how does he like that, hey?"

In spite of his drunkenness, Krisjan realised that he had said too much. He peered into Cyril Stein's face to try and read what was going on in Cyril Stein's mind. He felt sorry, now, that he had said all that. But then, what the hell did this man, Stein, just because he was school-board secretary, want to bring his brother Johannes into it all for? Because he was in a state of drunken anger with himself, Krisjan wanted to turn those feelings against Cyril Stein.

Cyril Stein sensed something of that. So he finished his beer quickly and left. Well, so that was what was going on between them – the school principal's wife and his brother, Cyril Stein thought. There was Willemsdorp for you, he thought to himself. But that young Krisjan must have been mad to make mention of it. Not mad, Cyril Stein said to himself immediately afterwards, but frustrated – through having got that tuppeny-ha'penny job through his brother's influence. And he himself was frustrated in the same way. And what, come to think of it, was being school-board secretary in Willemsdorp but also a tuppenny-ha'penny job? But to think what was going on in Johannes Erasmus's house. . .

Cyril Stein didn't feel quite so bad about himself, then. There were worse things than to be a dagga-smoker, he thought. And it gave him a reasonably elevated opinion of himself for a while, then – thinking that he couldn't fit into the life of Willemsdorp.

3

This time, too, when Marjorie came into Charlie Hendricks's flat, she came in without knocking.

Charlie Hendricks was not altogether surprised to see her. He had been expecting her. For one thing, he thought she would come again because he owed her money. As soon as she was inside he went to the door and turned the key in the lock. He remembered, uncomfortably, the last time Marjorie had been for, as far as he could remember, the door had remained unlocked, then, throughout the period of Marjorie's visit.

"Sit down," he said. There was now none of the embarrassment that had characterised the first stages of her previous visit. She seemed calm and self-possessed. So she had been last time, too, for that matter. It was only he who had been flustered, Charlie Hendricks remembered. And in reply to his invitation she now went and seated herself, without speaking, and very naturally, and with a good deal of grace in her movements, on the bed.

She again wore that silk square on her head – striped, gay; oh, gay. But she had on other shoes. Pretty smart-looking shoes they were, too, Charlie Hendricks reflected. He didn't need to have a particularly agile brain once more to associate Marjorie's change of footwear with Detective Sergeant Brits's remark about the coloured woman with three pairs of shoes. He found himself getting interested in Marjorie. It was nothing in the way of a personal interest, of course. It was just that she was there. And her job in life was going around whoring with white men. And she must have a good deal of contempt for white men, by now, Charlie Hendricks thought. Just about as much contempt as one white man who lay with her would have for another white man who did the same thing – if he got to know about it, that was.

Charlie Hendricks remembered the contempt he had felt for his editorial predecessor, Esselen, when the suspicion had first entered his mind that Esselen had had illicit intercourse with Marjorie. There was a lot of hypocrisy about it, and all that, Charlie Hendricks realised. But all the same it was a real feeling. It was something you couldn't get away from. You just *felt* there was something low about a white man that went to bed with a woman that wasn't white. And even if you yourself were also that kind of white man, it just didn't make any difference. Maybe you despised yourself even more than you did that other white man who also carried on with coloured women.

But that wasn't the point. It was human nature for a person to be hardest of all on somebody who had the same weakness that he himself had. And to call that sort of thing by ugly Greek names like hypocrisy didn't help matters much. Charlie Hendricks despised himself for having sexual relations with Marjorie, a coloured woman.

But he had come to reconcile himself to having that opinion about himself. He was just low, that was all. And he always had been low. And he had tried to conceal his lowness from himself. But it had all come out now. Good. He was a dirty, lousy, shabby creature. He wasn't fit for decent human company. Well, he could accept that about himself. Lena Cordier, for instance, must have thought him pretty low. Otherwise she wouldn't have turned down his advances like that. She must have felt, with that feminine intuition that they talked about, how low he was.

But that didn't mean to say that he was going to stand for any other man being just as low. For a white man – any white man – who went around with coloured women Charlie Hendricks now had only unbounded contempt. He felt much worse about that class of man than he had felt ever before. For a white man that slept with a nigger moll hanging was too good, Charlie Hendricks felt now –

And so he could not help but wonder what Marjorie, the nigger skirt, must be thinking of that class of white man to which he himself now belonged. It was on the tip of his tongue to ask her. But at the last moment his courage failed him. It would be best not to bring that question up at all.

In any case, it was just possible that that was the kind of white man that Marjorie admired, Charlie Hendricks thought. Because, where would she be, without that kind of white man that would take her and give her money? It would mean that she would have to go and hang around with kaffirs. And where would she be, then? *They* didn't have any money. But it was because of the falseness and the self-deceit that this sort of thing was wrapped in – it was because of that that Charlie Hendricks refrained from questioning Marjorie. He knew how much insincerity and humbug there was inside himself on this question – humbug that he believed in, what was more. And so he didn't feel that it would be fair to ask a coloured girl to say what she *really* thought.

Suddenly his thoughts went to Jones, the compositor on the *Northern Transvaal News.* A dry old stick, Jones was. But you couldn't but feel that he was straight, somehow. And it must have been that Jones had detected that about him – about how low he was, and weak, Charlie Hendricks thought. That was why Jones had all along treated him with disdain. Maybe there was some sixth sense that Jones had that told him when a man was low. The same kind of intuition that Lena Cordier had, perhaps. Maybe Jones had already come to suspect that he, Charlie Hendricks, was not above going to bed with a coloured woman. Perhaps it was a bit far-fetched, an idea like that. . . but there was no doubt about it that Jones did make him feel inferior, all right. There was something about him, some weakness in his nature, Charlie Hendricks felt, that Jones the compositor had tumbled to, all right. Otherwise Jones would never have been able to make him feel so inferior. It was because Jones had made him feel a swine that he started thinking of Jones, then – one association of ideas evoking another.

Seated in a chair opposite Marjorie, a glass of brandy in his hand, Charlie Hendricks surveyed her steadily for some moments. There was much that he wanted to ask of her. There were a good number of questions, too, that he felt he dared not put into words.

So he contented himself, for a start, by asking her where she lived. And before she had told him, he knew what her reply would be, also. In the location was where she lived, Marjorie said. But he didn't ask her why she didn't go to Johannesburg. For that would be the obvious thing for her to do. In Johannesburg she wouldn't have to live in any coloured location. Not with her looks and her knowledge of men, she wouldn't have to. She could be fixed up in almost any Johannesburg flat – provided that she combed out her hair first with a hot brass comb and smeared hair-straightening cream on it.

And then, for a moment, the interest Charlie Hendricks took in

Marjorie was a personal interest. But he hadn't meant it to be that. And in the very next moment he switched the line of talk, directing it into a quite different channel. But the fact remained that, for several instants, there had been that personal side to it. It flickered, that personal side. It looked as though it was going to catch hold, too, almost. But, flickeringly, the flame died.

For Charlie Hendricks had asked her how she was doing.

"I get by," was how Marjorie answered.

Not a bad answer, Charlie Hendricks reflected. It showed that they did have a cinema for Coloureds in the location, for one thing.

And it was then that Charlie Hendricks had it on the tip of his tongue to ask Marjorie what her surname was. But he didn't ask her. He was afraid. He was afraid that it might be a surname like Mletshwa. Marjorie Mletshwa. Or Umzimkululu. Marjorie Umzimkululu. That would be just too awful.

On the other hand, she might have a white surname. Like Smith. Or Malan. Or Labuschagne. Many Coloured people did have White surnames, deriving from a White ancestor. But Charlie Hendricks was afraid to ask Marjorie in case, with her, it was different. In case she was Marjorie Bwanu-Bwanukwlapu. He was afraid to ask her that before he went and sat on the bed next to her, and started taking her in his arms.

But afterwards, when she was ready to go, and she had taken up her handbag, and she was looking at her reflection in the mirror to see if the brightly-coloured doek was sitting straight on her head, then, because he didn't care any more, Charlie Hendricks took the liberty, straight out, of asking Marjorie what her surname was.

And when she told him he was surprised. Surprised that he hadn't seen the resemblance before. Why he hadn't seen it before, of course, was because she was pretty. What was rugged in her father's countenance had, in her own features, fallen into place. So rough was the paternal mould that you could hardly believe that a few softening touches could make all that difference. But when Marjorie told him her surname, the resemblance was there as clear as daylight, for Charlie Hendricks to see. He was only surprised that he had not detected it earlier. But he realised that it would actually make it more *difficult* to see the resemblance – seeing that, when she smiled, Marjorie was, well, radiantly pretty. If you knew her father, the White man, it would be even more difficult to realise that Marjorie could be his Coloured daughter. You wouldn't think that her mother, the nigger woman, could transfer to her daughter so much prettiness.

But Charlie Hendricks was sorry that he had asked that question. It made him feel more uncomfortable than ever, when he heard the answer. For he thought of that kaffir woman living in the location, taking in washing and living on mieliepap so as to be able to bring up a white man's baby. And he felt that, instead of despising Marjorie as a whore, he was beginning to admire her. And he couldn't stand for that. For where would he be then? As it was, he already felt degraded enough.

"My surname," Marjorie said, "is *Jones*. I am Marjorie *Jones*."

After Marjorie had gone, Charlie Hendricks remembered that he had thought of the compositor Jones earlier on. And he hadn't been quite sure as to why he had thought of him. He had attributed it to a somewhat obscure association of unconscious ideas. But the reason for it was clear enough, of course. Something in a gesture or a trick of manner on Marjorie's part must have reminded him of her father, without Charlie Hendricks having been aware of it. Something in the way she had said or done a certain thing must have reminded him of Jones. That was the link.

Charlie Hendricks wondered, for a moment, whether she had ever told her father. But in the next instant he knew the answer. Jones was a respectable White artisan. It was inconceivable that he should be on speaking terms with his illegitimate Coloured daughter. It was quite on the cards that he didn't even know that he had such a thing as an illegitimate Coloured daughter.

4

Lena Cordier had made all arrangements for leaving Willemsdorp. Quite soon now she would be setting off for Johannesburg. She already knew the school she had been appointed to in Johannesburg for from the beginning of the new term.

She had given up thinking of Jack Brummer. Or, at least, she had partly succeeded in convincing herself that he meant nothing in her life any more, and that she wanted nothing more from him, and that life would go on for her just as it had been before she met him. But there were times when she wasn't so sure. There were lonely nights in her room in Hex Buildings when she was not too certain as to how she would act if there was a familiar footstep on the wooden floor of the passage, and if there came a knock at her door that she knew.

There was a circumstance that puzzled her, though. She wasn't nearly as worried about her condition as she might have been. That would get fixed up, she felt. Lots of girls had had the same thing happen to them. They had faced it. So could she. Not that she didn't get frightened, sometimes, of course. Supposing things didn't turn out the way she hoped. . . She had known moments of almost overpowering terror. But she had mastered those fears. It would almost seem as though her condition, while being the cause of her anxieties, also gave her in some strange way the strength to overcome them.

Now, sitting on the bed in her room, an American magazine in front of her and a pair of scissors in her hand, Lena Cordier turned over the pages on the look out for an article of feminine interest that she could snip from the magazine for the next woman's page of the *Northern Transvaal News*. This would be almost the last issue that she had to assemble copy for. Her eye was interested by a bold headline: HOW DOES IT FEEL TO DIE? – BY 19 AMERICAN DOCTORS. You had to hand it to these American doctors, Lena Cordier thought. Well, she had got over that. She wasn't brooding on suicide any more – as she had done at the beginning, when she first realised that Jack Brummer had left her, and that she had been dropped in the cart. At the same time, she had not gained so complete a control over herself that an article with that title did not hold a morbid interest for her any more. And she felt pretty sure that more than one reader of the *News*, living out on the veld or in a Northern Transvaal village, would, for personal reasons, intimate reasons, feel impelled to peruse more than just the headline. She snipped out the article. She didn't read it. She would read it and sub it after dinner.

A little later she put on her hat and went out. A quiet stroll down the jacaranda avenue and then further on along the road that led out of the town would do her good, she felt. She was almost happy, walking on the purple blossoms that had vanished from the branches overhead and now made a carpet for the sidewalks. She walked further than she had meant to. Quite soon she was beyond the last houses of the town and was following the road in its lazy winding over the veld. In the distance she could see the first of the whitewashed stones placed there to indicate to travellers using the road at night that around the bend was a bridge. She thought, then, unwillingly, of the past. Unwillingly she remembered the times when she had seen those whitewashed stones in the night, sharply defined in the headlights of Jack Brummer's car.

She must forget all that, she told herself fiercely. If her feelings were going to start playing havoc with her like that, she had better turn back at once. Right now, she had better turn back. Even though her heart told her that it was already too late. Even though she knew from the whitewashed stones that it was too late – those stones swimming as though in mist. She bit her lip. She hated herself for being so weak. In another minute – no, no, not that. She would turn back. She would not allow all her sternly formed resolutions to dissolve just in a moment of blinding memory. It was as though – no, she dared not allow herself to think, to feel. Her heart was not going to sway her head again. There was a ringing in her ears, when she told herself that.

The car was almost upon her before she recognised it. She had turned back by then. And when she saw whose car it was, and she saw the occupants – saw them clearly – all her feelings suddenly crystallised into fury. The car, and Jack Brummer at the wheel, and Mavis Clark sitting next to him – there was no nonsense about having mist in front of her eyes, then. And Jack Brummer put on speed.

"I suppose they think I've come walking out here to spy on them," Lena Cordier thought. Well, let them imagine what they liked. It was sure to worry her. By the side of the road she saw a cake of cowdung. But somehow she resisted the impulse. Afterwards she wondered how she restrained herself. For the car was still near enough, then, when she thought of it. But it just so happened that she didn't do it. She didn't yield to the impulse. She didn't pick up the cake of dried cowdung and throw it at Jack Brummer and Mavis Clark in the car.

She was walking back to the town, now – walking quite fast. Other cars passed her. She shouldn't have walked out so far, she said to herself. It must look queer to people passing her in cars, seeing a woman walking out so far on to the veld alone. Alone. Yes, and that was why she was alone – because Jack Brummer had left her. Had got her into trouble and had left her to walk along the road over the veld alone. She felt at the same time sorry for herself. And at the same time anger. Her emotions were all mixed up. She was glad when a car drew to a stop and the driver offered her a lift back to town.

She was already in the car before she took it in, properly, that the driver was Charlie Hendricks. And suddenly, of all the people that she could have picked at that moment to have sitting next to her, it seemed to her that Charlie Hendricks was the one that she would have been most eager to have.

She wondered if he could guess in any way how she was feeling.

"Let us go into the hotel, into the lounge, and let us sit together at a table, just you and me, and let us get drunk together," was what she hoped Charlie Hendricks would say.

But he didn't say that.

He cleared his throat several times, trying to screw up the courage to invite her to tea, but he couldn't bring himself to blurt out the invitation. Because he knew that was how it would sound in his ears – as though he were blurting it out. He felt that he could not talk to Lena Cordier without betraying his eager desire for her. And he was afraid to risk being snubbed again. And also, because of the coloured girl, Marjorie, he felt low at the moment – he felt he wasn't worthy of Lena Cordier. So he dropped her at the door of Hex Buildings with hardly so much as a word.

When she got back to her room Lena Cordier started reading that article that she had clipped from the American magazine.

Chapter Ten

1

"I CAN'T help thinking – well, that he's queer," the Reverend Thorwell Macey was saying in the Willemsdorp club. "Don't think I'm so narrow-minded as to take exception to the way he dresses. I mean he can wear all the striped scarves and sandals he wants to, and also all the rings with stones in them the size of – oh well, I don't care what size – and I don't care what stones, either: opal, turquoise, emerald, topaz. I don't know and I don't care. But I say the man is queer. And what's more queer is that he's got quite a responsible sort of a job, too, hasn't he? This Cyril Stein, I mean. He appoints teachers to the staffs of the government schools around here, doesn't he?"

"Provincial Council schools," Johannes Erasmus explained. "We call them government schools, but actually they fall under the Provincial Council. Not that I've got anything against Mr Stein, myself, you'll understand, but it is sort of generally understood that he got the position through – that is – family influence."

"Oh well, that I wouldn't hold against him," Reverend Thorwell Macey said, with an airy wave of his hand. "Can't do anybody harm to come of a good family – that's what I believe. And I don't care how he dresses, either at work or in his spare time. – Yes, thanks, I don't mind if I do have another brandy. – But what on earth does he want to come and talk to me about his soul for?"

"Perhaps, Mr Macey," Charlie Hendricks remarked, "because he thinks you're a clergyman."

There was general laughter.

"Well I'm blessed," Mr Macey said after a pause. "You know, that's the last thing I would have thought – that he was coming to me for spiritual guidance. You see, for one thing, he's not a member of my congregation. What church does he belong to, anyway?"

"Dutch Reformed Church," Johannes Erasmus said, adding that Cyril Stein was not a regular church-goer.

"And another thing," Reverend Macey said, "is that it is not as usual a thing as you might perhaps imagine for a man to come and talk to a clergyman when he's in trouble or doubt. With a woman I'll admit that it's perhaps different. But take your own cases now. If you were in distress, any one of you, you wouldn't come and talk to me about it, would you? You'd go into a bar and get drunk. Or you'd – "

"Go and see the Provincial Councillor about it," Jack Brummer interjected brightly. For it was at that moment that the Union Party candidate for the Provincial Council, Robert E. Constable, accompanied by his election agent, Piet Fourie, entered the club. Johannes Erasmus resented their arrival. He had wanted to take the parson up on the remarks he had just been making. He wasn't going to be unfriendly. But he felt that a little man-to-man talk with Reverend Macey might do both of them a bit of good. And Johannes Erasmus didn't know when he would again get such a chance for a tête-à-tête.

What he wanted to say to the parson – not in so many words, perhaps, as much as by inference – was that in this regard a great deal depended on the individual minister of religion: on his personality and his outlook and his mode of life. There would not be so many people visiting psychiatrists, Johannes Erasmus wanted to tell Reverend Macey, if those people felt that they could freely, and in an open-hearted way, and in confidence, approach their minister with their troubles. There was a difficulty of his own, too, that he would have liked to talk about. And he would not have minded making mention of it within the hearing of others, either. It might perhaps have done good, even, if he had aired, in the precincts of the club, this personal problem of his own: this inability of his to fit smoothly and naturally into the pattern of speech and thought that was accepted and recognised by the other members of the club. He would not have been shy to have spoken about it, then, at that moment, when the atmosphere and the circumstances were just right for it. But with the entrance of Robert E. Constable he had missed his opportunity. And he didn't know when he would get a chance again.

"Rooivlei," Robert E. Constable announced. That was where the meeting had been held that he and his election agent had just come back from. Both men looked tired. In addition, Robert E. Constable sported a fairly respectable sample of a black eye. But those present in the club sensed that he hadn't got it at the Rooivlei meeting. So nobody made any mention of it. They couldn't send his photograph to the Rand newspapers. It was no use Hershberg the chemist doctoring his injured eye in such a way that it would look a lot worse photographed. Even the process man who made the block for the Rand newspaper would sense that the caption "Union Party candidate assaulted by backveld hooligans" was phony. You could *feel* that it was the kind of black eye that a man could sustain in only one way – through slipping and striking his eye against the doorknob of his hotel bedroom after he had had one too many.

So, as though by common accord, nobody spoke about how Robert E. Constable's face looked. Nobody even remarked on the fact that the pastel shade of face powder he had applied to his eye served but to accentuate the more lamentable features of his injury.

Charlie Hendricks was in the meantime pondering Jack Brummer's wisecrack: "Go and see the Provincial Councillor about it." Well, if he himself were ever in trouble, Charlie Hendricks felt, then Robert E. Constable was the last man he would want to go and talk to about it. Rather would he go and see Dap van Zyl, the Volksparty man. Then he remembered that he had before had a similar idea. It wasn't a healthy way for his mind to work, Charlie Hendricks said to himself. He didn't like it. It was almost as though he were accused of something and he were looking for somebody to take his part. He had to stop getting ideas like that. What was the matter with him?

He knew, of course. It wasn't that there was anything wrong per se with his relations with Marjorie. At least, it was rotten, and all that. Stinking, and all that. But it wasn't just *that*. He was, in spite of all kinds of liberal and even egalitarian views that he might hold, still, at heart, a Boer and a Calvinist. Charlie Hendricks knew that about himself. He was the editor of a Union Party newspaper. And intellectually he recoiled from the Volksparty tenets. But in his blood he was a Boer. And he was sleeping with a kaffir woman. The generations of Boer ancestry were stronger than he was. He felt a lost soul.

It wasn't Cyril Stein but he himself that had to go to a parson for help and guidance. And he saw Dap van Zyl, for that reason, as a man that could help him. He felt he needed help. If he wasn't a Boer in his blood he wouldn't need help. But you could do nothing about the things you were convinced of in your blood. The brain was nowhere in such things. And he had no illusions about Dap van Zyl. Superficial, cheap, all the rest of it Dap van Zyl certainly was. But in the last extremity there was something about Dap van Zyl that Charlie Hendricks felt he could cling to.

135

Hell. . . Charlie Hendricks thought, suddenly. He must be going mad. What the hell. . . Hey, steward, another brandy. Yes, make it a double. . . What the hell, Charlie Hendricks said to himself. Anybody would think he was a criminal, the way he was feeling about himself. And for no reason. Enough of that! Let them all come – only, he must not start making a fool of himself, now.

Piet Fourie, Robert E. Constable's political agent, was holding forth: "We *should* win," he was saying in confidential tones. "I don't see why we *can't* win. But they're so bloody ignorant, on the backveld. They keep on asking our candidate will he sleep with a nigger woman. Just think of that. Asking Mr Constable a question like that. As though Mr Constable would ever want to sleep with *any* woman, as long as he's got a bottle."

2

Johannes Erasmus put his car away in the garage. Then he walked up the gravel path to the front door. He had got home rather late from the club that night and, although the light was still burning in the dining-room, he thought it possible that his wife was in bed. She often went to bed, leaving the dining-room light on. Johannes Erasmus unlocked the door with his latch key with a minimum of noise. He did not wish to disturb Malie. But he need not have taken these precautions. Malie was reclining on a settee in the dining-room, waiting for him.

"Sorry I'm a bit late, Malie," Johannes Erasmus said somewhat mechanically. "I got talking at the club. You know how it is, one thing leading to another, and all that. Before I knew where I was, it was eleven o'clock. The time just passed."

It wasn't usual for her husband to make such long explanations – and over nothing at all. Malie started getting suspicious. What was Johannes up to, she wondered. It was when he went on talking that she knew.

"I was talking to Bayfield first," Johannes Erasmus went on. "And then to Macey. Jack Brummer was there, too. And so was the editor of the *News*, that chap Hendricks. And then afterwards – "

But Malie wasn't listening, any more. How foolish of her. Of course, Johannes would know that his brother had been there. The stink of his hairoil. You couldn't miss it. It was all over the place. She would have to talk to Krisjan about it. Not that Johannes had guessed anything, or was likely to, even. She was satisfied on that point. But there was no sense in Krisjan calling on her when his brother was away, and then leaving behind him a smell of hairoil that was as good as a visiting card. She'd make Krisjan stop using that cheap, greasy stuff. It was a common class thing to do, in any case, plastering that muck on his hair.

"No, you're not really late, Johannes," Malie said, making an effort to keep her voice calm and level. "But it's a pity you didn't come earlier, though. Because then you wouldn't have missed Krisjan. He seemed disappointed that you were out. I suppose he must get pretty lonely, at times. Being strange to the town. And I don't imagine he'd have many people to talk to. He should have a girl. It shouldn't be difficult for him to find one. He's got something about him that quite a lot of girls will get attracted to, I imagine."

Inwardly, Malie was beginning to feel amused. She was pleased with her own recklessness. For, in a way, it was reckless of her to talk like that, seeing that she knew so well – from long experience – how bitter Johannes would get to feel whenever she spoke about a young man being attractive to girls. Even though Johannes had so far succeeded in schooling himself that he did not always betray his resentment straight away, he always, in the end, revealed what he really thought. Sometimes he would let a whole week pass before letting on that some remark she had made had been to him like a blow. And it seemed to her that of late he was getting better at it – hiding from her, at the moment, the gnarled part of his jealousy when she spoke about some young man in a friendly fashion. But when his anger broke out afterwards, through having been pent up so long, Johannes would of a sudden look black as thunder. But even then he wouldn't storm. He wouldn't rage. Almost, Malie would have preferred it if her husband did let himself go at such times, and raised Cain.

Secretly, she began to wonder, sometimes, if she wasn't growing afraid of him. She knew him so well, Malie told herself. She could manipulate him with such ease. He was a born sucker for a woman's wiles. He was a natural. He was putty in her hands. She could do with him what she would. Look how simple it had been for her to get him to bring his brother Krisjan to Willemsdorp. She had worked it all so easily that Johannes was one hundred per cent convinced that it was a matter of his own planning and volition.

But, all the same, Malie wasn't feeling quite so sure of herself, any more. Especially lately. It was as though she could sense that there was awakening in Johannes some side to his nature that hadn't been there before. And she was frightened of that. It was something that she couldn't handle because it was something she didn't know about him. This long explanation of his as to why he was late, for instance. When all the time he had known that his brother had been there – and he had said nothing about it. And it had taken her longer than it should have, to put two and two together. In this case, putting two and two together meant remembering about the hairoil. But there would almost certainly be a time in the future when putting two and two together would be something quite different. And would she be quick enough then? Yes, Malie reassured herself, she would.

Tonight, for instance, now. Her mentioning that Krisjan was attractive to girls. Well, you couldn't beat that for clever, Malie said to herself. Of course, she had said it only on an impulse. For a joke as much as anything else. But just see how it would work out, she thought. Even in the unlikely event of Johannes having entertained any sort of suspicion as to what might have been going on between her and Krisjan, she had headed him off by having spoken about Krisjan in those terms. Pretty smart, Malie thought. Now Johannes wouldn't know where he was. And served him right, too, she told herself. He had no business to be so jealous. If your husband was jealous, then you surely had the right to do what you could for yourself, Malie reasoned.

"Afterwards, the Union Party candidate, Robert E. Constable, came into the club," Johannes Erasmus went on. "What does that 'E' stand for, I wonder? He's got a black eye. He must have got it when he was drunk again. How a man can have the nerve to get on to a public platform with a black eye that he's got from being drunk is something that beats me. And he had the cheek to say that he thinks the platteland will vote for him. If he gets five hundred votes above the couple of thousand that he'll get in any case from the English and renegade Boers and foreigners in the town – well, then you can call me a cuckold."

Johannes Erasmus laughed when he said the word. Malie, after hesitating for a second or two, laughed also.

"You," she said, eventually. "Really, I don't know what you're going to say next."

She laughed again, trying to make her amusement at his remark sound unforced. How much did he know or guess? Malie found herself groping in the dark. There were certain things that she had, until now, regarded as certainties. She didn't know how much reliance she could place on those certainties any more. To herself she admitted that what she had said, ringing her words with an artificial laughter, was no more than the truth. She didn't know what her husband was going to say next. More, she didn't know what he was going to do next. And 'next' did not mean merely the following couple of seconds. It meant the next week or two. Or month or two. She would in the future have to be much more circumspect in her relations with Krisjan. That cheap, stinking hairoil of his was definitely out. And Krisjan would only be permitted, in future, to come round on nights when it was certain that Johannes could not come home suddenly and unexpectedly. She was getting almost as much afraid of what he came out with as of what he suppressed.

"You," Malie said again, and laughed. Her laughter was clear, bell-like, prolonged. It was not really infectious, though.

3

So that was that, Charlie Hendricks said to himself.

He said it almost as though he was wiping his hands of something – of something unpleasant. And the fact that he said it to himself and not to an audience made very little difference, then.

He was back in his office. It was night time. He had gone back to his office to write the leader for the next edition of the *News*. And in the passage between the administrative section of the building and the printing works he had come across Jones the compositor. What Jones was doing there at that time was, to Charlie Hendricks, a mystery. One thing Charlie Hendricks was certain of: Jones hadn't come around there out of love for his job. The very suggestion of that would be silly. The most likely explanation of Jones's presence there, at an hour far later than what the Typographical Union would countenance for a journeyman to be on his employer's premises, was that Jones had come back to do an under-the-lap job. He had probably got an order for visiting cards or for letterheads from some local firm – a small job that didn't need much setting or running off, and that he could do on the quiet and for which he could pocket the proceeds. . . without the proprietors of the *Northern Transvaal News* knowing anything about it – or caring much, either.

But in that passage Charlie Hendricks and Jones had had an altercation. And what Charlie Hendricks preened himself about was the fact that it was Jones's nerve that had given way first. It was Jones who had first become insulting. It was Jones who first spoke words that he would, no doubt, during the next few days come to regret. Why Charlie Hendricks was happy about it was because he imagined that, what with one thing and another, his own nerves were more taut than most people's. Therefore the discovery that Jones was an even more unstrung sort of person that he himself came as balm to Charlie Hendricks's ego. Charlie Hendricks would not have imagined readily that a workman, a compositor, an imaginative member of a trades union, would have exposed sensitivities of a sort that he himself bristled with. A workman, Charlie Hendricks would have imagined, was by the nature of his day to day activities cushioned against that sort of thing. A workman wasn't *het up* all the time, every moment, like an editor was, Charlie Hendricks had thought.

But he realised, now, that he was mistaken about all that. And he was pleased about it. It gave him a lift to think how balanced he was, really. And it was not without significance, Charlie Hendricks thought, that it should have happened in the passage – that it should have been there that he had the *passage* with the compositor Jones.

"Editors – I've seen them come and I've seen them go," Jones had said. It was clear from that just what a state Jones must have been in, Charlie Hendricks reflected. Because with that remark Jones had come his whole guts. He kept nothing in reserve. That was what made it so easy for Charlie Hendricks to score the final victory.

"Oh, really, Mr Jones," was all that Charlie Hendricks had said, then. And it was all that he had needed to say.

Back in his office, behind his typewriter, Charlie Hendricks was smiling to himself. It seemed as though the leader was going to be easy to write. At last he had exposed Jones for what he was – a hollow fraud. So Charlie Hendricks thought. Maybe he would not have been able to handle Jones in that cool, effective and infuriating way, Charlie Hendricks thought, if he hadn't known that Jones was Marjorie's father. And he wouldn't be surprised, even, if Jones didn't know that he was Marjorie's father. That was how funny the situation was. It was quite on the cards that Jones would be the most surprised man in Africa if he were suddenly confronted with his illegitimate Coloured daughter.

Jones would probably get the shock of his life if he were to be informed that there was a flesh-and-blood memorial – she in her twenties and filled with gusty being – of his surreptitious visits to the kaffir location in the days of his turbulent youth.

Charlie Hendricks slipped a sheet of copypaper into the typewriter. In no time it was covered with resounding phrases that were respectable because they had had their day. He put in another sheet. He filled it with lined-up clichés. Something made him look up from the typewriter. He started to smile.

For standing in front of him was that queer looking little Coloured man, old and yet ageless, youthfully wrinkled, willowy in a joint-creaking fashion. Josias, his name was, Charlie Hendricks remembered. Well, he was glad to see Josias. He recalled Josias's remarks about something that made you forget all your troubles. And there was some girl's name that Josias had mentioned. Nellie somebody, he had said.

"Any more news about that girl, Josias?" Charlie Hendricks enquired affably. "Nellie, I think you said she was called."

The Coloured man did not smile. Last time he had come round he was all grins.

"Nellie Pope was the name I said, master," Josias answered, "but it's not about that I've come to see master now, tonight."

He spoke earnestly, sombrely, almost. It was as though he were compelling himself not to smile.

"Well, you don't seem very happy about it, Josias," Charlie Hendricks continued in the same tone of levity. "I hope there's no trouble about your Nellie. I mean, I hope she's not *in* trouble. You didn't do wrong by Nellie, perhaps, hey?"

It sounded very funny to Charlie Hendricks, all those things he was saying. He was really enjoying himself. What seemed even funnier to him was the set expression on Josias's face – such a striking contrast to the way he looked last time he came round at night.

Charlie Hendricks put his hand in his trousers pocket. "Here, Josias," he said, taking out half a crown and putting it on the edge of the desk for the Coloured man to pick up. "See if that will make you feel different." Charlie Hendricks recalled the eager dexterity Josias had displayed on his previous visit. How he had made no mistake in catching the coin flipped in his direction.

But this time Josias made no move. He glanced at the half crown reposing on the edge of the desk. He looked at it once, disdainfully. Then he fixed his gaze full on Charlie Hendricks's face. Charlie Hendricks felt, directed straight at him, a pair of surprisingly young eyes with an age-old message in them. He couldn't think, immediately, what the message was. But he felt that, given time, he would be able to work it out. It was a sinister expression, anyway, that Josias had in his eyes.

"That is not enough, master," Josias said.

Then Charlie Hendricks realised what that message was. It was old enough, God knew. It was, God knew, also sinister enough. It was blackmail.

"Get out," Charlie Hendricks started to say. He scuffled his feet underneath his chair and started to rise. One quick step round the side of the desk and he'd be able to land that impudent Coloured a kick up his backside. But Charlie Hendricks did not get up out of his editorial armchair. There was something white and quivering inside him. Even before Josias spoke again, he knew what the Coloured man was going to say. He didn't know it in actual words. But that wasn't important.

"Her name isn't Nellie Pope, this time, master," Josias said. "Her name, master, is Marjorie."

And the Coloured man began to say more things about Marjorie. He communicated the information to Charlie Hendricks in the crude, earthy language of the kaffir location.

Stunned, Charlie Hendricks felt in his inside jacket pocket for his wallet. Licked and frightened, he pulled out a number of banknotes. His fingers trembled. He let Josias see that there were no notes left in his wallet. He passed the money over to Josias. The Coloured man took the money and went out of the office and into the night without a word.

What was Josias to Marjorie? – Charlie Hendricks wondered when he was once more alone. Josias was her ponce, possibly, her pimp. Maybe he was her husband, even. But how was all this going to end? It was quite a while since Marjorie had last come round, Charlie Hendricks remembered. Her visits had been weekly. Then they had ceased. And it was hell for him to have to admit it to himself – but he had missed her, those weeks when she hadn't shown up. He was ashamed to have to acknowledge that truth to himself. That he had missed Marjorie's visits.

But he didn't blame himself for it. The person that was to blame was

Lena Cordier. She must have guessed just how he felt about her. And she was like a cold piece of stone. If Lena Cordier had given him even the slightest hint of encouragement, Charlie Hendricks said to himself, he would not be in the position that he was in now. It was Lena Cordier that had brought him to this shameful condition. There was nothing that Marjorie had to worry about – to be ashamed about. She would take it all just in her stride. She would bring an illegitimate coloured child into the world in just as casual a way as her own mother had brought her into the world. No, it wasn't Marjorie's trouble, Charlie Hendricks realised, it was his trouble. It was he who would have to do something about it. Of course, the chances were that it wasn't his child, even. Marjorie was no doubt sending the Coloured man, Josias, round to every white man she had ever slept with, just to extort money from them.

Nevertheless, Charlie Hendricks could not bring himself to take so easy a way out. No doubt that was what Jones the compositor had done years ago. Jones had as likely as not said that there was nothing to prove that he was responsible. There were other white men involved. Why pick on him?

Charlie Hendricks couldn't take it that way. He *felt* that it was his child.

And so something had to be done about it.

He was not prepared to go through life with the feeling that there was that illegitimate coloured child – born into the world without hope and without opportunity. Born into a world in which all the doors were shut. *His* child, his own child. Begotten in sin and disgustingness. And that child a human being. And that human being a coloured bastard. Bred in the nigger location because there was no other place for a part-white child to grow up in. And with no future – for no matter what talents that child had, where was there an avenue that would afford a part-white, part-coloured child any hope of self-expression?

That wasn't going to happen to any child of *his*, Charlie Hendricks said to himself. He sat staring out blankly over the top of his typewriter. The leader for the *News* wasn't getting written.

He would stick at nothing to prevent that, Charlie Hendricks said to himself, eventually. He had nothing against Marjorie, of course. But he felt satisfied in his own mind that it was his child that Marjorie was pregnant with. It was a feeling he had that was more positive than any ideas that Marjorie herself could have about the child's paternity. For Marjorie was somebody with a light nature, somebody living from day to day, taking life as it came, not profoundly stirred by anything, really, since she had no depths. If there was anything to Marjorie at all, she would long ago have quit the Willemsdorp nigger location and have gone to Johannesburg. Because in Johannesburg she would have been able to palm herself off as white. All she needed in Johannesburg was some hair-straightening cream and a brass comb, heated. Instead, she preferred to remain in Willemsdorp, a nigger woman with three pairs of shoes. Like hell he would allow her to bear his child, Charlie Hendricks said to himself, seated at a blank typewriter.

The leading article that had started off so well with inanities and stereotyped tags had suddenly jelled. It wouldn't stand up to real life. But, anyway, Marjorie was not going to bear his child, Charlie Hendricks told himself. To prevent that, he would stop at nothing. Illogically, he put the blame on Lena Cordier.

4

Election day came and went. The ballot boxes were brought from polling stations all over the district and a couple of nights later the counting of the votes started in the magistrate's court of Willemsdorp.

After the hectic nature of the election campaign, the actual announcement of the result came almost as an anticlimax. There was a high earth embankment at the back of the courtroom, on a level with the large, old-fashioned sash windows. A fair-sized number of Willemsdorp citizens had congregated on the embankment. Through the windows, the curtains of which had been drawn aside because of the heat, they could see the two candidates and their scrutineers and the magistrate and the magistrate's court clerks counting the ballot papers. In the glare of the electric light the faces of the persons in the courtroom wore a look of nervous intensity. Even the expression on the magistrate's face bore evidence of strain. And as the piles of counted ballot papers mounted, so did the air of excitement in the courthouse.

Robert E. Constable, neck and ears darkly flushed, started fidgeting with his tie. The Volksparty candidate, Dap van Zyl, sat stiffly forward over the table. He looked as though he had not had a wink of sleep for several days. Handsome in a full-blooded fashion that was in keeping with his oratory, Dap van Zyl seemed, in the electric light that came from overhead, to have grown suddenly old. His face looked then as it would look in about ten years' time. The disproportion between the long-curved-chin lower part of his face and the upper part was cruelly accentuated.

The crowd of watchers on the earthen rampart, their numbers increasing with the passing of the hours and half-hours, began to share in the feeling of tension that came from the garishly lit courtroom. The atmosphere of repressed excitement communicated itself to those standing outside in the dark. The younger element – Volksparty-supporting adolescents, in the main – had ceased their horseplay activities of pushing each other down the side of the embankment. Nobody called out any more, "That's my vote, there," when a ballot paper of whose cross-marked implication the scrutineers were doubtful was passed to the magistrate for adjudication.

Among the members of the public on the rampart was Eloise, wife of Dap van Zyl. She wore a dark, smartly tailored costume and a small hat with a feather. She was dressed differently from the other women who were there. For it was a hot night. Most of the women were bareheaded. Most of them wore flimsy summer frocks. She stood apart from the crowd. Her manner was aloof. Only, when somebody came up and spoke to her in the dark, the corners of her mouth would go up in a set smile. And to whatever inanities were addressed her she would reply in a voice that was hard without being unfriendly. Eloise van Zyl was a politician's wife. Gazing fixedly through the sash windows, she saw neither her husband nor Robert E. Constable. All she saw were the heaps of ballot papers, momentarily growing in size. It seemed almost as though, from that distance, she could read what was on them.

Eventually the time came when the magistrate, after consulting his clerks and the candidates and their scrutineers, wrote something on a piece of paper and rose out of his chair. Everybody else in the courtroom got up, too, then. The big gamble of an election conducted on the lines of Western democracy was over. The magistrate with his entourage moved towards the door of the courthouse. The crowd on the embankment rushed round into the street. Among those that slipped and fell, descending the steep side of the embankment at speed and in the dark, was Eloise van Zyl.

But the actual announcement of the result was not exciting. The magistrate opened the door slightly. He kept the door ajar until the stampede had stopped, and the crowd was standing breath-bated, hushed. Then he came out on to the steps. And because Dap van Zyl came out immediately after him, with Robert E. Constable following a few paces in the rear, the crowd knew that Dap van Zyl had won. Dap van Zyl was Willemsdorp's Provincial Councillor.

After the cheering had died down, the magistrate read out the figures. That was the only part of the result that was really unexpected. The Volksparty had scored a landslide – and at a by-election.

At the foot of the rampart, Eloise van Zyl heard the cheering. In the dark, she was looking for her small hat with the feather in it.

Chapter Eleven

1

IT was either that Lena Cordier had suggested that she would be glad if Charlie Hendricks would drive her to the station on the night that she left Willemsdorp by train for Johannesburg. Or else it was that the offer had come from Charlie Hendricks. At all events, they were there. And because the train was, as usual, late, they had gone into the station tearoom for a coffee.

"I have taught in Johannesburg before," Lena Cordier was saying in reply to a question by Charlie Hendricks. "So I won't be altogether lost, there. Another thing is that last time I was in Johannesburg I got appointed to a school in Newlands. And I couldn't possibly go to a worse school than that was. Right in the slums. The principal had years before given up having any sort of educational idealism. That part of it wasn't so bad, of course. It's when a principal still tries to carry out the things they've taught him at university and normal college – things about esprit de corps and the theory of education and child psychology and laying the foundations for the future of the nation – it's that kind of school that it's just too awful to be a member of the teaching staff of. And all the time you know that the principal is either the biggest fool out or the biggest hypocrite out. Mostly, he's both. I've noticed that when a person is pompous and hypocritical and all that sort of thing, then it's because he has found out that, inside himself, he's very stupid. He hasn't got a brain that's as good as the next man's brain, he's found out. And so he thinks he'll make up for it by *pretending*. He thinks he'll get by through being solemn and playing the hypocrite. That kind of school is just too awful to teach in."

It was a strange thing for Charlie Hendricks to listen to Lena Cordier talking in those terms. She was revealing a side to her nature that he had not, until then, suspected. A harshness. A brittleness. A disillusionment with life that he had not gathered from the comparatively few conversations he had had with her. An underlying bitterness that, reading between the lines, even, he had not detected in the woman's page articles she had written for the *Northern Transvaal News*.

He hadn't known that there was this side to Lena Cordier's nature, Charlie Hendricks thought, sitting in the station tearoom opposite her, stirring his coffee. And yet, most of the time it wasn't Lena Cordier that he was thinking of. Dominating his thoughts was the information that the coloured man, Josias, had communicated to him about Marjorie Jones. That was something that really did get him worked up. If only Lena Cordier hadn't treated him so badly, Charlie Hendricks was thinking. Then he wouldn't be in this jam, now. Almost he wished that he could tell Lena Cordier about it. It was only a woman that would be able to help him, he felt. But he didn't have the guts to talk to Lena Cordier about Marjorie. Even though he sensed that of all the people in the world Lena was the one person that would have been able to help him.

He couldn't just picture the way that Lena Cordier would recoil from him, if he were but to mention once that he was in the most awful kind of trouble through sexual relations that he had with a coloured woman. How Lena Cordier's mouth would curl, then, he felt. How she would despise him. How the light in Lena Cordier's eyes would grow with each moment more cold when he tried, haltingly, to explain that he wouldn't have lain with the coloured girl, Marjorie, in the first place, if he hadn't been drunk. And that he wouldn't have got drunk, either, if it wasn't because of the way that Lena Cordier had treated him.

"But that school in Newlands, now," Charlie Hendricks heard Lena Cordier continuing. "There was a government school for you, all right. With every child, almost, you could feel that that child was going to turn into a criminal. You could feel it. You could sense it. And when you knew the home background of that child, through your having had to go round to that child's home before you could fill in the Social Welfare card for him, then you didn't blame the child at all for going to turn out a criminal. You knew that there was nothing you could do about it. You knew that there was nothing anybody could do about it. And the headmaster of the school was tired and disillusioned. He didn't care anything, as long as the discipline didn't get so bad that it would get into the Sunday newspapers every week.

"But why I wouldn't, more than anything, like to go back to a slum government school of that kind in Johannesburg is because of the few children, here and there, that you could feel weren't really criminals. There were a few children that you could sense had something to them.

They weren't dishonest. They weren't vicious. They didn't tell lies. They came of very poor families. And you could see that their parents tried to keep them decent. And that was what seemed so awful about it, because it was so hopeless – poor whites trying to keep up a show of respectability. Your people and my people, there in the slums of Johannesburg. You've got no idea how awful it is. There were times when I actually wished that those children wouldn't keep up trying to be decent, because they had been taught that way, uselessly, in their homes in the slums. I would be almost glad when I saw one of them starting to get low – starting to tell lies or starting to steal. It seemed less terrible like that, somehow."

Lena Cordier went on talking. It was something he hadn't known about her, before, Charlie Hendricks thought to himself. That she could talk like that. That she could feel like that. That she could reason like that. She had really revealed nothing of her true self to him, until now. Now that she was on the point of leaving Willemsdorp – now that she would already have been miles away from Willemsdorp if the train hadn't been late – she was giving him an insight into herself of a sort that intrigued and puzzled him.

He remembered that he had had daydreams about her. For quite a while his waking times and his dreams had been obsessed with pictures of Lena Cordier. His waking times had been taken up with thoughts of Lena Cordier that had not differed essentially from the lush daydreams of first manhood – gorgeously coloured visions of girls brimming over the bubbly edge of a beer glass. His rushing in to save Lena from under the galloping hooves of runaway horses. All that kind of thought that he had had about her. Rank, overgrown vegetation thoughts, with just a dash of starkness introduced by the years that he had dreamed about her. And now, to this different Lena Cordier that he was meeting now for the first time, he felt more drawn than ever.

Only, it was too late, now, Charlie Hendricks told himself. The thing that had happened with Marjorie Jones, the coloured girl, had come in between them. It was too late. Just like that train was late.

But the Willemsdorp-Johannesburg mail train, although not strictly punctual, was not as late as all that. A whistle and a far-off rumbling came out of the night-veld and penetrated to the inside of the station tearoom. Lena Cordier and Charlie Hendricks got up from their seats. There was something symbolical in their rising. It marked the end of an epoch. It had a link with the way the magistrate had got up out of his chair in the courtroom when the last vote in the Provincial Council by-election had been counted.

Charlie Hendricks lifted Lena Cordier's luggage through the window of her compartment. A bell rang. The train shuddered through its whole length. Away it would speed, across the Highveld and through bush, winding around the sides of koppies, onward under the stars, chooook, clickety-clickety-clack, the engine sending up smoke and sparks into the sky, the engine sowing almost invisible cinders over the plain. . . shedding cinders on the newspapers on the platform bookstalls of Johannesburg station.

As the train drew out of Willemsdorp station Lena Cordier leant forward and kissed Charlie Hendricks on his mouth. She kissed him very naturally. And Charlie Hendricks knew that she meant it all, just like that. All, for the first time, plainly and nudely and ungarnishedly and unadornedly.

But he also knew that it was too late.

2

"Remember, now," Commandant Roelf Kolyn, head of the South African Police for the Willemsdorp district, said to Detective Sergeant Brits. "Don't mention his name to me. Don't tell me who the man is. Just talk of him as the suspect. If it comes into court I want to be able to say absolutely honestly that it was just a routine investigation that you carried out, and that I had no idea as to the identity of the parties involved. I don't want any rubbish about a political prosecution. *In case* they hint something about a political prosecution, afterwards that is."

They were, Roelf Kolyn and Brits, ensconced in the commandant's office. Because of the overwhelming victory gained at the Provincial Council by-election by the Volksparty candidate, Dap van Zyl, Police Commissioner Kolyn was prepared to give a measure of serious consideration to Detective Sergeant Brits's report of his investigations into local miscegenation. It was, after all, in line with the policy of any Volksparty government that this sort of thing should be stamped out. And now that it looked, from the magnitude of Dap van Zyl's election victory, as though the Volksparty was going to get a mandate from the nation, it was up to the commandant to be more active in this particular matter. He didn't want to be left out on a limb.

"And what's more, she's got four pairs of shoes, now," Detective Brits was saying. "Think of that. A nigger woman with four pairs of shoes. But it don't matter how many pairs shoes she's got. I'll track her footprints in the sand part of the pavement as good as she's walking barefoot. *And* as good as she's a Mchopi nigger woman carrying one of those beerpots on her head to press her feet down into the sand still more."

The commandant and the detective both laughed. It was quite a jolly sort of an incongruity – picturing that Coloured girl as a raw tribeswoman from the kraal, wearing a goatskin skirt and with a baby fastened on her back.

"But the man, now," the commandant continued. "What we have to do now is to work out a plan to get him dead to rights. You know that we can't afford to slip up. And from what you've told me, I can see he's as foxy as they make him."

Detective Brits had not yet told the commandant, in so many words, as to who the white man was. But from a couple of hints that the detective had dropped the commandant had gathered that the suspect was somebody pretty high up. And there was a thrill of the chase in the thought of bringing down that size of game that the commandant could not readily resist.

"Four pairs shoes is more than what my wife can afford," Brits said. "What with the prices that things is today."

"Forget that side of it," Commandant Kolyn said. "If we can pull this off, I'll buy your wife a pair of shoes. That's how good it is. But let me try and think, now. The one thing we mustn't do is to make this white man suspicious. We mustn't let him guess that we're on his trail. Especially if he's as foxy as all that. We can't be too careful."

The commandant reflected, for some minutes, deeply.

"Of course, there's one way," he said, after a while.

Detective Sergeant Brits nodded. He knew what was coming. "I've thought of that, too, sir," he said. "But you know how it is, sir. That's the bloody worse of this Tielman Roos Ack – excuse me for saying bloody, sir. But they doesn't allow one accused to turn King's evidence under this ack, sir. You got to gets them both dead to rights, sir."

The commandant agreed that it was so. "When I think that a man

151

can be so low – so cunning and crafty and all that," he pursued, "I don't mean so much sleeping with a kaffir woman, but sleeping with a kaffir woman in such a low way that you can't catch him at it. . . *that's* what I mean about a man being so low. . . then I just feel like pinching him anyhow. Even if we don't get a conviction. I feel like arresting him just to teach him a lesson not to be so low as to sleep with a kaffir woman in a crafty way that we can't catch him at it. Because it will ruin him, all right. Even if he gets acquitted, it'll ruin him just as much as a conviction. Just to be mixed up in such a kind of a case will finish him off, all right. Even if, as I have said, he gets away with it.

"But there will be a comeback, all right. They'll come back on me for it, right enough. I'll get transferred and I won't get promotion and they'll as likely as not send me out to some shitty post like the Caprivi Strip. Because, even though the man is ruined, it'll look as though I brought the prosecution for spite. But I feel almost like *doing* it, there you are. I mean, Brits, to think that a man can be so *low* as to sleep with a kaffir woman and then to cover up his tracks in a way that you can't produce any evidence against him that will go in a court of law – as you've made it clear to me that this man is doing. I'm almost tempted to work a roughie on him. Just so his name will stink all the same even if he gets found not guilty. Just because he's so low, I feel I'd like to deal with him. Even if the Attorney General jumps on me like a ton of bricks, afterwards."

It was Detective Sergeant Brits's turn to be reflective. "That other thing, now, sir, as you've spoke of, sir," he remarked diffidently, "perhaps we could. . . You know what I means, sir. Locking the Coloured woman up in a cell and scaring the guts out of her. Hitting her over her arse with a short piece of belt fastened on to a stick, even, sir."

"She won't fall for that," the commandant said shortly. His tone sounded even more brief than the concise piece of belt mentioned by the detective. "With four pairs of shoes, she'll know a thing or two, all right. She'll probably even go and see her lawyer, next day. In any case, her King's evidence wouldn't go under the Tielman Roos Act – as you yourself have mentioned."

It wasn't that, that he was getting at, the detective explained. He wasn't thinking of anything as crude as merely extorting a confession from the white man's illicit partner. He had planned something slightly more intricate. But on maturer reflection he had come to the conclusion that that project would not work out, either. Satisfactory though his scheme appeared to be on the surface, Detective Sergeant Brits acknowledged it could not, in practice, be relied on to produce the hoped-for result.

"What I means is for us to scare the living tripe out of the Coloured woman in a cell with a piece of short belt fastened on to a handle and laid across her backside," Detective Sergeant Brits said, "and then for her to trap the white man. I takes it you knows what I means, sir."

"You mean that she'll arrange for that white man to go to bed with her in a place and at a time that she'll notify the police beforehand, so that you've just to go and pull them out of bed and have a clear case?" the commandant enquired, looking suddenly interested.

That was the general idea, Detective Sergeant Brits said. But, on thinking it over, he realised that it wasn't certain to work out that way, exactly. That exact same plan had miscarried once before, to his knowledge. It had miscarried through a circumstance that had been overlooked in one respect. Just as easily, he reasoned, could it miscarry in some other way – through some unlooked for circumstance that might not be apparent at the moment but that could, unexpectedly, defeat the ends of justice in some other way, right at the last moment. And the upshot of it would again be that the white man would get away. It was too risky, taking it by and large, Detective Sergeant Brits thought.

A policeman was a superstitious mortal. His was not the nature that proceeded by trial and error. A policeman did not believe that failure could be merely a stepping stone to success. If a particular kind of strategy had been found to be a washout once, a policeman was not likely to go and apply it again, adding to it sundry improvements in the hope that a perfect technique would ultimately be evolved. Once bitten, twice shy, was how a policeman saw life. And there was a good deal of plain sound common sense in such a point of view. That it was a Weltanschauung that did not lead to the dizziest kind of heights was a matter of minor importance. The stunt that Detective Sergeant Brits had in mind had proved a flop once. That was enough for him. There was no point in trying it out again. You were just liable to burn your fingers in some totally different way next time.

"How it went wrong was when they tried it on in Bloemhoek," Detective Sergeant Brits said. "They walloped that Coloured woman up a bit, and then they tells her a couple of lies about they'll let her off easy in court. That's why they says to her in the Bloemhoek police cells after they done finished walloping her, all she's got to do is to go to bed just like usual with that Bloemhoek town councillor. Only, she's got to tip the police off first, see? Well, so she agrees. And nobody could say afterwards as she didn't done her share properly. Only, just before he gets into bed with her, that town councillor sights all the belt marks on her backside. And because he's got a pretty quick brain, the town councillor tumbles right away that the police has been giving that Coloured woman a bit of a doing. So he just grabs his trousers and ducks. And it's night time in the street and so before the first policeman spots him, the town councillor has got his trousers on again. And so they can't bring a charge against him of public indecency, even. And next month the Bloemhoek commandant of police gets shifted."

Meanwhile, as the detective was talking, Commandant Kolyn's mind reverted to the question of the local suspect. Who *was* it, the commandant wondered. Somebody pretty high. That much he knew. Moreover, there were several men that he could think of whom it *might* be. Eventually his curiosity got the better of him.

"Look here, Brits," the commandant said, "on second thoughts, it wouldn't do any harm if you did tell me who that man was – who that man is, I mean, that we're after."

"Oh, you means as you wants me to tell you what his name is, sir, the name of this white man as I suspects with that Coloured girl, her that's got the four pairs shoes? You wants to know what his name is, is that right, sir?"

The commandant nodded.

After a quick look round to make sure that the door was closed, Brits told him.

The commandant stared at the detective. Then the commandant whistled.

3

The further that Charlie Hendricks drove into the Native location situated on the outskirts of Willemsdorp, the more convinced he was that he was making a fool of himself. Only, he was determined to see Marjorie. The news that Josias had communicated to him was beginning to disturb him beyond measure. He had to see Marjorie.

Something had to be done about it. No bastard, yellow complexioned child that he was the father of was going to grow up in the Native location. He had a conscience about it. He'd feel guilty for the rest of his life. Marjorie was not going to have that child. He was determined about it. She had to get rid of that child. He would do all he could to help. She could get some Native witch-doctor to help her. A white doctor, even, if it came to that. He'd pay for it, Charlie Hendricks decided.

But Marjorie hadn't come round again. Nor had he seen anything, since that night in his office, of the coloured man who might be her pimp or her husband. And he didn't know Marjorie's address. And he had no means of finding out. All he knew was that she lived in the location. And he couldn't go round asking white people where he could get hold of her. They would jump to a conclusion right away.

That was why Charlie Hendricks was driving through the location, now, driving slowly and keeping a sharp look out, in the hope of seeing Marjorie walking down a road or standing in front of a house. And the further he went, the more foolish he felt. He realised now that it was just as much out of the question to stop a Native man or woman, or child even, here in the location and to ask for Marjorie Jones. It would look just as suspicious as, in the town, asking a white person. And the mere fact of what he was doing, now – driving through the location – well, that in itself seemed pretty fishy, if you liked.

He was pleased to note, however, that the location inhabitants did not display an unusual measure of interest in his presence. And it struck him, then, that for all they knew, he might be there on legitimate business. He might be a friend of the white superintendent of the location, and he had come to visit him. He might be somebody from the Native Affairs Department who had an official reason for coming round. He might be an insurance agent or a collector for a burial society. Or a hire-purchase instalments man.

Charlie Hendricks breathed more freely when he found that he wasn't attracting an undue amount of attention. But there was still no sign of Marjorie. He saw only enormous numbers of children, their complexions varying from a high yellow to coal black. There were but few adults – and they were mostly elderly. The able-bodied male and female residents of the location were in the white man's town, working. There were lots of dogs, too. . . yellow, striped, spotted, mangy, dispirited.

The houses were a haphazard collection of wood-and-iron and

unbaked brick structures, with holes in the walls to take the place of windows. A lot of them were mud huts with flat roofs of corrugated iron held down with huge stones. But, because there was more space, the location didn't have the squalor of a Native area in Johannesburg. It didn't stink like a city slum. The smell that hung around it was not of poverty and dirt. There was an all-pervasive smell of stale wood smoke that was not unpleasant. And where dirty water ran from a tin shanty into the unmade road you didn't get a feeling of helpless misery about it, as you would if it was a city location. Above all, there was space. There was the sun, the sky. There were numerous garden patches devoted to mealies and pumpkins. There were pumpkins round and fat and golden. Some of the mealies stood up very tall. There were myriad flies buzzing around in the sun, and when they got tired of that they would go and alight on sore-eyed children.

But where abouts would Marjorie be, though?

That was when Charlie Hendricks saw a car stop down the road. And he saw a man step out of the car. It was a white man. Even from that distance Charlie Hendricks recognised him. Of all the – Charlie Hendricks started thinking. For that white man wasn't a hire-purchase furniture salesman. Nor was he an official from the Native Affairs Department. And he wasn't, either, canvassing for a burial society. Charlie Hendricks couldn't turn back. It was too late. That other white man had probably already seen him.

But what on earth could Dap van Zyl be doing there, drawing up in front of a tin shanty in a Native location – coming there on his own? It couldn't be there that Dap van Zyl's washerwoman stayed, and that he'd come round to see about his laundry. It couldn't be that he'd come round because he was a Provincial Councillor. In a strictly academic sense the Natives in the Willemsdorp location might be Dap van Zyl's constituents, seeing that they lived in the district that he represented in the Transvaal Provincial Council. But they only lived there. They didn't have the vote. Charlie Hendricks felt that he would give just anything, then, if he could turn back in time, so as to be able to avoid the imminent meeting. For it suddenly struck him that, if he was entertaining all sorts of mistrustful notions about Dap van Zyl's presence in the location, what must Dap van Zyl not be thinking about him? And for all he knew, Dap van Zyl might have a perfectly innocent and perfectly legitimate reason for being there.

But Charlie Hendricks realised that he couldn't turn back now. The road was too narrow for a U-turn. And it was almost a certainty that Dap van Zyl had already seen him. All he could do would be to drive on and then, when he got to the bottom of the road, to pretend surprise at the encounter. Only, he mustn't overact the surprise, Charlie Hendricks told himself. And then he would get out of his car, and he would exchange a few words with Dap van Zyl, standing talking to him there, next to the tin shanty, and then he would drive off again, in a perfectly natural manner, as though there was nothing more to the meeting. As though it was as matter of fact a thing to run into Dap van Zyl in the middle of a kaffir location as to come across him in the club. All the same, Charlie Hendricks could not but feel that it would take a bit of acting, all right. . .

Dap van Zyl had personality. That was what Charlie Hendricks felt above everything else about the politician when the two of them shook hands. He had a kind of self-assurance that made the person he spoke to feel completely at ease as well. Something magnetic about him. A man-of-the-world air. A sound brain – which was a lot better than to be brilliant. Easygoing good looks.

"Looking for a story for your paper?" Dap van Zyl asked of Charlie Hendricks. "Well, the editor before you – what was his name, again – ?"

"Esselen," Charlie Hendricks said. Well, of course. Why hadn't he thought of that before? Naturally, that was what he had come round to the location for. An article on it. With photographs.

"Yes, Esselen," Dap van Zyl said. "He did quite a snappy series on it, I remember. He had some good photographs, too."

They went on talking and Charlie Hendricks found himself getting more and more sick. Esselen, he thought. Photographs, he thought. A snappy little series, he thought. He had no doubt what had brought Esselen there, into the middle of the location. The same thing that had brought him, Charlie Hendricks, round there. The same thing that had brought Dap van Zyl there.

For, through the partly open door of the tin shanty that they were standing talking in front of, he had caught a glimpse of a skirt that he remembered. The outlines of a woman's figure that he knew. And fastened around her head a scarf with a bright pattern that he would recognise anywhere.

And here was all this dirty make-believe going on between Dap van Zyl and himself.

"I say, you look pale," Dap van Zyl remarked after a little while.

157

"The heat getting you down, I suppose?"

"Yes," Charlie Hendricks said. "The heat, I think, and – and other things."

They parted a few moments later, Charlie Hendricks getting back into his car and driving off, leaving Dap van Zyl still standing there, solid and good-looking and infinitely sure of himself, by the side of the unmade road in the Native location in front of the tin shanty of which the front door was slightly ajar.

But there was one thing that Charlie Hendricks had positively made up his mind about. Marjorie Jones was not going to bear a child by him. He was not going to have a share in awakening into living a creature whose first view of the world of men would be obtained from the interior of a tin shanty in a negro location.

He had at least found out, now, where Marjorie stayed.

4

One would be wrong to blame Cyril Stein for having put through that phonecall. For the fact of the matter was that Cyril Stein had nothing to do with it. It was the pretty sizeable volume of Indian hemp which he had inside him that evening when he passed the Town Hall that prompted him to indulge in what seemed to him a harmless bit of fun. Cyril Stein had made quite a praiseworthy effort to lay off the dagga. And until a day or two ago he almost believed that he had cured himself of the habit. Indeed, he *was* cured. Whatever the drug is that you are addicted to, you *are* cured, until the next time.

And because he was properly steamed up with dagga that evening, walking under the jacarandas on the Town Hall sidewalk, it just had to happen that his eye had to alight particularly on one prominent citizen of Willemsdorp who was attending the civic reception accorded Dap van Zyl. And it was purely in a spirit of frolic that Cyril Stein sidled off to a public telephone booth, then, and picked up the receiver and asked for the Town Hall. "Tickey, please," the telephone operator said. When Cyril Stein slipped in the coin, he was just about convulsed with laughter. It was so funny, he felt he wanted to let the telephone operator into it as well. But on second thoughts (on Nellie Pope's second thoughts, rather) he decided not to. The caretaker at the Town Hall answered the phone.

"Hello," said the caretaker.

"Hello," Cyril Stein said, feeling he wanted to choke, it was such a scream.

("Put your handkerchief over the mouthpiece," the fumes of the dagga smoke inside him said to Cyril Stein. "Otherwise he might recognise your voice, silly." Cyril Stein did what Nellie Pope told him.)

"I'll see if I can get him," the caretaker said after Cyril Stein had told him who the man was that he wanted called to the phone.

"He's sitting just over the door – " Cyril Stein started to say.

("You stupid," the Indian hemp hissed at Cyril Stein, putting a hand over his mouth that felt like – and might have been – a piece of sacking. "Tell him this man *said* that he would be sitting near the door, in case he got called. If you tell the caretaker you can *see* that gentleman sitting there, near the door – and you *were* going to say that: don't deny it – well, then the caretaker'll say why don't you go and call him yourself. Really, you know, you are a silly. Where you'd be without me, I don't know.")

"All right, I'll go and see if I can find him," the caretaker said, after Cyril Stein had told him the things that the dagga made him say. "Just hold on for a minute."

The drug known as Indian hemp or dagga or cannabis indica or hashish or Nellie Pope or msangu, that which grows by the gate (and a lot of other names), had Cyril Stein completely in her, its, his or him's sway, then. He was completely befuddled. He felt that he was walking on air when he was staggering. He felt he was a god when a worm with any kind of aim in life wouldn't look at him twice, the worm not seeing him even as potential nutriment. With the dagga inside him he felt that his brain was soaring to sublime heights. Actually, it wasn't even up to the level of a university professor's brain. And any racecourse tout could make rings round him. But those are the illusions of grandeur that you get from smoking dagga.

Standing in the phonebox, waiting, Cyril Stein, sheltered from the world of external reality by the warm embraces of a narcotic drug that in India they called bhang, saw the whole universe, moon and people and church towers and jokes about sex, reduced to a single pinpoint. And he was happy about it.

"Hello," he heard at the other end of the line.

("Put back that handkerchief over the mouthpiece," the goddess residing in dagga whispered to Cyril Stein between her teeth, nudging him at the same time in the ribs.)

159

"Look here," Cyril Stein heard himself saying. "Yes, look here, I'm just a friend. But I felt I had to give you a tip. Your wife. . . What's that? No, not my wife. . . I haven't got one. . . Perhaps you should go and see who's with her."

("That's enough. Put down the receiver," Nellie Pope told Cyril Stein.)

Chapter Twelve

1

THERE was no more to it than that Cyril Stein had been smoking dagga again, when he had done his best to give it up. And when he had passed the Town Hall and through the open door he had seen, sitting stiff and straight up and pompous, the principal of the Afrikaans-medium school, he could not restrain the impulse of wanting to laugh. And in a flash Cyril Stein remembered, the narcotic helping him to remember something useless when it would very surely have betrayed him if it were something worthwhile that he had had to recall. Cyril Stein remembered what Krisjan Erasmus, brother of the school principal, had said to him in the pub. "What's more, my brother wouldn't think he was somebody. . . yes, every time he's away at night, there am I on the bed. . ."

It was as though Cyril Stein could hear those words being uttered right then, when he was passing along the sidewalk in the dark, and he saw Johannes Erasmus sitting in that seat near the door, looking important and solemn, at the civic reception to the new Provincial Councillor. If he had to remember a date in history, say, or a Latin tag that he had learnt at school, "quisquis id est, timeo Danaos," even, or something to do with the hypotenuse of a square, Cyril Stein, filled up with dagga, would have been nowhere. Nought out of ten would have been all he could bank on. But when it was something else. . . well, he could hear almost the exact intonation of Krisjan Erasmus's voice when he had proclaimed his brother, Johannes the school principal, a cuckold.

The next step, for Cyril Stein, had been very simple. The telephone booth was right there. To find a threepenny piece in his pocket did not require much rummaging. And, for the rest, the angel of what the Indians called bhang was at hand to guide him in everything he said.

Johannes Erasmus parked his car by the side of the road. The light in the dining-room was still on. He went up the garden path on tiptoe, angry with himself and ashamed of himself for having those suspicions. He was walking up the garden path on tiptoe, a disgusting anonymous phonecall leading him up the garden path. Through a filthy anonymous phonecall he was treading gingerly, walking on his toes out of fear of the filth that he was walking on. No matter what his wife, Malie, might be up to, Johannes Erasmus thought – and quite likely she was up to nothing: quite likely he would find her as he had done the last time he came home and the dining-room light was on: quite likely he would find her half-asleep on the couch, alone. . . but for something stinking, he felt, there was nothing to touch that low thing he was doing now, coming in sneakingly, to catch his wife unawares, because some dirty skunk had phoned him. It was himself he was walking on, Johannes Erasmus felt, and that was why he had to be careful where he trod. Each step he took polluted his shoes. No shoepolish advertised over the commercial radio programme would get them clean again.

But thinking like that didn't help to make Johannes Erasmus act differently. When he inserted the key in the front door it was with a furtiveness that a burglar using a key made from a wax impression would have envied. Johannes Erasmus was entering his own home like a thief in the night.

But Malie was not reclining on the couch in the dining-room.

It was an old set-up. The situation was old. So was the sequel. Johannes Erasmus hadn't been quite noiseless enough. In coming up the garden path. Or in opening the front door. Or in crossing the floor of the dining-room towards the passage leading to the bedroom. And Johannes's brother, Krisjan, wasn't quick enough, either. It must have run in the family. Krisjan got his trousers on. But not quick enough. He also got out of the bedroom window, but also not quick enough. Johannes dashed to the window. He saw his brother Krisjan sprinting across the lawn, pulling at his pants. He saw him start to climb a wall. In a flash Johannes divined where his brother was heading. He was going to cut through the grounds of the Church of Christ Scientist and make for the back of the Education Department buildings where his truck would be parked.

He would get him, Johannes decided. He would have to drive round several blocks to reach the Education Department buildings. But he felt that he could just make it. First he would have to get at his desk in the study. He couldn't get the drawer open straight away. That wasted a few precious seconds. All the time he pictured his brother Krisjan tearing over the grass towards his lorry.

Malie, who had followed her husband as far as the dining-room, screamed when she saw him come out of the study. He looked dazed. As though he was coming out of a *brown* study. Malie screamed again when she saw Johannes make for the front door.

Her second scream seemed to waken Johannes to some sense of reality. For he darted back from the door towards where his wife was standing with her belly pulled in and her head forward and her arms bent up. He kicked out at her. That was a few more precious seconds wasted. Completely wasted. Because he missed.

And then he had trouble in getting the car to start. He didn't realise at first that he couldn't start the car with one hand. So he put down the revolver. But he put it where he could find it again. It was an old rendezvous, the Education Department buildings. . . Johannes Erasmus had called there often before in the past, on business – serious business. And his driving there now, too, in the night, also had something to do with education. He was going to teach his brother, Krisjan, something.

The school principal swung his car round the last corner. Those few wasted seconds made all the difference. A truck was careering down the road, making for the outskirts of the town. Johannes had one foot down flat on the petrol. And one hand on the wheel. And one hand on the revolver. It was a straight run, on the road to the north. The street was empty. Sometimes Krisjan, in the truck, got a bit ahead. At other times Johannes gained on him.

They were approaching the bridge. Johannes saw the row of white-washed stones. The truck was going fast. It looked as though Krisjan would get away. Johannes brought the revolver down level over the steering wheel.

The first shot shattered his own windscreen. He fired again. Then again. Then two more shots.

Gradually he eased up on the accelerator. He brought his car to a stop. The truck was disappearing round the bluegum plantation in the dark.

There were two people parked in the car in the shadows of the trees. Johannes Erasmus didn't know they were there. Slowly he started up his car again. He turned back, homewards. He was glad his brother had got away.

Driving back home, Johannes Erasmus was sobbing. The revolver shots had brought him to his senses. He was glad he hadn't killed his brother. But he felt as though his own life had gone to hell, had been dissipated in ruin. He felt as though his own life had trodden a gallows path up the gravel of his front garden and had then rushed to final destruction along the road over the bridge that was lined with white-washed stones set apart at regular intervals.

Johannes Erasmus got back home. This time, when he entered the dining-room, Malie was on the settee, waiting for him. It might have been that all the in between things were just a dream. That he had never got the phonecall. That he was only coming home now for the first time, the reception to the Provincial Councillor over.

"Would you like me to make you some coffee?" he heard Malie ask.

Instead, Johannes Erasmus went and knelt at Malie's feet, where she was sitting on the couch. And he laid his head in her lap and his body shook with great sobs.

"No good could have come of it," Johannes Erasmus said, at length, his voice strained with crying, "getting Krisjan a job through influence – family influence."

Malie stroked Johannes's hair, petting him, seeking to comfort him. But they both of them realised, inside themselves, that it was useless.

They both knew that nothing would be the same again.

2

The reason why it was pretty bad for the Coloured man, Josias, locked up in one of the Native cells of the Willemsdorp gaol, was because there was nothing that the police had on him. And while they could have trumped up any one of a dozen charges against him, such as vagrancy, or not having a pass, or resisting the police when a police-man asked him for a pass, the fact of the matter was that they weren't interested in him as a customer for one of their stupid suits with broad arrows on it. They didn't want him in gaol. All they wanted from him was information. They only wanted him to talk.

And Josias wouldn't talk. He was afraid that if he talked he would incriminate himself. And it was no use policemen coming into his cell and explaining to him that as soon as he made a statement they would let him go. He'd been caught that way before – in just exactly that same way, the policeman using the identical words. "We don't want you," policemen had said to him in the past. "Why do you want to make things bad for yourself? And look at that blood running off your back. I don't know where to hit any more, hardly. There are almost no more fresh places to hit. All used up, just about. Is it *worth* while making a fool of yourself like this, Josias? And we know why you won't talk. It's because you're trying to cover up somebody else. But where will it get you, being staunch like that, big-hearted like that? Would they do that for you – keeping quiet?"

More than once, in the past, Josias had yielded. He had made a long statement, telling the police everything he knew. And it had always ended the same way – he had got time for it. A long stretch, too, the last one was.

Whereas, on this occasion, the police were genuinely not interested in him. All they wanted was for him to talk. They knew all about him, how he made his living and one thing and another. But he was just small potatoes. They wanted to know who the heads were of the dagga-ring from whom he got his supplies that he retailed in small parcels. The police were after the heads in the traffic. They wanted to lay the *heads* by the *heels*.

The police also wanted some down to earth information about White men that were consorting with Coloured women. And they knew that Josias could also give them that information. And it could all be done in a nice way, too, without any unpleasantness. He could even go and sit down in the commissioner's office, if he liked. And a short-hand writer would take down everything he said. And he could go immediately afterwards – go back into the street and peddle some more narcotics, if he felt like it. The police didn't want him. They wanted the big shots in the game. And after he had made his statement, they would gladly have given him a packet of cigarettes as well, as he was going out. It could all have been done in such a nice way.

Instead of which there was. . .

Josias, with his clothes off, was spread-eagled across a table. It was a small table. His wrists and ankles were shackled to the tablelegs near the floor. At a cursory glance – and if you'd had a few drinks – it would have looked to you as though the table had eight legs.

"Look at the filthy mess he's made on the floor," the sergeant said. "Give him a few more for that. . . No, not on the same place, Pelser. Hit him on another place. He doesn't feel it if you hit him on a place that's

165

already cut open. Give me that strap for a bit. You're tired. . . Yes, have a beer. . . Yes, thanks, a small one."

The work of reasoning with Josias went on in the half-light of the prison cell.

After about five minutes the sergeant, exhausted, handed back the sjambok to the constable. Swish – theeeak – whoosh. . . the lash rose and fell, making comical sounds, leaving broad weals on human meat.

"You know, Josias, old man," the sergeant said, after a while. "It's so unnecessary, all this trouble you're giving us. And it can't be too pleasant for you, either. I mean, just take a look at your back – oh, I forgot, you can't see your back, of course – the way you're lying. But perhaps you'll take my word for it. Now, Josias, maybe you think this is all very funny. Maybe you've got no idea what we've been doing to your back. . . seeing you've just been lying down there taking it easy, all the time the constable here and I have been working our guts out on you. Don't think I feel sorry for myself for having to put all this hard work into you, and getting no extra pay for it, either. *I'm* not squealing. It's part of my job. But it's just like you – you being so soft-hearted and all – to feel sorry for me the way I got to sweat and carry on, and without any proper space to swing this sjambok, either, the way I'd like to swing it. But don't feel sorry for me on that account, either, Josias. I just got to make the best of it, I suppose. I know you must think it's a very hard life, being a police sergeant. But that's your trouble all over. You're too kind-hearted. Sorry for people when you don't *need* to be sorry for them. And sorry for the wrong people, too, as likely as not.

"Now, all we want from you is a couple of names. And a couple of statements to go with those names. But no, you're too tender-hearted to split on your pals. Too staunch, that's your trouble. Always thinking about other people. I'm sure you're even thinking about the constable, now. He's got his sleeve well rolled back, now, Josias, and he's got a firm grip on the handle of the sjambok, and he's sort of getting ready to take a step back. But I don't want you to give us this information for the constable's sake, Josias, just because you feel sorry for him, him being so worn out and all. If you think perhaps he's had too long a spell at it, I could go and fetch another constable out of the charge office that's fresher than this constable. . . What do you say, Pelser, would you like a relief?. . .

"But it's you yourself I'd like you to think of, Josias. You mustn't just think of other people, all the time. I know you believe I'm only joking, but your back – it's like raw liver, your back is, in places. But there are other places that are not so bad."

In the end, Josias yielded. He made the statement lying where he was, the sergeant being reluctant to let him get up in case he turned soft-hearted again, halfway through his statement. A clerk from the office took down what Josias had to say.

And nobody was more surprised than Josias was when the sergeant informed him he could put his clothes on and go. He was on the verge of collapse when they released him from the table. When they told him he was free to go, the shock was too much. He realised then that the police had told him the truth. So he had got the hiding for nothing. He fell across the table once more. He had fainted.

"Hasn't he had enough?" the constable asked. "What's he lying on the table again for?"

"'S a funny thing," the sergeant said. "We're letting him go. But you wouldn't think it from his back, you wouldn't. Looks like he's wearing a striped jersey – and like he'll be wearing it a good long time."

Back home in his khaya in the location, Josias did not sleep very easily that night. Arrested, flung in a cell, thrashed to within an inch of his life, and then released again – it was a good deal to happen all on one summer's day. And more than one white man in Willemsdorp, if he had known what had gone on record about him in Josias's statement, would have had a pretty disturbed sort of sleep, also.

3

Lena Cordier had been appointed to a school in Orange Grove. She went to school backwards and forwards by bus from the building in Eloff Street in which she was staying. The flat she had rented was on the third floor of Repton House, a decent class building with the rent somewhat higher than she could really afford to pay. But when she was walking about looking for accommodation in the centre of the city (and having a particular aim in view) there was something about the look of Repton House that told her it was the right place. And when she spoke to the landlady she knew that she was not mistaken.

"I like my tenants to conduct themselves respectable," the landlady said, showing Lena Cordier over the flat. "This is a decent class building. And I get my rent regular. Some of the young ladies in this building gets their rent by – well, you'd be surprised to know what big mining men some of them are. You know what I mean – no Syrians and tha' kine-uv trash. I don't stand for no nonsense here. Tha's what I mean that Repton House is a respectable building. Decent class is what we have here. And I just got t' take one look at you to know you're decent class. . . No, no, I don't want t' know who's keeping you. Just as long as I get my rent regular, and everything goes on decent, and no Syrians. . . that's all I need to know. . . Thank you, I might's well have it now. . . Yes, that's right *and* ten shillings. Thank you again. And I'll push your receipt under the door sometime when I've made it out. I hope you get on 'll right here, dearie."

That was that. And Lena Cordier felt that she would get on all right in that building. She was extremely hopeful of meeting some girl there who would be able to put her on to somebody – preferably a qualified medical practitioner – who was not averse to turning an honest penny. And Lena Cordier was perfectly correct in the conclusion she had come to about Repton House. You could *see*, just to look at it from the outside, that Repton House was a decent class building. You could also see that it wasn't a bloody convent.

It took a bit of getting used to, though, Lena Cordier realised, the transition from the country town life of Willemsdorp to the physical and spiritual conditions of the city dweller's being. For one thing, there was no wide, open veld at your door, almost, that you could walk out on to.

But, in a city, Lena Cordier reflected, every road did not lead inevitably to a bridge the approaches of which were marked out clearly with whitewashed boulders placed at specific intervals apart: that, at least, was something to be grateful for. In the city they didn't make such a fuss of your having crossed a bridge. . . all right, you crossed it, so what? That was how they regarded a bridge in the City of Johannesburg. There was nothing to get all worked up and excited about. Or, all right, you didn't cross the bridge. You walked only as far as the middle of that bridge. And it was a railway bridge. And you didn't walk all the way over the bridge because you decided to jump over it just as the signal was going for the 9.15 local from Brakpan. Again, so what?. . . Maybe those whitewashed stones standing in rows on each side of the bridge in Willemsdorp were headstones. Maybe, Lena Cordier reflected, they were whited sepulchres. . . One thing, she realised, was that although there was much that was frightening in the

City of Johannesburg, she had none of those fears, living in Repton House, Eloff Street, that she had had in Hex Buildings, Willemsdorp. . . It seemed that it was not in itself important as to whether or not a thing was frightening. What mattered was to what degree you yourself were afraid of it.

Maybe there was no veld that you could take long walks across, in the city. But the veld was still there, of course. At least, the earth that the veld was made of, was. Was and is and will be, ever more, meaning existence. Only, in a city, the topsoil and subsoil and rock formation part of the veld were present in a more stylised form – in the tall straight up and down of buildings. The soil of the veld was compressed into bricks and tiles. A whole stretch of what had been virgin Highveld was telescoped into concrete.

There was Repton House, now, for instance. Repton House was a koppie standing right in the middle of Eloff Street, right in the centre of Johannesburg. Or, at least, a good deal of the red sandstone that had been excavated from a koppie and that was amenable to being dressed as building stone was standing there, perpendicularly, in Eloff Street – the individual stones chained together in a mortar more binding than anything they had known when they were merely part of an antisyncline in a geological stratum of the Karoo system. Repton House was, by reason of its origins, a concentrated piece of African hill. And on the four perpendicular sides of this piece of African hill that had been transported into the centre of Eloff Street, Johannesburg, there sprouted windows, the thorny panes catching at the garments of the passing sun, tearing off bits as the sun went by, holding fragments of yellow rag spiked for brief moments.

Within the first week of her living in Repton House, Lena Cordier got friendly with a girl with bleached hair called Molly. Molly lived on the fourth floor of Repton House. And when she first learnt that Lena Cordier was a schoolteacher, teaching at a government school at Orange Grove, Molly thought that it was a new lark. A game that she herself had not been let into, so far, Molly thought. Well, what will they think of next, had been Molly's first reaction. But within half an hour – because hers was not a suspicious nature – Molly accepted Lena Cordier simply as a girl that had gone wrong. And to Molly's ideas where Lena Cordier had gone wrong was not in having got herself in the family way – because that was something that everybody could understand – but in having become a schoolteacher.

Well, there was an Indian doctor, Molly told Lena Cordier. His name was Something Peewelaswamy. It was a name nobody could pronounce. They just called him Dr Pee. He was very good, of course. Not only at *that*, but also at his job. But when it came to *that*, there was no White doctor in Johannesburg to touch him. No matter how far gone you were, inside a week you'd be sitting up laughing. Yes, if Lena liked, she'd fix it up with Dr Pee. She'd phone him to come round, Molly said. Only, of course, Lena had to be careful. There was the landlady. Dr Pee would have to come up the back stairs, when the landlady didn't know about it. The landlady wouldn't allow even Syrians into the building – let alone anybody as Coloured as an Indian. But Dr Pee was *good*, Molly insisted. No matter how many months, he could fix you up.

Orange Grove Government School – a decent school. Every school day Lena Cordier arrived on time. And she wrote words on the blackboard. And she corrected school exercise books. And she walked up and down in the aisles of the classroom. And she showed the pupils, each of them, where they went wrong. And there was not a single pupil but could point its little finger at Lena Cordier and announce to the whole world where she, Lena Cordier, had gone wrong. That was what Lena Cordier thought. But she was surprised to find that no schoolchild in the lower standards pointed its finger at her and lisped "Whore." It seemed that the world was like that, the world outside of Willemsdorp. All that the world outside of Willemsdorp seemed to be concerned about was that you should do your work all right. As long as you did your work all right, it seemed that the world – outside of Willemsdorp – didn't care what you did in your spare time. At least, no eleven year old child got up out of its seat and denounced Lena Cordier, proclaiming, "Bitch! Harlot!" Not that eleven year olds didn't use that kind of language, of course.

But what Lena Cordier did think, when she was back in her flat after school, and Molly was visiting her, and Molly was putting her wise about how she should not allow Dr Pee to charge her too much, then it seemed to her that it was really Molly, the professional prostitute, that was the schoolteacher, and that it was she, Lena Cordier, that was the pupil – the schoolchild sitting straight up in her desk, her arms folded and her face expressionless.

There was also one stage at which – when Molly got to some of the more lurid details about how Dr Pee did a job – Lena Cordier felt she wanted to put up her hand in class and ask the teacher could she please leave the room.

4

In terms of straightforward, all-out sensation, with no holds barred, there was little that anybody could take exception to in the piece of news that swept Willemsdorp like wildfire. Even before it got into the newspapers – both the English *Northern Transvaal News* and the Afrikaans *Nuus* – everybody knew all the details. At least, they knew as much as the police did. And the police knew everything except who the murderer was.

But sensation – hell, there was just nothing like it. A bombshell was tame next to that. Just about anything you could think of was tame next to that. Just as the more startling events of real day to day life must of inevitability be much more terrible and grotesque than the most far-fetched kind of fictional invention. It was as though, from the moment that piece of news was bruited abroad – before it got into the newspapers, even – life in Willemsdorp had changed. It was as though the substance of being, the inner content of getting up in the morning and going to your work, the material thing of taking your clothes off at night and slipping in between the blankets, had become charged with an altered nature and quality.

The public knew as much as the police knew. Which was that a Native, walking across the veld at night, had made a report to the Kleinberg police. The Native reported that he had witnessed something unusual. He had seen a man, the Native said, climbing through the barbed wire that was around the Wondergat. And from the look of things it was a White man, seeing that there was a motor car parked by the side of the road at the time.

The Native had not been able to observe much more than that, owing to the darkness of the night. But what the Native seemed pretty convinced about was that what the man threw into the Wondergat was the body of a woman. From the size and shape of the bundle that was precipitated in the dark into the depths of the Wondergat the Native witness could come to no other conclusion but that it was a woman. He couldn't see very much, owing to the night being somewhat dark, but his *feeling* about the whole affair was that it was a woman's body that went plunging down into the frightening depth of the Wondergat under the starlight.

Detective Sergeant Brits was on the scene early next day. He borrowed a crane from a nearby corundum diggings that had progressed to the stage of investing in a two-ton crane. Rope he got next, and a Native police constable who was sufficiently intrepid to allow himself to be let down into the Wondergat on the end of a rope. There was something antiquely symbolical in the situation, something of an ancient whimsicality in the thought that a policeman had to be tied on to a rope first before it would be possible to tie the murderer to the rope. Give a policeman enough rope to hang the murderer with.

And they needed a lot of rope. A good deal more than they had brought to the Wondergat with them. They didn't know that the hole was all that deep. When they had let out all the rope they had to the end, the Native policeman was still suspended in mid-air – as the murderer would be, yet, at the conclusion of the case, after the judge had passed sentence and Detective Sergeant Brits had put a tick in blue pencil next to the name of the accused in his dossier.

When they found out that the rope the Native policeman was tied to was too short, they sent into Kleinberg for more rope. That was an indulgence that they would not accord the murderer on the morning of his execution. To the murderer's complaint that the rope was too short they would attach little importance, just so long as the murderer was attached to the rope. They would certainly not send out for more.

The Native police constable located the woman's body floating on the water at the bottom of the Wondergat. The two of them were brought up together – the dead woman reaching the surface in the arms of the police constable who held her very tightly – in marked contrast to the manner in which she had descended the Wondergat. For when he had her suspended over the mouth of the shaft, the murderer did not hold on to her as tightly as he might have.

But in Willemsdorp. . . was it a sensation? Brother, don't talk.

Chapter Thirteen

1

CHARLIE Hendricks, his work on the newspaper done for the day, was on his way up the stairs of the building where he had his flat.

That was when he encountered Cyril Stein. Charlie Hendricks knew by then that Cyril Stein was the occupant of the flat on the other side of the landing.

Charlie Hendricks was not in the mood for company. Nor did he particularly feel like going into his flat and sitting there on his own. More especially as he felt that it was not very likely that anybody would come and visit him. There was one visitor from whom he could very certainly not expect a call – a visitor who had come round in the past at fairly regular intervals; clandestinely; surreptitiously. Even though she had always come in without knocking.

But that was the sort of thing a ghost did, Charlie Hendricks reflected – coming in without knocking.

No, he mustn't think along such lines, Charlie Hendricks said to himself. And then he realised, with an overwhelming clarity, that the one thing he didn't want was to be alone with his thoughts. That was how it came about that he invited Cyril Stein into his flat for a drink.

And because that was the subject everybody in Willemsdorp was discussing, it wasn't long before, seated in Charlie Hendricks's flat, glass in hand and with a jug of water and a bottle on the table between them, the two live men were talking about the dead woman that the Native police constable had brought up from the dark pit of the Wondergat.

"Of course, it's mostly hearsay, I believe," Cyril Stein remarked, "but I understand that she wasn't quite white. And that her murderer is a white man who got her into trouble. A bit shocking, isn't it? I mean, I can't picture myself going there at night. Even if it's without a dead body to dispose of. Just the thought of *going* there at night makes me feel shaky. Not that I'm superstitious or anything like that, of course, but I've seen the Wondergat. And all I can say is that the murderer must be a man with an iron nerve."

"Either that, or it's somebody completely desperate," Charlie Hendricks replied. "It's amazing what the most timid person can do if he's really got the wind up."

Cyril Stein laughed. "But all the same, the Wondergat," he said. "It's a bit too profound for me, if you get me. At least a couple of thousand feet, according to what they say and, what is worse, according to how it *looks*."

"A bit out of your depth, is it – the Wondergat?" Charlie Hendricks answered, deciding to join in with Cyril Stein's attempt at being facetious. It was about as good a line as any, he reflected.

"And they say it's some man that's quite well known," Cyril Stein continued. "At least, it appears that the police are suspecting someone quite well known. What evidence they've got I can't say, of course. But it would be dashed funny if it turned out to be the Police Commissioner himself, say. Or this Provincial Councillor, Dap van Zyl. Or what about that red-faced man that stood against him – what's his name – Robert E. Constable? That would be a laugh, wouldn't it? What makes me also think it might be Constable is that he's left town. Sounds suspicious, I must say – his making a getaway like that. Or what about Johannes Erasmus, the principal of the Afrikaans-medium school here? There's very little I put past him, you know."

Cyril Stein had been smoking dagga, that afternoon, and in fair quantities. So that almost anything could make him laugh. And the thought of Johannes Erasmus flinging a girl into the Wondergat seemed excruciatingly funny to him – especially taken in conjunction with his telephone call of the evening of the reception.

"For that matter," Charlie Hendricks said, trying to sound airy, "it might be one of us two – you or me, say. Have another drink?"

"After that," Cyril Stein replied, "I think I will. . . After all, even if we are innocent, it doesn't mean to say that the police are not suspecting us. Take me, for instance. I'm sure I'm under a cloud, at headquarters. I've never been able to fit into the life of the town. Who's a more likely suspect? What's more, I absolutely don't *know* where I was on the night of the eighteenth – or the eighth, even."

"As for me," Charlie Hendricks said, "I'm somebody that hasn't been here long from Johannesburg. And anybody from Johannesburg always is distrusted in a small town, just as a matter of course. And what is the first thought that will occur to the police? Why, just this:

there was never any trouble of this sort in Willemsdorp before I came here. What sort of a leg have I got to stand on?"

"On the gallows trapdoor," Cyril Stein acknowledged, "none."

"And another thing," Charlie Hendricks went on, "it seems to me that the police are strangely uncommunicative about this thing to me. In the past, I could always go round to Detective Sergeant Brits and he would show me his dockets and dossiers and what-not. He'd give me all the inside dope he had. And if there was something he knew and that he didn't want me to publish right then, he'd tell me, and he'd trust me that it was strictly off the record. But there's nothing like that now. All I get from him are just the bare facts. Maybe that's all he does know. I can't tell. Maybe he has given me all the information he's got, and he just doesn't tell me any more because he's still casting around in the dark, and he genuinely doesn't know any more. Perhaps I'm just imagining things – "

"I know," Cyril Stein interjected, "a guilty conscience."

Charlie Hendricks sniffed. A smell of something burning. No, not quite. It was something coming from Cyril Stein's cigarette. It was acrid. Yet sweetish. A very individual fragrance.

With the rapidity of a right hook Charlie Hendricks felt his mind being carried back into the past. That smell gave him a jolt. He found himself in Ferreirastown, as a cub reporter. There was a sack of green leaves that a couple of members of the Narcotics Squad were destroying in the back yard of an Indian store. Yes, he knew, now, what it was that Cyril Stein was smoking. So that was what he had felt about Cyril Stein. Anyway, he knew now. And he remembered how the Narcotics Squad detectives had, for fun, rolled a cigarette out of a few of those green leaves. And they had offered him a draw, and he had declined. He was afraid of the stuff.

All right, he knew all about Cyril Stein. Even though he had had quite a few drinks inside him, and even though he had a good deal in his own mind to accuse himself of, Charlie Hendricks was not able to rid himself entirely of the prejudices that every decent white South African had in this regard. He liked Cyril Stein, and all the rest of it. But a white man that smoked dagga – well, such a one was rather outside the pale.

"I notice you're sniffing," Cyril Stein said. "You can't understand what the cigarette tobacco is that I'm smoking? Well, I'll tell you. In for a penny, in for a pound. I might as well be hanged for a sheep as for a lamb, I suppose. But next to murder, this is just small potatoes. What I'm doing is, I'm smoking dagga." Cyril Stein laughed.

He expected Charlie Hendricks to take his statement as a joke – as a cheerful bit of fantasy, in line with the ribald remarks they had been making about the Wondergat murder. He never for one moment thought that Charlie Hendricks would really believe that he was smoking dagga. Of all things. . . He had expected Charlie Hendricks to accept it as a flourish on his part. He didn't think Charlie Hendricks would take him seriously.

"Yes, I recognise the smell, now," Charlie Hendricks said. "You know, I don't feel it's right that a white man should smoke dagga. Western civilisation. We've got to set the Coloured races an example. You know what I mean – White superiority. If we start going in for their degenerate practices like smoking dagga, then the next is we'll be wearing a striped blanket with a top-hat, like a Bakwena chief, or we'll be drinking kaffir beer out of claypots or – or – "

"Or doing a spot of ritual murder to bring rain," Cyril Stein declared, desperately trying to force his brain along the paths of make-believe that he and Charlie Hendricks had wandered a couple of moments before. But it was hard. It was tough going. The machinery grated. He took a plunge.

"And maybe, what that Wondergat murder was for, was just to bring rain," he said. "Perhaps, why that white man let the girl drop into the Wondergat was because he had fallen so low that he was also going in for Native tribal practice. After all, there is a drought on. And he didn't mind how low he let the girl fall, seeing that she was Coloured."

No, he wasn't getting the right vein. He was being flat-footed. The ideas and the words were eluding him. Persiflage – that was what he wanted. But all he was saying now merely sounded clumsy. He took another plunge. And this time it seemed, from the effect it had on Charlie Hendricks, that he had tripped right over and fallen deeper down than the Wondergat.

"You should be the last man to talk about low habits," Cyril Stein said, winking, "because what you have been doing is much worse. I mean, you must have slept with a Coloured girl in the first place, to have the police after you, now, for this thing."

Charlie Hendricks gulped down more brandy. No, it couldn't be, he said to himself. What this man was saying to him, across the table, with the jug of water and the bottle of brandy between them – hell, what was he getting at? Charlie Hendricks felt a slow fury rising in him. It was as though he were getting hot at the back of his neck. In a few moments he would be seeing red. Then purple. . .

"Damn you, what do you mean?" he demanded of Cyril Stein. "Don't beat about the bush, man. Come straight out with it."

For a moment Cyril Stein got frightened. As quickly his fear left him. One thing, at least, he was satisfied about, and that was that he was a match for the next man. Never mind how the Philistines in a dorp like Willemsdorp treated him, as a man he believed himself to be as good as any man. Just let this Hendricks try and start any rough stuff with him, and he'd show him pretty quick. Already Cyril Stein was eyeing the bottle, now no more than half full, on the table between them. Just let Hendricks try anything, and he'd have that bottle right on his head. Or he'd smash the top of that bottle and stick the rest of it into Hendricks. How would Hendricks like that? At the thought that he could hold his own, Cyril Stein suddenly grew self-confident. And, in consequence, relaxed.

"Look," he said to Charlie Hendricks, speaking very quietly, "I honestly thought you had a sense of humour. That's why I said that I was smoking dagga. I was saying it just for a joke. In the same way that we were hinting to each other that we were, the pair of us, a couple of murderers. It was all just for a laugh. Just for talk. Just for the sake of moonshine. Or. . . say, *wasn't it?*" Cyril Stein laughed.

His sense of humour appealed to, Charlie Hendricks laughed also. "Oh yes, of course," he said. "It was all just a joke. Everything we've been saying and hinting here in my flat has just been a lot of balls. The very suggestion that what you're smoking might be dagga is as absurd *as anything else we've been saying.*"

The equivocal in Charlie Hendricks's remark did not escape Cyril Stein. And so it became his turn to be serious.

"I'll tell you something," he said. "I know that it's only a decadent white man that will talk to you like I'm talking now. But I'm not too sure if I would not rather *be* a decadent white man than some of these solemn frauds, brainless as they make 'em, that pass as pillars of society. I wouldn't be with them for anything. And, all right, I know that if a white man starts smoking dagga he's a lost soul. He's degraded. He's finished. Don't think I haven't got a conscience about it, because I have. That's why I've tried hard to break myself of it. Sometimes I think I didn't try hard enough. I think that if I had really *wanted* to save myself from becoming a dagga addict, I could have. But then I'm not too sure on that point, either. But, anyhow, I did try, and it was no good. The dagga beat me. The dagga was my master. And I've surrendered. And I know that I'm the lowest kind of white man that there is. And I won't argue about it. Only, the funny part of it is that I don't *feel* any lower than any white man sitting in the Willemsdorp Club tonight. That's how good it is. For one thing, I'm not a fraud. I'm not a hypocrite. I don't pretend I'm any better than what I am. And as far as *brain* goes, I can make rings round any one of those dolts. And it's not the dagga talking, either, when I say this. And if it is, I don't care."

Cyril Stein looked pale. He paused. In his eyes you could read an overstimulation – or a near-exhaustion.

Charlie Hendricks was interested. "Tell me, what does it do to you," he asked, "dagga?"

"It's the oldest drug in the world," Cyril Stein answered. "And the most widespread. In the Arab countries they call it hashish. In the East they've got lots of names for it. Here the coloured addicts call it Nellie Pope. But what's in a name? The important thing is that it severs the bonds of time and space. You are transported into a dream world. And nobody can see it on you – nobody can say you're a drunkard, look how you're staggering, look how you're lying on the pavement. You go on in your dream world. And you do your work. And you meet and talk to people who are not in a dream. And they don't know that you are full of dagga. And you laugh a good deal. And colours are very bright. And sounds seem very distant. And a second seems to get the length of half a century, or so. And you imagine the most incredible things. Even as you walk about the streets you imagine – oh, anything: that you're an emperor. Why, you *know* that you're an emperor. That the street is a desert wider than the Sahara, and that it'll take you days and weeks and months to cross it. And the street *is* all that. And it does take you all that time to cross it. And don't you yourself know of streets like that – wider streets, even: streets that you can never cross? And I suppose if you keep on smoking dagga you start losing grip. You go to pieces. You go mad. That's the price you've got to pay, I suppose.

"Well, there it is. Like any drug, it'll let you down in the end. But I know lots of people who have never smoked dagga that have also been let down. Anyway, I tried to break myself of the habit, and I couldn't. So I know I'm rubbish. But I wonder if I shouldn't be grateful to the dagga for having taught me that. Maybe, if it wasn't for the dagga I'd never have found out I was rotten. I would have gone to the grave with illusions about myself. I would never have faced up to myself, maybe if it wasn't for the dagga. I would have gone on kidding myself that I was something that I am not. And I would also have missed all the sensations that I get from smoking dagga. With your permission I'll light up another one. Care to have a pull? Mind you, it doesn't always work the first time. The name we addicts give to a dagga cigarette is a 'zol', by the way."

Cyril Stein passed over the smoke to Charlie Hendricks.

Charlie Hendricks hesitated. He remembered the time in the back yard of the Indian store when the two members of the Narcotics Squad had, for a joke, rolled a dagga cigarette out of that sackful of dagga that they had destroyed, and they had, also just for the fun, offered him a draw, and he had declined. Well, he had come a long way since then, he reflected.

"Okay," Charlie Hendricks said, eventually. "As you said, earlier on, in for a penny in for a pound. I might as well be hanged for a sheep as for a lamb."

"It makes you forget all your troubles, for one thing," Cyril Stein said as he passed the zol across to Charlie Hendricks.

Charlie Hendricks, puffing deeply, remembered when somebody had last expressed that same sentiment, in almost the identical words. It was that queer coloured man who had called himself Josias.

Charlie Hendricks went on smoking.

In one respect, Cyril Stein had not been strictly accurate. That was when he had said that dagga did not necessarily work the first time. For in Charlie Hendricks's case it did.

It was late that night that Charlie Hendricks got up out of his chair to see Cyril Stein to the door. In departing, Cyril Stein slipped an envelope into Charlie Hendricks's hand.

"There's enough in there for a couple of dozen smokes," Cyril Stein said. "Just mix it with tobacco and roll it in a piece of paper, like I told you."

Makes you forget your troubles, Charlie Hendricks thought. But what troubles could anybody have in the world, if he felt like Charlie Hendricks was feeling then?

"All the same, I am afraid of dagga," Charlie Hendricks had said to Cyril Stein as Cyril Stein was on the point of leaving. "I'm not worrying that it might lead me to commit murder. What I am afraid of is that it will bring me down to wearing a blanket with a top-hat, and no shoes."

Trouble, Charlie Hendricks thought, when he was alone in his flat. *N-thick trouble* was a bit of university slang that he recalled from his student days. But he could think of no trouble that was not very far away now – further away in the future than his student days were in the past. That was one thing dagga did for you, anyway. Past, present, future were all one, and all alike meaningless. Quite pretty things, they seemed, troubles – if you got a proper faraway perspective on them. Slender leaves nodding in a grey night, very distant and nodding in the wind. And he had a brain powerful enough to deal with any problem, he told himself. Even if it was only the dagga that made him tell himself that, Charlie Hendricks didn't care.

2

As for being in trouble, well, Lena Cordier was no longer in trouble. The Indian medical man, Dr Ranjit Peewalaswamy – whom his white patients addressed as Dr Pee because they couldn't get their tongues round his name – had come round at Molly's bidding, and because he was good at his job, Lena Cordier was up and about again, back in her classroom, inside of a week. But what Lena Cordier didn't like about it, altogether, was that Dr Pee, a tall, thin, youngish-looking Indian, had performed the illegal operation free of charge. He wouldn't take any money for it. Molly's warning to Lena, that Dr Pee might overcharge her, had been superfluous. Another thing was that, after Lena Cordier was well again, Dr Pee kept dropping in at intervals. Every so often he came round ostensibly to see how his patient was getting on – when there was obviously no further need for his visits.

Dr Pee's calls were embarrassing to Lena. She felt immeasurably grateful to him, of course. She was infinitely indebted to him both as a person and as a medical man. But she wished he wouldn't come round, any more. She would gladly pay him almost anything he asked. It would give her pleasure to hand over to him her entire savings. But she wished he would stay away. After all, he was an Indian. And she could not help but wonder what the landlady of Repton House was beginning to think of his visits. Lena was sure that the landlady would be prepared to overlook Dr Pee's presence in the building if she knew that his coming round was connected only with a matter of procuring an abortion. But she would never tolerate his paying social calls in the place. If the landlady drew the line at Syrians – and rightly, Lena Cordier felt – it was obvious that an Indian would get pretty short shrift.

Then there were Lena Cordier's personal reactions. Surely, Dr Pee did not think. . . He couldn't possibly take her to be the kind of white girl that associated with Indians. . .

Lena Cordier had been back from school several hours. She felt lonely in her flat. She started thinking of Willemsdorp. The people she knew there. No, there was nobody there that she would particularly want to see again, she thought. Except, perhaps, one person, she reflected. And that person wasn't Jack Brummer.

Her fountain pen was lying to hand. Next to it was the writing pad. She reached forward for the writing materials. She scribbled a brief note. She sealed it in an envelope and wrote on the address. The letter was to Charlie Hendricks. Just a few words, polite and non-committal, thanking him for driving her to the station on the night she left Willemsdorp. It could have been no more than a bare formality, her dropping him a line. What made it different from a mere formality was that it was so belated. The time interval between when he had taken her to the station and her sitting down and penning that note gave significance to the letter. Anyway, he would know her address, now, Lena Cordier thought, as she put a stamp on the envelope and went out to post it.

Alone in Johannesburg, Lena Cordier felt, by the time she reached the pillarbox, that she would be glad to see Charlie Hendricks again.

Of all the people she knew in Willemsdorp, he was the one she would most like to see again. And she would be glad to see him soon.

3

It did not take long for police investigations into the Wondergat murder to reach the stage where they effected an arrest. And while to more than one white man in Willemsdorp, perhaps, it came as a personal relief to think that somebody had been laid by the heels, at the same time the general reaction on the part of the public was of a character amounting almost to consternation. The police had not yet officially disclosed the identity of the woman that had been dredged up from the water at the bottom of the Wondergat: a piece of flotsam, jettisoned by a white man who had felt himself in danger of steering on to the rocks.

But those citizens of Willemsdorp who experienced a direct easement of the tension in their own mental state when they learnt that somebody had been apprehended for the crime were only a handful. They were very much in the minority. The general public was aghast. The man in the street shuddered. It was as though the ground under him was no longer stable. In the Middle Ages people would probably have painted some sign on the front door and have stayed inside, keeping that front door barred.

The reaction of the average inhabitant of Willemsdorp was understandable. The ordinary person was reasonably honest, reasonably hard-working, not tempted to the extremes, either in terms of his day to day behaviour or in his imaginative speculations. And so it was only to be expected that he would be not only perturbed but speechless, not only startled but dismayed, when it got about – as it did like wild-fire – that the man who had been caught in the police net, who had been escorted by Detective Sergeant Brits and a plainclothes constable to the cells of the local gaol, who had had his fingerprints taken and had had the charge of murder read out to him, who had been warned that anything he said might be taken down and used as evidence against him, who had been asked (unofficially) by the plainclothes constable if he was not ashamed of himself, who had been recommended (unofficially) by Detective Sergeant Brits to come along and make a clean breast of it, who had been lodged in the local gaol under a magistrate's warrant, who had been issued with a card bearing his name and number and the details of the charge preferred against him, who had been given two grey prison blankets and a prison stretcher and had a cell on his own because he was up on a murder charge, who had to leave his shoes and tie and braces in the corridor outside his cell, who had to surrender his watch and money and valuables and cigarettes and matches to the section warder, who had had his attention drawn by the section warder to the clause in the prison regulations empowering the officials charged with his custody to place him in chains if he offered violence, whose request to be allowed to send a message or write a letter had been received with a stony, half-pitying, half-contemptuous silence, who had been issued with a tin dish and a wooden spoon and a slop pail. . . that that was none other than Dap van Zyl, who had been returned for Willemsdorp by an overwhelming majority at the Provincial Council by-election, who was the white hope of the Volksparty for the Northern Transvaal, who had the respect even of his Union Party opponents, who had a political following and a political personality that was considered to be the equal of that of any legislator in the country, who was reckoned as being in line in, say, twenty years time, for the premiership, who was already being referred to, in the press and from the hustings, as – undissemblingly by his supporters, satirically by his adversaries – the King of the Bushveld. . . he it was that had had a noisome-smelling latrine bucket kicked into his cell by a section warder and that had slammed on him a cell door bearing the temporary, chalked inscription: "Charge – Murder."

If Dap van Zyl, elected by public vote to high office, had had as great a mind as the job to which he had been voted, he would have reconciled himself to the paradox in his position. He would as likely as not have said something about the mighty brought low, in between putting the sanitary bucket to the use intended by the authorities.

Instead of which, face to face with the time-honoured appurtenances and psychological devices connected with penology – no communication with the outside world and a stinking pot – he panicked. He couldn't really think of himself as the mighty fallen, because inside himself he had always known that he did not amount to much. He knew that everything he had achieved in life had been through the medium of cheap tricks. And so for that reason he was vulnerable to other cheap tricks.

He saw himself standing in the shadow of the gallows. A bluffer himself, he didn't recognise the gallows as also just another bit of common legerdemain. He didn't perceive that a crossbeam with a rope tied to it ending in a knotted egg-shape for a head to go through was also a piece of frippery, a paper pellet kind of knick-knack that only a humbug would be humbugged by. He didn't realise that that was the last thing any man with principle, with a single cardinal belief, could ever be impressed by. He didn't have the spiritual resources to be able to say, "Well, they can only hang me. And so what? And on a piddling, laughter provoking thing like that, too." He didn't even know – and that was something that any professional convict that had done time in prison with a gallows as part of its architecture could have told him – that a gallows was not even a very effective instrument of execution. If the rope was too long it was liable to jerk your head right off, so that they would have to sew it on again on to the roughly dissevered skin and flesh round about the second cervical vertebra of the upper part of your torso from which your head had been pulled off, before they handed your body over to your legal next of kin (wife, mother, father – *or son or daughter*) for decent Christian burial.

Or else the drop that the hangman had worked out for you was too short, with the result that the hangman's assistant would have to undertake the unpleasant task – and with no proper sort of light to help him, either – of clambering down a lot of wooden steps to where the sawdust was and kick you enough times in your belly for, when you were hoisted up again on to the trapdoor platform, the prison doctor to be able to certify that life was extinct. (Or, at least, extinct enough for the rough and ready demands of everyday prison usage.) Dealing with a lot of long-timer isolation cell convicts, some of them having served twenty years and more, it wasn't naturally easy for the prison doctor to determine as to which were alive and which weren't. If a man's neck was sewn on to his head again, neatly, it would puzzle the doctor somewhat – did that convict come round because he wanted to be put on the jam diet, or was he standing in line there as the next on the list – certified by the hangman – as being in need of burial? It wasn't too easy for the doctor to work it out, sometimes.

Anyway, Dap van Zyl was not so far developed, intellectually, as to be able to realise that the whole idea of stringing a man up on a piece of rope that was too short for him was so much bull. All you could achieve with that was to deprive a family of its breadwinner. The judge, in his wig and red robes, would deliver himself of certain remarks, pontifically. And because he had made those remarks, in his wig and red robes, pontifically, in C Court, High Court, Central Criminal Assizes, Autumn Sessions, under God and under King, it would naturally be of small concern to the judge, in his wig and red robes, that small children should ask of their mother, trying to cook porridge on a fire made of newspapers because there was no money for coal, "But where *is* Daddy, Mummy? Why doesn't Daddy come home? Why is

Daddy so long away, Mummy? Is Daddy living with a woman again, Mummy?"

Maybe it's not such a bad home, taken all in all, the particular part of hell in which Daddy is. Maybe he deserved all he got, being hanged and getting the stray left-over lights (that resided in his body through some mistake about the length of the rope) kicked out of him by the hangman's assistant.

But Provincial Councillor Dap van Zyl was in mortal terror of the rope. He lacked the philosophical background that would enable him to laugh at his predicament. Held incommunicado, and with an evil-smelling latrine bucket for company, he panicked. He did not have the spirit to say to himself, "Well, one thing, my conscience stinks a lot worse than this harmless old crap container." He simply got dread-stricken. He tried to pace up and down in his cell. But it worried Dap van Zyl, with his florid good looks and his man of the world, man to man personality, no end to find that there *was* an end to how he could walk. The confined nature of his cell accommodation made a farce of his pacings, seeing that he could only take a step and three-quarters in pacing lengthways, and the better part of a step and nothing if he were feeble-minded enough to want to pace up and down the breadth of his cell. For the first time in his life Dap van Zyl discovered that he was a victim of that poltroon kind of neurasthenia that is linked with claustrophobia.

Just because he was a tall man, and he was locked in a concrete cell, iron-doored, that measured six foot two inches in height and slightly less than six foot in length and that was hardly more than three foot broad, Dap van Zyl got hold of the silly idea that he was locked up in a kind of Black Hole of Calcutta and that he couldn't breathe. This was very foolish. For one thing, there was an air-hole at the top of the ceiling that was at least the size of a child's fist. And there weren't any Black-Hole-of-Calcutta warders holding lighted torches in front of it. Moreover, it happened on only very rare occasions that a fellow convict, with a misguided sense of playfulness, would go and put a tin dixie on the upper level aperture of the air-hole.

Be that as it may, Dap van Zyl, Provincial Councillor, white hope of the Volksparty for the Northern Transvaal, started getting the wind up, just because it was dark in his cell and because he had the ridiculous idea that he couldn't breathe in his cell. He wasn't able to reason that, seeing his cell was airtight and that Detective Sergeant Brits had probably stationed a Native policeman above his cell's air-hole – with meticulous instructions to the Native policeman as to where to put his foot – it was right on the cards that he wouldn't be able to breathe quite as freely as he would like.

Dap van Zyl, with all his manly good looks – asymmetrical, though, in a certain respect – hadn't enough philosophy to take it all in his stride. Just because he couldn't take a proper stride, lengthways or breadthways, he was flummoxed. He went too much by physical, material factors. He couldn't laugh when he didn't have enough carbon monoxide-free air to laugh in. He went by the scientists. He got frightened when he was shut in by an iron door, between walls of concrete. And he remembered, too, the chalk inscription he had seen on the door. The words MURDER CHARGE chalked on the door of his cell in a prison warder's illiterate capitals. Dap van Zyl hadn't the poetry and the philosophy inside himself to say, to himself, "Huh! Written in chalk!. . . Chalk rubs off, don't it?"

The Provincial Councillor, Dap van Zyl, locked up in a local gaol cell, had much less fortitude even than the coloured man Josias, a comic character and a dagga peddler and a low-grade pimp. For Josias had to have half the backside flayed off him before he would talk. Whereas, the Provincial Councillor, Dap van Zyl, made a statement before they had done anything at all to him. It never seemed to occur to him that the police never would do anything to him. All they would do would be to prefer a charge against him and to take him into custody and to release him, soon afterwards, on bail, and then to lead whatever evidence they had against him, in court.

Held incommunicado, with a stinking piss pot, Provincial Councillor Dap van Zyl went to pieces. He had far less sense, even, than the coloured man Josias. All that Dap van Zyl needed to have said, in terms of South Africa's common law procedure act, was "Get me a lawyer. I reserve my defence."

But because he was himself a legislator, a man who had a share in making the country's laws, he was himself suspicious of the law. He did not trust the law to help him. He wanted to live – just to stay alive. And he felt that there was nothing – keeping within the strict letter of the law – that they couldn't do to him, if they had a mind to. The Magna Carta Act only laid down that the body of the accused person

186

had to be produced in court within forty-eight hours of his arrest. The Magna Carta Act did not lay down how alive the accused's body had to be. And Dap van Zyl, with all that extrovert get-there force in him, wanted only one thing. He wanted to stay alive. And he had the uneasy suspicion – strengthened by that tendency towards claustrophobia that he had now detected in himself for the first time – that the law wasn't worried very much as to how the accused person fared during the period between when he was first taken into custody and when he appeared in the dock.

Dap van Zyl panicked. As Detective Sergeant Brits had guessed that he would panic. As any man at all, who didn't have the sages and the poets or a previous conviction to sustain him, would panic.

Dap van Zyl pressed the bell in the corner of his cell quite a number of times without a warder appearing. He shouted and banged the lid of the evil-smelling chamber pot against the iron door of his cell quite a number of times without a warder appearing. And so the result was that, when a sleepy-lidded warder did eventually make his appearance, and unlocked the door of Dap van Zyl's cell, so that the half-light from the gaol corridor streamed into the cell as though, by comparison with the interior murk, it was summer noon-time, Dap van Zyl was one hundred per cent ready to come his guts. He made a statement. He made it gladly. Even though his whole political career went to hell, he didn't give a damn.

"I slept with her, but I didn't murder her," was what Dap van Zyl said and what he put his signature to.

He made a long statement, that was typed out for him to sign in triplicate. He described all his movements in detail. He acknowledged freely that the Coloured woman – the deceased in the case – had been his mistress. He knew that in making that statement his political career was at an end. But he insisted, volubly and with wearisome repetition, that he hadn't murdered her.

4

That night Johannes Erasmus came back from the club.

He was deep in thought. When he arrived in front of his house he sat a long while in his car before starting it up again and driving it into the garage. The light was on in the dining-room. But he wasn't interested.

187

He was thinking of his boyhood. In between that, he was thinking of Malie. It was all over between them, he knew. It had always been all over between them. And Malie had known it. He hadn't. He didn't know if Krisjan was in the bedroom now with Malie. He didn't think it very likely. But he cared not at all.

That kaffir path over the veld that he used to walk along backwards and forwards from school, with his brother Krisjan walking beside him, came very vividly into his mind. A long, narrow path winding between the tufts of grass that were yellow with the winter and the sunshine. A path winding silently through the years. The wind blowing through the grass was muted. The noise of the insects in the grass was stilled.

It was late when Johannes Erasmus went in at the front door of his house. He crossed over to his study. He pulled out the top drawer of his desk. He did not close it again. There was a narrow couch in the study. The couch was covered with a leopard skin kaross. Johannes Erasmus lay down on the couch, pulling the kaross over him. He pulled it to above his head. He gave a long, restful sigh. He was back on that path through the yellow grass. From underneath the leopard skin kaross the report of the pistol was not very loud.

Chapter Fourteen

1

D AP van Zyl's appearance in court was brief. The charge of murder was read out to him and he was remanded back in custody for two weeks. His lawyer applied for bail. The prosecution opposed the application. The magistrate reserved his decision, pending instructions from the Attorney General in Pretoria. So, in the meantime, Dap van Zyl had to go back to gaol. To the intense disappointment of the large crowd, both inside the courthouse and outside, the proceedings were entirely formal and lasted barely ten minutes.

In the meantime, Willemsdorp was being swept by rumour. The headmaster's suicide, people said, proved conclusively that there were two of them in it – Dap van Zyl and Johannes Erasmus. They were accomplices in the murder, and when Johannes Erasmus heard that his accomplice, Dap van Zyl, had been arrested, he realised that the game was up. There was even a story to the effect that a warrant for the headmaster's arrest had actually been taken out, and that the police were on their way to his home when Johannes Erasmus shot himself. The police were actually knocking at his door, according to another account. And it was when he heard them knocking and shouting "Open up in the name of the law!" that he turned the revolver on himself. With the furnitures and backdrop of high drama did rumour invest the headmaster's taking of his own life, lying in his study on a couch that was the length and width of a grave, drawing over himself a cover made of the skin for which a leopard had no more use, on that day when he, too, had died by a bullet.

The atmosphere in Willemsdorp was electric. First the woman's murder – and the gruesome circumstances attendant on her corpse having to be windlassed all that way into the sunlight from the black depths of the Wondergat. And as a match for all that starkness, here was the Provincial Councillor for Willemsdorp in gaol and under the gibbet's shadow – a tenebriousness even more forbidding than the shadows at the bottom of the Wondergat. And here was the respected headmaster of the government school dead by his own hand to escape arrest.

That Dap van Zyl's arrest and Johannes Erasmus's suicide were linked, no one doubted.

Where was it all going to end?

And, as is so often the case at such times, it seemed as though Nature was also waiting in suspense. The drought continued. The heat was oppressive. Nature with bated breath was standing by, expectant – one with doom and yet outside of it. It was maddening. The drought. The heat. All life hushed, on tiptoe. In dread. There were few in Willemsdorp who were not to a greater or a lesser degree unnerved.

One such was Jack Brummer, the mining commissioner. He knew there was nothing they could touch him for. He had never had anything to do with that woman. And he could prove it. But what could he prove and what couldn't he prove? What was evidence, anyway? Supposing somebody said they saw him there? It seemed that the police were as jumpy as everybody else over this business. Ever since he had got so scared that time over Lena Cordier – even though there was nothing in it, of course – any small thing could upset him. And he knew something that nobody else knew. Even Mavis Clark didn't know. She heard the shots, of course. She was in his car with him under the trees by the side of the road at the bridge, on that night when the motor car came tearing along the road behind the lorry. And so she heard the shooting. But she hadn't recognised the car that the shots came from. She didn't know that it was Johannes Erasmus's car.

Now, should he go and tell the police about it, or shouldn't he? If it came out afterwards that that shooting on the road at the bridge had something to do with this whole ugly mystery that lay over the town, how would he look if he didn't report it? Wouldn't it seem as though he was mixed up in it, somehow?

Jack Brummer started imagining things, building up things out of fear. The more baseless the edifices were that he created out of his thinking, the more terrifying they seemed. He was at the mercy of shadows. And this time it wouldn't help for him to go into the Kleinberg bush area and try and shake it off. This time it wouldn't work. This time he wouldn't get a new perspective on things, out in the open air, talking to people, drinking with people. It would only make it worse. He wouldn't drive down that road past the Wondergat again. No matter that he knew he had nothing to do with the murder, he just wouldn't dare. And as for talking to those people – the people on the diggings and at the hotel: that prospector, Clinkwood, for instance – why, all the time he was talking to them he would think that they were looking at him with suspicion. They would look at him as though they felt he knew something. Or he would imagine they were looking at him in that way.

Even because he had been with that journalist, Charlie Hendricks, to the Wondergat, he felt uncomfortable in Hendricks's presence. He had come across Charlie Hendricks only that morning, and he could have sworn that Hendricks had looked at him suspiciously. All imagination, of course. But there you were. And then this awful heat, that made you get the craziest sort of fears and fancies. And in the Kleinberg area the heat would be a great deal worse.

His trouble was that he didn't have any roots, Jack Brummer said to himself. He was just drifting along, from one woman to another. He had no anchorage. Any kind of awful thing could happen to him, the way he was. He was unprotected. Through that affair with Lena Cordier his guts had given in. He had felt as guilty as hell over that, and after that everything made him feel guilty. Even if it was something that he could *prove* his innocence about. But could he prove anything?

And those shots, there, fired in the dark from Johannes Erasmus's car. What if it came out that he knew about it? And what if that had an important bearing on the murder, and everything else? How would he look in court if he admitted that he had kept quiet about it? And it was just possible that Mavis Clark might let it slip out, some day, that she had sat there in the car with him and that they had heard the shooting. . . although Mavis had promised him that she wouldn't mention it to anybody. But you never knew. It might just slip out. And what did he want to make her promise that for – unless he was in it up to the neck?

"Up to the neck." Jack Brummer didn't like that expression. He reached his hand to the top of his shirt and undid his collar button. The heat – it was too awful.

Jack Brummer struck the bell on his desk. Mavis Clark came in with a pencil and notebook. Jack Brummer told himself that here was where he was going to stop fighting shadows. Gallows' shadows.

"Mavis," Jack Brummer said, "will you marry me?"

"Yes, Jack," Mavis said, not very surprised. She went round to behind the desk and kissed him.

Detective Sergeant Brits had come into the office so quietly that he was already sitting down opposite him before Charlie Hendricks, looking up from his typewriter, was aware of the policeman's presence.

"Oh – ," Charlie Hendricks said, with a faint start, "oh, good day."

"Good day, Mr Hendricks," Detective Sergeant Brits answered.

For a while they sat in silence, Charlie Hendricks and Brits, observing each other across the four-foot width of the editorial desk.

Charlie Hendricks felt the sweat breaking out on his forehead. With a quick involuntary movement, he brushed off the beads of moisture with the back of his hand.

"Yus, hot, isn't it, Mr Hendricks?" the detective remarked.

No, on the contrary, Charlie Hendricks could have said – it was cold. Cold sweat.

"Just as hot as that, Mr Hendricks, we police is on the trail of the murderer," Detective Sergeant Brits said, proud of his wit.

Charlie Hendricks found himself wanting to smile. Well, he only hoped it was so – hoped that the trail the police were following was as cold as the sweat that was coming out of him. He said nothing, however. He wasn't going to talk. Let the detective do all the talking. Let the detective take the initiative. He only wished that he had had a few puffs of the dagga that Cyril Stein had left with him. That he had had a smoke of Indian hemp about half an hour ago, say, instead of just when he had woken up in the morning. It was good stuff, that dagga, but the effect of it wore off after a couple of hours. Charlie Hendricks had already rolled and smoked several cigarettes – mixing the green leaves with tobacco – out of that brown paper parcel that Cyril Stein had left with him. And it was a first class cushion against the shocks of reality, dagga was – so Charlie Hendricks had found out. With a couple of puffs of dagga smoke inside you, the world took on quite a different look. You rode the bumps of life with an easy resilience, airily – finding time to adjust your hat-brim to a natty angle in mid-air. He could do with a smoke now, but hardly with a policeman looking on. So he picked up his cigarette case lying beside the typewriter, instead. He passed the case over to the detective.

Brits took a cigarette and lit up. Charlie Hendricks followed suit.

Pity he hadn't loaded the cigarettes in his case with dagga, Charlie

Hendricks thought. That would have been a lark. To have had Detective Sergeant Brits smoking a drugged cigarette. It would be interesting to watch the effects on him. Well, perhaps next time. But Charlie Hendricks had the uneasy feeling that there mightn't be a next time.

He wished the detective would talk, though. Would give some sort of hint as to what he had come about. If it was on the most dreadful errand possible that he had come, let him at all events get it over and done with. Let him do his worst. The strain was killing. Charlie Hendricks dabbed at his forehead again. And there was Brits's awful grammar. Charlie Hendricks found that he couldn't stand it, suddenly. For God's sake, why couldn't the man talk decent English? It suddenly seemed to Charlie Hendricks that it was an affectation of the detective's, talking that way. It was all put on. Brits must know better. He had knocked about a bit. No matter how unlettered he might have been when he joined the police force, he must have picked up as he went along. No raw recruit from the platteland talked like that – and Charlie Hendricks had met plenty of them in the course of police court reporting. It must be a stunt, he decided, Brits talking that atrocious kind of grammar – like something he had invented himself to work on the nerves of the person he was talking to.

But when was Brits coming to the point of all this?

"We's got him, Mr Hendricks, the murderer; I thinks as how we's got him in the bag," Detective Sergeant Brits went on, his weakness of syntax lending colour to Charlie Hendricks's suspicions. "Does you thinks as we got him, Mr Hendricks?"

Charlie Hendricks took a deep puff at his cigarette. More than ever he wished it was dagga. He noticed that his hand wasn't steady. Nor was his voice when he answered, "Well, I've got no facts to go on, have I? No data."

"Here's the facts, Mr Hendricks," the detective said. "A kaffir seen Dap van Zyl throw that coloured woman down the hole. He's not sure, quite, seeing how it was dark, him not too near at hand, and not anxious to get too near at hand. But we can fix that, I thinks. Yes, I thinks we can fix that. And there's that prospector Clinkwood. He's seen – oh well, it don't matter what he *seen*. But he reckons he'll identify that man. He reckons he's seen him before in a pub and in a car. Anyway, Clinkwood will be here inside the hour. And I *think* he'll say as it was Dap van Zyl he seen getting out the car that night by the side of the road for a – . Well, never mind what he *seen*. He don't know Dap van Zyl. But when he sees him I think as he'll say that's the man he *seen*, see? And there is a whole lot more evidence I got. But that evidence *might* be that it's Dap van Zyl or it might not mean him. It might be some other man that went with the coloured moll. But it just *could* be Dap van Zyl. But then there's the jacket."

"Jacket?" Charlie Hendricks asked. Dreading he knew not what. He couldn't guess what it was all about. But the thought of it made his blood run cold.

"We found a kaffir wearing a jacket," Detective Sergeant Brits said, "at least, it was me found that nigger with the jacket. And I wants you to put that in big headlines the moment we've checked up. Because it's that jacket as is going to hang the murderer. And I wants the credit for it. I got that jacket only this morning on a kaffir wearing it. And I wants you to put that big in the paper. That's how I'll get promotion. The murderer when he clumb through the barbed wire done left most of the arse part of his trousers sticking on the wire. And the jacket of them trousers I found a kaffir wearing right this morning. What you think of that, hey? Pretty smart, hey? And a couple of wallops with a piece of hosepipe and the kaffir comes his guts and he says he stole the jacket out of a motor car on the way to Kleinberg. And that kaffir says we can put him in jug for stealing the jacket. He don't mind going to jug for stealing the jacket, he says, just so long as we don't hang him for murder, he says, and never mind that piece of hosepipe, either, he says, just so long as we doesn't hang him for murder, he says. And we knows that Dap van Zyl was in Kleinberg for the Kruger Day business *on the same day* as the kaffir says he stole the jacket. You'll put it in big headlines, hey? Just so I can gets promotion, hey? You do me a good turn, see? Next time I do you a good turn, too, see?"

Charlie Hendricks was groping for another cigarette.

"You chainsmokes, hey?" the detective remarked.

Charlie Hendricks ignored that. "But you can't expect me to publish all that now, right away, I mean," he said at length. "You've first got to prove that it is Dap van Zyl's jacket."

Detective Sergeant Brits laughed.

"Yes, you got some brains," he said. "You should also be a detective. But I thinks as I can prove that it's Dap van Zyl's jacket. Today, still, I'll know. And that's why I came round here, before Clinkwood turns up and before I finds out about the jacket. I wants to put you wise, so the moment I tips you off you can write it all in the papers. There was laundry marks in that jacket. At Johannesburg headquarters there's a branch has got a list of all the laundry marks in the Transvaal. How you like that, hey? They already got my telegram. How long do you thinks as it'll take them to find the laundry and to find out who is the customer that had his jacket drycleaned. Coming?"

"Where to?" Charlie Hendricks asked.

Detective Sergeant Brits got up out of the chair.

"Gaol," the detective said. "Where else?"

In a half daze Charlie Hendricks started to patter after him.

"Better get your hat, Mr Hendricks," Brits continued. "I would like as you must be in the gaol yourself when Clinkwood turns up. I wants you to see how Clinkwood identifies the murderer. I also wants you to hear for yourself the name of the laundry and the name of the customer. That will give you a laugh. You can write it all in big letters."

Charlie Hendricks, on the way to get his hat hanging from the wall, paused. It was a desperate chance.

What if everything the detective had been saying really was just straightforward? What if in his ungrammatical utterances there were no hidden allusions, no lurking innuendoes, nothing in the nature of sly double-entendre? It seemed hardly possible – just as it seemed impossible that Brits really didn't know any better when he talked that kind of grammar.

Charlie Hendricks cleared his throat. "Look, there's an article here I've got to finish that's rather urgent," he said, trying to sound matter of fact. "Perhaps I could come round a little later."

Detective Sergeant Brits looked disappointed. "Well, just as you likes, Mr Hendricks," he said, after a pause. "Well, you better just does what you likes. You knows your business. Like I knows mine."

A few moments later he had gone. And the grammar in Brits's last remark did not jar on Charlie Hendricks. In fact, he did not notice that the detective had used bad grammar at all. What he had said did not sound uncouth.

3

Charlie Hendricks waited in the office of the *Northern Transvaal News*. He waited several minutes. Detective Sergeant Brits must be a good way towards police headquarters by then, he reckoned. So Charlie Hendricks got his hat, after all, and went, for the last time, out of the editorial office of the *Northern Transvaal News*. But when he reached the pavement he did not, in terms of Detective Sergeant Brits's invitation, proceed in the direction of the gaol.

Instead, he took the exact opposite direction. He went along a sidewalk that led to his flat. He went just the opposite way from gaol. For the first time, Charlie Hendricks realised that he was on the run from gaol. It gave him a thrill, somehow, the thought that he was on the run. There was a perverse delight in the thought. Something had happened to him, he felt, something new. It was as though a strange and magnificent life was opening to him. Something he had read about in books. And it had, incredibly, come to him at last. It was a new life – being on the run from gaol and the police. It was a colourful sort of life. And a kindly sort of life, it seemed. The pity of it was that it didn't seem that it was going to be a long sort of life. But then, anything that was supreme never lasted long. There was some Chinese proverb about it, too. Charlie Hendricks wondered if the Chinese poet who had coined that adage had thought it out when he was also on the run from gaol and the police. Quite likely. A lot of the writers and poets had done a bit of running from the police in their time.

And the queer thing, Charlie Hendricks thought, as he hurried along the sidewalk on his way to his flat, the sweat pouring off him by that time, on account of his fear that he might still, after all, be too late – the queer thing was that he was enjoying a mystic excitement. The thrill of the chase. It was like wine. He had never been a hunter. All his life he had hated hunters, despising them as cowards, pitying them as beggarly sadists. This was the first time in his life that he had been hunted. And it was fun. . . he was running from the gallows. . . If Death was the King of Terrors, the gallows, in the starkness of a rope and a crossbeam, was the King's most purpureally apparelled messenger. No, the King's agent. A trapdoor and a short hempen cord and a bar horizontal with the earth – primitively antithetical to the verticality of the rope – no! (as the person to be hanged would cry, "No!") – this was almost the King himself.

Charlie Hendricks, pale with fear, packed a suitcase in his flat. He was in a state of near panic. He was surrounded by a sense of doom that was yet exhilarating. A sense of impending destruction lapped round him like blue, deep waters. He was the most miserable of mortals, and yet elevated above all the petty anxieties of mortality. His *fear* had cast out all fear. He was shit-scared and yet he felt cock-a-hoop heroic.

He had his suitcase packed. Pyjamas and a couple of shirts and socks and handkerchief and toothbrush. What else? No, he couldn't straight away think what else. For his rendezvous – ultimately – with the hangman, was there anything else?. . . Oh, yes – razor. When he had that black sack pulled over his head, it had to be over a cleanshaven face. There was to be no stubbly growth on his chin. Sunken-eyed he might be, perhaps, on that morning. And villainous looking. Who isn't villainous looking, after all, on such an occasion? Meeting the King of Terrors, like that, face to face, rope to chin, it was only natural that, of the two, the King of Terrors should look the more presentable – having had a proper night's rest and a decent shave, no doubt. But Charles I, from all accounts, seemed to have been pretty spruce in the Banqueting House at Whitehall on Jan. 30, 1649. But then, Charles met the King of Terrors on an equal footing, almost, as a peer, almost – one king encountering another king half by chance, each king bidding the other king welcome. Never mind, Charlie Hendricks said to himself, if it was only for the impression that he would make on the prison governor, and the prison doctor, and the hangman and the warders – never mind any more Exalted Personage – he was determined to be hanged cleanshaven. He wasn't going to be another blue-jowled, open-hearted, rough diamond, wouldn't-hurt-a-fly kind of murderer. He was going to be trim and cleanshaven and sinister, and if they didn't like it they would have to lump it. So he put the razor and a packet of blades in his suitcase.

When he came out of his flat, carrying the suitcase, Charlie Hendricks ran into Cyril Stein. They exchanged swift greetings. Cyril Stein made certain signals. Charlie felt that, if he had time, he would like nothing more then than to sit down and laugh. For he knew what those signals meant. Cyril Stein was inviting him to come into his flat and join him in a dagga smoke. That was very funny, Charlie Hendricks thought. He must be getting very popular. Two invitations in such quick succession. Detective Sergeant Brits inviting him to step along to gaol. Cyril Stein seeking, with blandishment, to lure him into his flat.

"Sorry," Charlie Hendricks called out, dashing down the stairs, "I'm on the run. No time."

He was almost out on the sidewalk before he got the full gist of Cyril Stein's answer. "Can I run with you?" Cyril Stein had shouted back.

Not bad, Charlie Hendricks reflected. No, not bad at all. You had to give Cyril Stein credit for having a quick brain. Thinking out a reply like that, right on the spur of the moment. What was more, he knew that, if put to the test, Cyril Stein wouldn't have backed out, either. He would come along. Say what you liked about Cyril Stein, he did have a brain. And he did have guts. Not in the orthodox meaning that those words had, perhaps, but in a pretty real sense, all the same. What was more, Charlie Hendricks felt, he could have done worse than to have Cyril Stein as companion when he was on the run. But it was too late now. There was no time for him to turn back and say to Cyril Stein, yes, he could come along, too. There were no minutes to waste. A few moments of dawdling and there would be no sort of run for anybody.

Charlie Hendricks got into his car and drove towards the bank. He parked his car in front of the bank. He pulled out his fountain-pen and his cheque book. Fifty pounds was the sum that he filled in, payable to cash. If he made it more it might excite suspicion. Seated in his car, with the engine running, he was afraid of nothing. In a few seconds he could be tearing along the open road. With the veld and the sky around him he could thumb his nose at the whole world. But inside the bank he wouldn't feel too good. They could trap him, in there. Inside the bank there would be no petrol for him to step on. He would be hemmed in.

At that moment Jones the compositor came past.

"Hi!" Charlie Hendricks called out. "Hi! Hi!"

Jones did not realise, at first, that it meant him. And then he felt that to have his attention drawn in that way was derogatory to his dignity. Furthermore, when he found that it was Charlie Hendricks calling him, he felt just a little peeved.

But Charlie Hendricks was all worked up. And when you are in that state you can do things that are way beyond your normal capacities.

"Will you just slip into the bank for me and cash this cheque?" Charlie Hendricks asked of Jones, easily and glibly. "If I stop the car I won't be able to get it started again. I'm taking it to the garage to have the distributor fixed."

"Sure," Jones said, taking the cheque and going into the bank. For the moment he had been bowled over. But when he studied the amount of the cheque he started wondering whether Charlie Hendricks had the money in the bank to meet it. Maybe that was why Charlie Hendricks was keeping his engine running, Jones thought – so that in case there was trouble about the cheque he could make a quick getaway. A moment of reflection, however, convinced him that his suspicions were absurd. And when the cashier counted out ten fivers without even going to the back to look, Jones felt ashamed of his unworthy suspicions.

In the meantime, Charlie Hendricks was on tenterhooks. Especially when he saw, at the far end of the street, Detective Sergeant Brits emerging from the police station in the company of the man that Charlie Hendricks had seen at the corundum diggings and in the pub, and that he now knew was Clinkwood. Brits was carrying a jacket over his arm. Charlie Hendricks felt pretty sure that he knew that jacket. But they didn't walk towards him. For in that case he would have put his foot down on the accelerator and made for the open veld. They walked off together in the opposite direction, Detective Sergeant Brits and Prospector Clinkwood.

Well, he believed he knew whose jacket it was, that Brits was carrying over his shoulder, and in connection with which he had sent a telegram to the police department that specialised in laundry marks. Thus Charlie Hendricks reflected. But did Jones the compositor know whose coloured daughter it was that had been fished up from out of the depths of the Wondergat? Charlie Hendricks had a shrewd suspicion that Jones didn't.

"Here," Jones said gruffly, coming out of the bank and pushing the fifty pounds at Charlie Hendricks.

"Thanks a lot," Charlie Hendricks said. He put the money in his wallet and started moving his car into the middle of the road. He changed gears. From second he changed into top. He pressed the accelerator down on to the floor. He travelled all out.

"Phew," Jones the compositor said to himself, without knowing that there was any profundity in his observation, unapprised of the fact that Charlie Hendricks had no intention of returning. "I've seen them come and I've seen them go. But I've never seen a *Northern Transvaal News* editor go as quick as that one, Gawd, you can't see him for dust."

Mile after mile Charlie Hendricks covered on the road to the north. It was the wrong direction, of course. Where he intended going was south, to Johannesburg. But he hadn't the nerve to turn back and pass through Willemsdorp again. As likely as not it was lies, all lies, that Detective Sergeant Brits had told him about how easy it was for the police to track down a man by the laundry marks on a piece of clothing. But he wasn't going to take a chance. More, if it was known that he had taken the road to the north, it would throw the police off the scent. They would be looking for him in the Northern Transvaal. All the time, under cover of night, he would have made a detour of hundreds of miles over sandy bushveld roads and veld tracks, swinging far across the west towards Bechuanaland, before he would again set the nose of his car in the direction of Johannesburg. It was only the next few miles that counted. Then again the next few miles. He came to a petrol pump in front of an Indian store.

A long, skinny Indian came out of the shadows of the veranda. Charlie Hendricks nipped his dagga cigarette quickly. He should be more careful, Charlie Hendricks told himself. He would get himself a bad name, smoking dagga openly like that. And he didn't want to get himself a bad name. No, he had to be careful of his reputation. With the dagga inside him, that thought made him laugh.

"Fill up the tank," he called out to the Indian. "And put two four-gallon tins of petrol in the back."

"Is the boss going to Egypt?" the long, skinny Indian asked, deciding that he could be funny, also, seeing his customer was jolly and laughing.

"Looks just like Jones, this Indian does," Charlie Hendricks thought to himself. "I wonder if he's also one of Jones's illegitimate children." That thought made him want to laugh again.

But then he realised that it was, of course, only the dagga that was making him think that there was any resemblance between the Indian and the compositor on the *Northern Transvaal News*. The recognising blues, he remembered, Cyril Stein had called it.

Mile after mile Charlie Hendricks traversed, swiftly, smoothly. The thought of Jones and Cyril Stein and the *Northern Transvaal News* made a strange kind of impression on his mind. They seemed to belong with a life that was already very far away. A life that had never existed, save in a dream. Or was this thing a dream – his flying over the miles along the road to the north? Anyway, both states of being couldn't be real. One was authentic; it had substance in time and place; it had actuality; it was a stubborn fact. The other was a dagga vision. But he wouldn't trouble to work out now which was which. It was equally fantastic anyway, his being the editor of a country newspaper or his being on the road to the bushveld, a fugitive from justice.

For all he knew, with all that dagga that he had been smoking, he might be imagining all this, that he had filled up his tank at the Indian store and that there were two four-gallon tins of petrol in the back of his car, and that he was on the run from the police. Perhaps he was really sitting in front of his desk, writing a leader.

Chapter Fifteen

1

T<small>HE</small> funeral of Johannes Erasmus was not well-attended. There was a good number of wreaths, but there was not a large crowd at the graveside. There were no children from his school singing hymns. His widow, Malie, had said that she would prefer it so. It was in the middle of a hot summer of terrifying drought. But perhaps Johannes Erasmus did not feel that part of it so much, seeing that he was being buried under a cloud. Everybody knew that he had committed suicide. And it was not so long ago that in Willemsdorp suicide was still regarded as a heinous sin. The older inhabitants of the town could well remember the time when a person that died by his own hand was refused the rites of Christian interment. He was buried outside the town, where the road forked. And there were no prayers. No sermon.

Today it was different. Still, there was a stigma about a man dying in the way Johannes Erasmus had done. And it was pretty generally believed that he had put a bullet through his heart in order to escape the rope.

The chief mourners at the funeral were Johannes Erasmus's widow, Malie, and his younger brother, Krisjan. Malie wore black and was heavily veiled. Krisjan had a piece of crepe sewed round his hatband and on his left sleeve. Unlike the time when he interviewed the secretary of the school-board, he remembered on this occasion to take off his hat.

Mutual grief did not have the effect of drawing Malie and Krisjan closer together. Indeed, they seemed to keep as far away from each other as was decently possible under the circumstances. They did not speak once.

When Malie bent down to pick up a handful of earth to cast into the grave, her arms and legs moved like sticks.

When they came out of the cemetery gates, Malie and Krisjan walked home separate ways.

2

Mile after mile.

This couldn't go on, Charlie Hendricks said to himself. Far into the Northern Transvaal he had already travelled. He had already journeyed a good way into the afternoon. He couldn't go on like that, he told himself – getting a flat feeling, and becoming desperately frightened, so that fear gripped his guts; and then stopping the car and pouring petrol from one of the tins into the tank, and lighting another dagga cigarette and starting off again. Given false courage by the petrol in the tank of his car and by the dagga fumes in his blood.

One thing he must do, he must eat. He was already just about to cross that ill-defined area serving as a borderline between the plateau-high-up Willemsdorp and the slope-of-the-escarpment bushveld that led to Kleinberg. He was between the desert and the sown. Between the rolling grasslands of the Highveld and the luxuriating jungle of the Lowveld. On the road that his car had brought him, he was just about midway between the two. On the dark, tortuous route along which he had been led by his brain, he was in pretty wild country – betwixt and between. On his left hand was sanity, on his right madness. Or it was the other way around. He wasn't quite sure, now, any more. He would find out later, maybe. Later, perhaps, it would be made clear to him as to what was lucid grass veld and what was bush lycanthropy. Afterwards it would all get sorted out for him. Although he must acknowledge that he had a sneaking affection for the sound of the word 'lycanthropy.' There was so much more of a ring to it than to a word like 'rational.'

But at that moment he knew that he was in a country of the brain that it did no man good to be in. He wasn't sure if he was a sage or a manic depressive, an oracle of light or somebody that had run amok. The right way to find out, of course, would be to go back to Willemsdorp, and to present himself to Detective Sergeant Brits.

But he didn't know to what extent Detective Sergeant Brits was himself normal. Indeed, from what he had observed of him, Charlie Hendricks could not but feel that Brits was pretty far advanced along the road to paranoia. Further than he had himself come on the way to Kleinberg, Charlie Hendricks said to himself. But all these things might yet straighten themselves out. Only, what was very necessary was that he had to find some place where he could get a meal. He wasn't hungry. Physically, he had no appetite at all. He felt as though he had just eaten. Ever since Brits had called on him in his office, he had had that feeling that his belly was surfeited with a large quantity of indigestible food. But he knew that his brain was in need of victualling. His belly wasn't important. It was his brain that was taking him through all this.

And Charlie Hendricks realised that his brain was going funny on him.

The hot sun of the afternoon, now. For he was entering the tropics, where the sun was hotter than on the Highveld. And his brain had begun to think of the hot, semitropical sun as a pipe that God was smoking. That flaming circle in the sky was the glowing top of the pipe that God was smoking – that He was smoking dagga out of, as likely as not: else how could the world be as mad as it was if God wasn't a drug addict? Well, just look at all the illogical things that happened in the world at times. And the awful things. The awful things happened, no doubt, at those times when God was trying to pull up His socks – when God was trying to break himself of the degrading habit of smoking hashish. And that spiral of pale blue cloud, reaching down out of the sky in the east to almost touch the koppies on the skyline. Well, Charlie Hendricks knew that shade of greyish-blue and those spirals. . . he was blowing the same kind of clouds out of the window of his car at that moment. And if it wasn't hashish smoke from God's pipe forming that vast column above the koppie in the eastern sky, well, then –

He had to eat, Charlie Hendricks told himself. The hot, copper sun, unrelenting, unwinking, was an Eye. It was an Eye fixed on him. From that eye he could not escape. Piece of impudence, that Eye looking at him like that. Why couldn't that Eye go and look at something else – or at somebody else? Why couldn't that Eye go and look at Detective Sergeant Brits instead, say? There would be a pretty fine collection of things that the Eye could go and look at Detective Sergeant Brits accusingly for. Of that Charlie Hendricks felt pretty sure. What did that Eye want to look at him for, like that? Charlie Hendricks found himself praying for the night to come. Even if there was a moon, the moon was different. The moon never looked directly at you. And as for the stars – why, there were myriads of *them*. *You* could go and look accusingly at the stars – at any star at all – and you would see that star squirm. That star had so much to hide.

Charlie Hendricks found himself hating the sun and praying for the dark. It must be wonderful to drive out under the night, into the moonlight and into the starlight. You couldn't get enough of that.

The direct gaze of the brass Eye of the sun was driving him mad. He had to find some place to eat. That would put him right. The dagga had carried him as far as it could. The drug had introduced a highly subtle system of shock absorbers between his raw heart-fears and the world of external reality. But the shock absorbers were wearing thin. He wasn't being cushioned any more the way he would like to be. It was that damned sun. Curse and blast the sun. Just bloody sanctimonious that sun was, with its one good Eye, with its one bigoted and hypocritical Eye, with its one impious and blasphemous and profane good Eye. Pretending that it was God's Eye. Well, then, where was God's other Eye? Looking at some place where it shouldn't be looking, no doubt. Looking slantwise at some female saint that was pulling up her dress to fix her stocking, very likely. Looking down into the depths of the Wondergat, maybe.

Bugger that round, brass Eye, Charlie Hendricks shouted, urging his car hell for leather onward.

But he had to eat, he told himself. Yes, he had to have food. He wasn't a scrap hungry. But his brain was starting to go queer on him. At the first roadside café or hotel he came to he would pull up and eat.

3

There was a thing for you, now, Charlie Hendricks thought.

He had finished his mixed grill and had sauntered out on to the stoep of the hotel at Witgat. The hotel was a low wood-and-iron building, much weathered. The veranda poles lined up on the edge of the stoep were much weathered. So were the proprietor and the handful of hotel loungers – corundum miners, by the look of them. And to think that here, on the stoep, he should encounter, of all people, the actress Sarah Wessels-Wessels. But what surprised him even more was that he should have gone into the dining-room and have ordered a meal, and have sat there eating it placidly, drinking his coffee, afterwards – and that during all that time he hadn't been worrying. He hadn't worried if his car was safe. He hadn't once looked over his shoulder when he heard footsteps. That was a pretty queer thing, he reflected. During all the time that he had sat in the dining-room eating, he had been completely at ease. He remembered that he had even complained about the soup.

But out here, on the stoep, sitting in a grass chair, he had suddenly started feeling shaky again. He was glad that his car was only a few yards away. He felt for the key in his pocket. In a matter of seconds he could dash for the driver's seat, insert the key, switch on, start up and head for the open road. Perhaps he should pull his grass chair a bit more to this side – yes, that would just about do – perhaps a shade more – that was better. . . now, if he had to make a sudden dive for his car, the veranda pole wouldn't be in the way.

"The sun too much for you?" he heard Sarah Wessels-Wessels ask.

"Sun?" Charlie Hendricks asked. He remembered the way he had felt about the sun, thinking it was an eye, when he was on the road in the hottest part of the afternoon. Half dagga-crazed he must have been then, he thought. But what did this woman want to mention it for, anyway? And what was she getting at? He started getting agitated again, suddenly, all over.

"I saw you moving your chair into the shade," Sarah Wessels-Wessels answered.

"Oh, that," Charlie Hendricks said, trying to smoke and feeling slightly more relieved. "The sun does get you down, doesn't it?"

"Drives you mad, too," Sarah Wessels-Wessels said. "Stone mad."

There were certain queer lacunae about the way he remembered things, Charlie Hendricks realised. Another effect of the dagga, no doubt. It was like when you had a migraine. One moment you could see a thing. The next moment you couldn't. It was the same with his memory – something the drug did to it. One moment he would remember a thing. The next moment he wouldn't. He couldn't, for instance, remember how or when, seated on the stoep, he had got into conversation with Sarah Wessels-Wessels. In the same way that he couldn't actually remember his arrival at the hotel. Somebody must have told him that the place he was at was called Witgat. Otherwise he wouldn't know the name. And that meant he must have asked somebody. But he couldn't remember nothing about that. At least, he couldn't *now*. Later on, no doubt, it would all come back to him. But, all the same, it was queer. Remembering a thing one moment and forgetting it the next. And afterwards remembering again.

"The sun gets you down," Charlie Hendricks repeated.

"It also goes down," Sarah Wessels-Wessels said, "the sun, I mean."

"So I pulled my chair a shade nearer the wall," Charlie Hendricks said.

"A shade nearer the shade, yes," Sarah Wessels-Wessels said, solemnly. "It drives you mad, the early afternoon sun. The sun puts its foot on the petrol and drives like mad. Drives you like mad, I mean. There's not a cloud that the sun can put its foot against. So it puts its foot against the petrol. That's how you get sunstroke – with the sun on your neck. And the only kind of cloud is the cloud that comes over your mind. That's what sunstroke is, and driving in the bush. There's no Go-Stop traffic lights for the sun. There's no Go Slow – School. There's no speedcop to give the sun a ticket. There's only – "

Charlie Hendricks was struck by a sudden thought. It seemed fantastic. But perhaps not really so fantastic, after all. Not when you reflected on the kind of person that Sarah Wessels-Wessels seemed to be.

"There's only the sun shining through the back of your neck like it's a piece of glass," Sarah Wessels-Wessels went on. "Once when smoke came out of the engine I thought it was my neck was a magnifying glass, and that the sun, shining through the back of my magnifying glass neck had set the engine alight. But I found that I was only talking through the back of my magnifying glass neck. Or is that what I'm doing now?"

Yes, Charlie Hendricks thought. She did have all the signs of it. He would take a chance. "Maybe," he said, "you're talking through the back of Nellie's neck."

He sat back in the grass chair to study the effect of his remark.

Sarah Wessels-Wessels did not turn a hair.

"I wouldn't smoke it here, though," was all she said. "Not on this stoep, with people coming and going. Have you got any on you?"

Oh Lord, Charlie Hendricks thought. I'm on the run. And here's this new thing, now – South Africa's leading actress asking me for dagga. And what is she doing here, anyway, in this hole? It seemed that life came to you only when you were on the run.

"I'm sorry," Charlie Hendricks heard himself saying, "but I haven't got the time. I've got to get going. I'm on the run."

Just through talking about it, the effect of the hashish he had been smoking earlier on came back to him. His voice seemed to be coming from far away. His voice seemed to be swimming and swaying, curving round dark mountainsides that gave out sparks for lamps – for stars to guide his voice to where Sarah Wessels-Wessels was. Old stars for old lamps. Rub your pocket handkerchief against a star and the genie of the Witgat Hotel is before you, waiting to do your bidding.

"Double gin and lime," Charlie Hendricks heard Sarah Wessels-Wessels say.

"Mountainside with sparks," Charlie Hendricks ordered.

"We haven't got those new Johannesburg cocktails here yet, sir," the genie said. "But if you leave it to me, I'll mix you something better."

Charlie Hendricks said all right. But the magic was gone. This wasn't a genie. It was a waiter. And a Johannesburg waiter, too, by the sound of him.

"I shouldn't have done that," Charlie Hendricks announced to Sarah Wessels-Wessels. "I shouldn't have been such a fool as to trade my old lamp for a star."

"I know, but people are doing that every day," said Sarah Wessels-Wessels, not knowing what the hell he was talking about and not caring: for what earthly difference did it make? "And they get sorry about it, afterwards. And so they go and put the star in hock. Any pawnshop you go into is just bursting with stars that people don't want. But you go into a pawnshop and try and buy an old lamp – any old lamp – and Uncle will just laugh at you over his counter. Wedding rings, he'll say, yes. Bucketfuls. Engagements rings? Take your pick. Medals? Solly, shovel some on to this counter, here: no, get the big shovel. . . But when you ask for an old lamp, he hasn't got as much as a wick."

As full of dagga as she could get, Sarah Wessels-Wessels was, Charlie Hendricks thought. And here was she asking *him* for a dagga cigarette.

4

Mile after mile into the night. It was better travelling in the night. There was no brass Eye of the sun, in the night, to give you a sense of guilt. He had made a wide sweep along into the west, by-passing Kleinberg. He was well on the way towards the Bechuanaland border. But the sun's place was taken by signposts, hands with mitred ends for fingers, pointing stiffly under the moon. And pointing at him. Names he read on the signposts: Hartbees, Ribbokrand, Blikwinkel, Kwaggafontein, Withaakdraai, Langpeul, Koekemoersrus, Wenplaas, Oliviersbult. The names were plain to read in the moonlight. But the hands of the boards were not pointing at those places with the restful sounding names: they were pointing at him.

He recognised the road. Something about it was familiar. So he stopped the car and lit another cigarette. That was better. He had no fears of passing the Wondergat, now. Blowing out a thin cloud of dagga smoke, he told himself that when he got to the Wondergat he would even leave his car and go up to that Phoenician mineshaft. Maybe he would even climb through the barbed wire fence and look down over the edge, looking down with the moonlight to help him. That would give Detective Sergeant Brits a headache all right, having more shreds of cloth to puzzle over – more bits of rag to fit into suits that had been to the drycleaners.

It was a good dagga cigarette. It was giving him all sorts of ideas. Had he really been on this road before, not so long ago, travelling in the night? Or was that just something he imagined? Was it reality or was it the dagga? Not that it mattered. With the dagga inside him nothing mattered. Still, it would be interesting to know. Was the finger of suspicion really pointing at him with every signboard he passed, or was this whole thing just a fantasy that his mind had conjured up? It was too late to bother about it now. Too late in the night for one thing. "The guilty fleeth" – or was it "The wicked fleeth"?: he wasn't sure – "where no man pursueth." He told himself that, if he were to turn back right now, and drive all the way back to Willemsdorp, getting there with the dawn, nobody would as much as notice that he had been away. He would go to his office and start work and everything there would be as it had always been. He had half a mind to do it, to turn back. And Brits would come in again and talk some more bad grammar.

No, Charlie Hendricks said to himself, no, on second thoughts he wouldn't turn back. There was just a possibility that Detective Sergeant Brits did suspect him. There was also the possibility that the detective might have good grounds for his suspicions. It might be that he wasn't imagining an earlier visit to the Wondergat. . . It might be that reality and dagga dream were one.

Well, he wasn't far from the Wondergat, now.

Another few hundred yards and he brought his car to a stop. There they were, a short distance off the road, solid poles of the barbed-wire fence erected around the Wondergat's edge. He took another pull at the cigarette. Phew, it was strong. He must have mixed too much dagga with it and not enough tobacco. It made his head swim. It gave him a lot of guts, too, though.

So he opened the door of his car and stepped out. It seemed to take him a long time, once he had got down out of his car on to the road, to stand up straight. He seemed to have grown miraculously tall. Up and up, he stretched. His spine, his neck, the joints of his legs. The bones of his body seemed strangely elastic. He could go on stretching up, up, up, like that, until his shoulders were on a level with the mountains. But he better not go too far with it, he told himself. The dagga had given him stature – not only had he become physically tall but he felt that, morally and intellectually too, he stood high up there, somewhere. He wished he had a good book to read, now, he thought, suddenly.

But, anyway, there was the Wondergat fence. In a few strides he would be there, carried over the intervening distance before he had really started walking. With this incredible length of limb he had float-ed through the air rather than walked. The next thing he knew he had bumped into a tree. So he wasn't so tall, after all. Otherwise he would have stepped right over the tree. He looked up. The tree soared above him, vast and bulky under the stars. So he wasn't really so tall, Charlie Hendricks told himself. He was just imagining it.

But at what he saw, then, the cold sweat broke out on his forehead as it had done when Brits had come into the office. For the first time he realised that it was a man standing there, under the tree, so close to him that he could touch him.

"Would have been funny, if I'd bumped into you instead of into the tree," Charlie Hendricks said, his voice coming from very far away, as it seemed to him.

"Yes, wouldn't it?" the man replied in cultured accents. But Charlie Hendricks wasn't taken in by the fact that he spoke like an educated man. He knew it was Detective Sergeant Brits.

"I have a warrant for your arrest," Detective Sergeant Brits contin-ued, "for the murder of Marjorie Jones. I must warn you that anything you say will be taken down in writing and may be used in evidence against you. Charlie Hendricks, you are under arrest."

Charlie Hendricks dabbed at his forehead. He didn't feel so tall, now, any more. Indeed, he felt much less than average height. He started to stutter.

"How – how – " he started to ask.

"That was very simple, my dear fellow," Detective Sergeant Brits interjected – and if his ungrammatical speech had in the past irritated Charlie Hendricks, his measured, cultured tones now exasperated Charlie Hendricks to the point of near madness, "I merely took the short cut through Kwaggapeul."

Brits pronounced the name 'Kwaggapeul' as though he had a cigar in his mouth – an imported cigar.

"No, I – that is," Charlie Hendricks stammered, "how did you know you would find me here?"

Detective Sergeant Brits laughed harshly.

"Elementary, my dear Hendricks," he declared. "Every tyro knows that the murderer always revisits the scene of the crime. . . If you want a good book to read, why not try *The Adventures of Sherlock Holmes?*"

Chapter Sixteen

1

MILE after mile. Hour after hour.

For a long while he had been driving due south. The bush had given way to scrub. The scrub had been replaced by the grass of the Highveld. He had made a great sweeping angle through the Northern Transvaal bush. His car was still running smoothly. With a bit of luck he should be within measurable distance of the West Rand in a couple of hours' time. With a bit more luck he should be driving through the outskirts of Johannesburg with the daybreak. He had kept the letter he had received from Lena Cordier. He hadn't replied to the letter. He would call on her instead.

He hadn't been smoking any more dagga, however. He was getting scared of the stuff now. He didn't again want to go through anything as terrifying as the thing that happened to him at the Wondergat. It had all been so real that he had difficulty, even now, sitting behind the wheel of his car, driving over a Highveld road, in believing that it was just another trick that his dagga-heated imagination had played on him.

At the Wondergat he had been afflicted with what Cyril Stein called 'the recognising blues.' He had himself experienced that phenomenon, when he had thought for a moment that the Indian at the country filling station had borne a resemblance to Jones the compositor. But that was going a bit too far – 'recognising' a shadow cast by a tree as Detective Sergeant Brits.

What was real and what wasn't?

Off-hand, Charlie Hendricks had to confess that he didn't know. Was it really the actress, Sarah Wessels-Wessels, that he had met at the Witgat Hotel, or was it some woman who had looked like her – or whom he had imagined had looked like her? Or was there a woman at all? And had she talked all that rot, all that aimless dagga-talk? For that matter, was there actually such a place as Witgat – such an hotel as the Witgat Hotel – or did that exist merely in his imagination? Hadn't he perhaps, when he was full of dagga, just made up the word 'Witgat' on the analogy of 'Wondergat'?

Charlie Hendricks didn't know. He felt, also, that he had no means of knowing. It would all get cleared up. But not immediately. That was what he felt. It was almost as though, when he left Johannesburg for Willemsdorp some months ago, to take up that job on the *Northern Transvaal News*, he had left reality behind. Come to think of it, everything in Willemsdorp had been pretty unreal – right from the start, even. The provincial council election. And the things that happened about it. And the people he had met in Willemsdorp. Why, to take just a few of them at random. . . Lena Cordier and Dap van Zyl and Robert E. Constable and his committee – and Jack Brummer and that English clergyman and that school principal, Johannes Erasmus.

And the detective, Brits.

And – yes, almost he had forgotten. And the coloured girl, Marjorie. As a matter of fact, she could easily have passed for white, he said to himself, then. She was on his conscience, all right. He didn't like to think that it was a woman of mixed ancestry he had got mixed up with.

But there you were, Charlie Hendricks said to himself, it didn't any of it seem real. The people he had met didn't seem to be people that you could feel and touch and smell. . . Not even Marjorie.

The people he had met in Willemsdorp. . . the things they did. . . the things that happened there. . . everything relating to Willemsdorp was pervaded by a sickly sense of unrealness. . . It was as though he had left Johannesburg and had arrived at a place that had no existence in terms of flesh and blood actuality. There was nothing corporeal; nothing substantial; nothing tangible and concrete. It was as though, the moment he had quit Johannesburg, he was plunged into a dagga dream. Take the announcement of the election result. Or the way he had walked a few yards into the bush, the time he had driven to Kleinberg – and when he came back it was to find his jacket gone. Then there was that Kruger Day festival – the people and the wagon and the horse commando and the volley fired at sunset; and the tableau: a woman actress taking the part of the Transvaal Republic's thick-set, bearded last president.

If that whole thing wasn't just a dagga dream, Charlie Hendricks said to himself, then he would like to believe what was.

But suddenly another idea occurred to Charlie Hendricks. And he didn't feel at all happy, then. After all, wasn't it just on the cards that the things that had happened at Willemsdorp were real-life things? And wasn't it just remotely possible that what went on in Willemsdorp might be the true pattern of existence? After all, wasn't that the way human beings did live? Take Cyril Stein, for that matter. Could you deny that Cyril Stein was a flesh-and-blood person? With his hyper-sensitivity, was there anything unnatural in his seeking to escape through the majestic portals of hashish, painted a grey-blue, with the legend 'Exit Door – Not Locked' picked out in electric lights? Was Cyril Stein the first secretary of a school-board anywhere in the world that had taken to drugs?

Anyway, that was Charlie Hendricks's problem now.

It suddenly struck him that, in the City of Johannesburg, that he had known all his life – the City of Johannesburg to which he was now returning along a road that went due south – in the City of Johannesburg life was a false thing that wore a double face. The back-veld town of Willemsdorp was a place where Life was still spelt with an upper case L. It was Life with the mask off. It was Life lived with an intensity that city dwellers had forgotten generations back.

The manner in which the people of the small town of Willemsdorp had their being was, on the surface, sufficiently placid. Under the surface it was an inferno; a maelstrom; a mad profluence, as life should be. It was rank with humanity, thick with humanity, heavy with lust, gusty with being. Everybody he had met in the small town of Willemsdorp – take those two prospectors in the pub; and the bartender, too, for that matter – had a place in life; belonged in life. The only person outside of life was he himself. In a city you don't live. You just show off.

Suddenly, Charlie Hendricks felt that he himself didn't have much to show off about. He wondered whether it would be better, after all, for him to return to Willemsdorp. What was he running away from, anyway?

But the moment he put the question, he knew the answer, too, of course. In the same way that he knew the answer right away when he had got the wind up, wandering into the bush above the cutting on the road to Kleinberg.

But he knew the answer, this time, before he ran. Before he packed his suitcase. Before he sent Jones the compositor into the bank to cash his cheque for fifty pounds.

214

All right, Charlie Hendricks knew that he was running away from himself.

And it's when it's yourself you're running away from that you can never stop running.

Notes on the Text

Deletions made in the 1977 edition of *Willemsdorp*, all restored here, are as follows: Detective Sergeant Brits's speech, in the present Chapter 9, beginning: "Anyway this one nigger. . . "; his speech about the beating-up of a Coloured woman in Bloemhoek in Chapter 11; the entire Section 2 of the present Chapter 12; and details relating to these omissions.

The point need not be overworked: these cuts all have to do with painful revelations of illegal brutality on the part of the South African police. Omitting them effectively got rid of all of the swingeing exposure Bosman intended of such routine practices. An element of tyranny, of menace, simply disappeared from the book – which to say the least is unfortunate, because solving the mystery at its heart calls for the full range of clues. To put this another way: one of the more sombre, sadistic threads was pulled from the weave of Bosman's embroidery, probably on the grounds that it was distasteful, leaving the design incomplete.

Otherwise, apart from typographical errors all routinely corrected here, there were only a few slips of continuity: Philip Steyn wobbles into finally being Cyril Stein; and is it the *Northern Transvaal News,* or indeed the *Willemsdorp News* as in the previous Human and Rousseau edition? – a frequency count would prefer the former.